BOSS DADDY

A SECRET BABY ROMANCE

NATASHA L. BLACK

COPYRIGHT

Copyright © 2021 by Natasha L. Black

All rights reserved.

JORDAN

"That's perfect. It's much better with the cheese like that."

I scooped up the last bit of the tasting Tyler brought me and put it in my mouth, nodding as I ate it like I was reaffirming the comment I just made. My brother was trying out several new items for that night's menu and was nervous about them.

That was one thing about my brother that never ceased to amaze me. Cooking wasn't ever something he'd seen as a potential career for himself. It wasn't like he ever dreamed of being a great chef or even just being a line cook. He'd tumbled into it when our oldest brother, Tom, bought this bar for us as a way to make money and support our parents as they both battled cancer.

All of us kind of fell into different roles and jobs we didn't see as part of our path when we looked into our futures. We picked them up and did the best we could do because it was what we needed to do. The bar was our saving grace, and especially when we were first starting out, we couldn't afford to hire anybody from the outside to help.

That had changed since The Hollow had gone from just a little neighborhood corner bar to a local destination. We got far too busy to be able to handle it all by ourselves, and we more than made up the money to compensate for payroll. But even as we added extra staff, Tyler didn't leave the kitchen.

In fact, he got more dedicated to coming up with menus that set us apart from all the other bars in the area. This was especially true for our theme nights. That was what we were known the most for among our customers. The brilliant idea of my brother Mason's wife, Ava, the theme nights transformed the bar with decorations, lighting, music, games and contests, and specialized food.

It was those that put us on the map and started drawing in the big crowds. Now some of them were so popular we had to give out wristbands to prioritize who was allowed in when we opened. Tonight's event probably wasn't going to be quite to that level, but that didn't mean we weren't going to be busy.

Board Game Night was something other places had done, but Ava was, of course, putting her own special spin on it. I was looking forward to seeing how the customers would react to the life-size versions of games being set up in the two back rooms and the speed-dating-style rounds at the tables in the front of the restaurant.

Opening time was just a few hours away, which meant we were all hurrying around trying to get the bar ready. The only one of the gaggle of us brothers who wasn't preparing for that night's event was Tom, and that was only because he lived and worked in San Francisco. He and his wife Amanda came to town fairly regularly, but it had been a couple months since we'd last seen them.

I finished cleaning the souvenir glassware we'd ordered

and had it set up behind the bar just in time for the shipment of supplies for the bar to arrive. As I walked outside to the back parking lot to start hauling in boxes and crates, a car pulled in. Ava and Mason got out, and I watched as they walked around to the back of the car. They paused for a kiss and grinned at each other before opening the trunk.

They had gone out in search of more games to have out on the patio and to break down and use in decorations for the night. I watched as Ava leaned over to get a bag out of the back of the trunk and Mason pinched her butt. She let out a little squeal and whipped around toward him.

Mason gathered her up in his arms, and they giggled, hugging and kissing again. Watching them flirt and then walk into the bar holding hands only reminded me of how badly I wanted that. Not Ava. She was like a sister to me and had been since they were just teenagers.

I wanted a relationship of my own. A family. There was a time when I thought I was almost there. Being in the military for nearly twenty years was hard and pushed me mentally and physically. But I always reminded myself I had a good woman back home who was waiting for me. And when I got out, we would get married and have a family of our own.

At least, that was what I had counted on. Then I found out my ex started cheating on me within just a few months of me leaving for one of my tours. She was carrying on with someone I had thought was my friend behind my back, all the while continuing to lead me on and letting me believe everything was great between us.

I didn't uncover the truth until I was back in town visiting during a leave and went to surprise her at her house. She didn't realize I was getting back so early. Obviously, or she wouldn't have been on a blanket in the backyard with the guy I thought was my friend.

That image in my head, I looked back over at Mason and Ava as they came out into the parking lot again and went for another load of the games. My brother waved at me but didn't let go of Ava's hand for a second. I waved back, not letting him see the emotion in my face.

I wanted what they had so much, but I wasn't sure I would ever find it. In my late thirties, I wasn't old, but I also wasn't the springy early twenty-somethings out in the dating market. Considering I had no intention of leaving my hometown of Astoria, the pool of options seemed pretty narrow and was getting narrower.

I carried a box inside and was unloading it at the bar when Ava came up.

"Hey, Jordan," she said.

I looked up from putting the bottles in place and smiled at her. "Hey, Ava."

"So, that new cocktail waitress I hired is starting tonight. She should be here pretty soon," she said.

"You have her starting on a theme night?" I asked, surprised. "Throwing her into the fire, aren't you?"

She laughed. "Well, I figure she better get used to it right off the bat. It's better to show her what it's like here when we're busy than to lull her into complacency with just a regular night and then have her freak out on us when we have another theme night. At least tonight isn't going to be as crazy as some of the others."

"True," I said. "You're being easy on her. Magnanimous, even."

Ava laughed. "Something like that. Her name is Hannah. When she gets here, will you show her around and let her know her duties and responsibilities? She says she has experience, so it shouldn't be too hard for her to pick things up, but I want to make sure that she is ready and can keep up tonight."

"Sure thing. I can do that," I said.

My sister-in-law walked away, and I went back to putting away the shipment and getting everything set up for the night. We had some experience with running the theme nights now and had learned that it was important to be set up and ready well in advance. Having things like the glasses positioned for easy grabbing and several of the most popular themed cocktails already mixed and set at the end of the bar for the waitresses to grab as they were ordered could save massive amounts of time and hassle.

A little while later, the door to the back of the bar opened. I looked up, expecting to see one of my brothers. Instead, my breath caught in my throat at the sight of a gorgeous woman walking in. For a second, I could barely think much less say anything. She looked at me, and I had to break my gaze so I didn't completely freak her out by staring.

"I'm sorry. We're not open yet," I said.

I was trying to think of a diplomatic way to tell her she wasn't allowed to come through the back door when she shook her head and smiled.

"I'm not a customer," she said. She held her hand out toward me. "I'm Hannah."

I couldn't believe this was the new cocktail waitress Ava hired. She was stunningly beautiful with a bright smile and a confident, unwavering gaze. She already looked completely comfortable in the bar. But she also seemed like one of those people who was probably comfortable anywhere she went.

Doing my best to keep my cool, I took the hand she offered out to me and shook it.

"Nice to meet you. I'm Jordan."

"One of the owners?" she asked.

I smiled. "Yeah. But tonight, I'm just a bartender. And I'm actually going to be showing you around and getting you familiar with the place and the job."

"Sounds good. I'm looking forward to getting started."

There wasn't anything overtly flirty or suggestive about that comment, and yet I felt it down to the depths of my belly. This might be a bit more of a challenge than I was expecting.

Still forcing myself not to stare at her, I opened my arms out to the sides to encompass the bar.

"This is the bar," I said.

Hannah nodded, playing up a deeply thoughtful expression like she was concentrating hard on remembering what I was telling her.

"Okay. We're just going to hit the ground running, I see. Should I be taking notes?"

She grinned at me, and I couldn't help but laugh. Walking out from behind the bar, I led her to the front of the space to start showing her around.

"This is actually the second location of The Hollow," I said.

"I heard that," she said. "The original one burned down, right?"

"Yeah. That was not fun. But it led us to this building, which is an awesome space and in a great location in town. I think I'll always have a soft spot for the original place just because that's where we got started and the one that our father got to see. But I do really like this one. It has a lot of potential, and we've been building it out and renovating since we got it."

"It's impressive," Hannah said, nodding as she looked around. Her big eyes met mine. "I'm sorry to hear about your father."

A little pang of grief hit my heart, but I didn't let it drag me down. It had been long enough, but it still hurt—I figured it always would—but I was able to live with it.

"Thanks. Thankfully, our mother is doing much better. I think having all the grandbabies around has made a big difference for her," I said.

We continued on through the bar, and I introduced her to everybody as we came upon them. I found myself laughing and smiling the entire time. Hannah wasn't just beautiful. She was friendly and confident and had a glow about her that I found myself drawn to.

Of course, I couldn't let myself dwell on that. It wasn't like I could act on it. Hannah was brand-new and a member of the staff. I couldn't cross that line. But there was nothing wrong with looking.

2

HANNAH

I swung by one of the tables I had been taking care of all night and scooped up the portfolio with the check in it.

"Keep the change," one of the men said.

"Thank you. Have a great night," I said.

"I hope to see you again sometime," he said.

I gave him one of my brightest, yet still generic, smiles. "I'll be working here just about every day."

"Sounds good to me. This place is lucky to have you."

I continued on through the bar without responding. He wasn't being inappropriate, but I wasn't going to hang around long enough for the tide to shift if it was going to.

Bringing the portfolio up to the cash register at the back corner of the bar, I opened it up and took out the money tucked inside. I handed it and the receipt over to Ava, who had jumped in behind the bar to help Jordan out. She read the receipt and counted out the money. Giving me an impressed look, she handed back several bills.

"Nice tip," she said. "You seem to be getting a lot of those tonight."

"People are trying to make my first night a good one," I said.

She smiled. "Somehow I think it's a little more than that."

I glanced over at Jordan as he walked up behind Ava to get another of the souvenir glasses on display. His eyes met mine, and we held each other's gaze for a brief second before he turned away. I had been catching him staring at me all night, ever since he showed me around the bar earlier and helped me get started.

Looking at him, it was hard to believe he was actually one of my bosses. He was old enough. I guessed he was somewhere in his mid to late thirties. But there was just something about him that seemed way more fun than a regular boss should be. Not to mention he was stupidly hot.

That was the part that really stood out to me. Ava was the one who hired me. She explained to me that the bar was owned by the Anderson brothers, and she was married to Mason Anderson. When she asked me to come in tonight as my first night, she told me to find Jordan, because he was the one who would be showing me the ropes and getting me started.

I came in just when I was supposed to and was taken aback by the man behind the bar. He was standing right there where Ava told me I would find Jordan, but he wasn't at all what I was expecting. Of course, I didn't really know what I was expecting. I was new in Astoria and hadn't met any of the Anderson family, except for Ava.

But from the very beginning, Jordan put me at ease. I felt comfortable with him as soon as we introduced ourselves, and he made sure I felt totally ready to jump into my new position. It was perhaps a little bit intimidating to find out I was starting on one of their theme nights and to hear that these nights often got crazy busy.

Jordan made sure I felt ready and told me that I was going to do just fine. That helped me relax and even get excited for what was to come. So far, he had been right. It was a great first night. All the customers were friendly and welcoming, the tips were flowing, and I was really liking all my new coworkers.

Especially Jordan.

Throughout the night I would glance over his way and find him staring at me. It didn't bother me. In fact, I found myself getting a little bit of a shiver from it. I was used to being stared at, and Jordan was not being at all creepy, which was more than I could say about a lot of guys. I'd had my fair share of creeps over the years, so I could sense these things.

By the end of the night, I was tired but happy. It was even more successful than I'd hoped it would be. I was looking forward to going back for another shift but was also happy that I would have most of the next day off to relax. I knew exactly what I wanted to do.

Though I got home well after two in the morning after my first shift, I was awake and ready to go by six-thirty. I was pretty sure working at the bar and keeping such late hours would eventually catch up with me and I would stop being quite as much of a morning person.

That day, I packed up my art supplies and headed for the beach. There wasn't anybody out there except for a couple of early morning joggers as I set up my easel and dispensed little bits of paint out onto my palette.

The view of the ocean and the rocks around it was beautiful. As I captured the image on my canvas, I found a calm I didn't know I could still achieve. It had been a long time since I'd felt anything even close to it.

I was glad to be so far away from everything.

My phone rang, and I carefully set down my paints to answer it. I smiled when I saw my best friend's name across the screen.

"Hey, Samantha," I said.

"How was your first day?" she asked.

"It was really great. I like the people I work with a lot, and the customers were super welcoming."

"That's awesome. I told you it would be good," she said.

"How about you? How's the family?"

"Well, Owen is walking on his own now."

"Already?" I asked, surprised. "He just turned one! I can't believe he's growing up so fast."

I was thrilled to hear about the little boy, the youngest of Samantha's two children, hitting his milestones. I loved children and missed being around them.

"You're telling me," Samantha said. "So, tell me more. How is it going out there in Oregon? I still for the life of me can't figure out why you would decide to move all the way out there."

I laughed. "Because it's all the way out here. It's going really well. It's beautiful out here, and I am really going to like working at The Hollow. I even have a boss that is not bad to look at."

That was the understatement of the century, but I didn't want to gush too much.

"Oh, really?" Samantha said, latching on to even the vague description. "What's he like?"

I told her about Jordan and how he'd shown me around when I first got to the bar. "And I caught him staring at me just about all night."

She let out a little bit of a squeal. At nearly thirty years old, she could still manage a schoolgirl squeal with the best of them. It always made me laugh.

"You should go for it!" she said.

"Go for what?" I asked, picking up my brush to start painting again.

"For him. You should just jump into it with him. Rip the bandage off."

I scoffed. "That is not going to happen."

"Why not?"

"I am definitely not ready for that, Samantha. Especially not with someone I work with, or I should say work *for*," I said.

"You should think about it. You can't wait around forever," she said, sounding a little disappointed.

Samantha loved her husband, a successful New York City banker, and she adored being a mother to their two children. But there were times when it seemed like she was missing the carefree days of youth and singlehood and wanted to live vicariously through me.

Only that meant she was also trying to turn my life into a Choose Your Own Adventure, with her at the helm of all the choices. It was all with my best interests in mind, but I wasn't ready to throw myself in quite the way she wanted me to.

After getting off the phone, I spent a while longer at the beach working on the painting. As it got later in the morning, more people started to arrive, and soon the sense of quiet and peace wasn't quite the same. Even then, it was good to see the families coming out to enjoy picnics and the little children running around on the sand.

I liked seeing them happy. It gave me a boost of optimism that one day I might be able to find that for myself.

I packed everything up and headed back to the little house I'd picked out almost as soon as I arrived in Astoria. It wasn't big or luxurious, but it was comfortable, and it was mine. And at that point, that meant more to me than I could put into words.

There was enough time for me to take a short nap and have lunch before I needed to get ready for work. I didn't actually have to be at the bar until later, but I was still getting the hang of the place, and I wanted to make a good impression.

It wasn't one of the theme nights, so it was already open for late lunch and early dinner by the time I got there. It wasn't busy, with only a handful of people scattered around at the various tables positioned throughout the space. I was amazed to see that there were no visible signs of the event the night before still there. It was like it had all magically disappeared in between the time I had left and the time I showed back up.

Ava was behind the bar when I walked in, and she waved me over.

"Hey," she said. "How are you doing today?"

"Doing great," I said. "Should I go check on any of these tables?"

She shook her head and smiled. "Don't worry about them. They're regulars. They pretty much take care of themselves. When they need something, one of the guys will take care of them. I wanted you to meet my best friend, Stephanie."

Ava gestured across the bar at a woman sitting on one of the stools with a beer between her hands. She smiled at me, and I smiled back.

"Hi," I said. "I'm Hannah. It's nice to meet you."

"You too. I've heard a lot about you."

I gave a slightly questioning look to Ava. "You have?"

Ava laughed. "All good things, I promise. Stephanie has been listening to all my complaints about this place since I showed back up in town and went to work for the guys. She hears all the dirt about this place. Not that you're dirt."

I laughed. "I've been called worse. Trust me. You said you showed back up in town? You haven't always lived here?"

I sat down on the stool beside Stephanie and listened to Ava tell me about how she had grown up in Astoria and been with Mason through most of her teenage years. When they broke up, she left and went to college, then settled in a different state. It wasn't until her father was seriously injured and needed her help that she came back. That was when she started working at The Hollow, leading to her reuniting with Mason.

I enjoyed sitting there talking with the women. I like how laid-back they were, and it felt like they didn't have any ulterior motives like most people did back home. Just before I got up to start my shift, another woman swept into the bar and went around to hug Ava.

"Hannah, this is Becca, Tyler's wife," she said.

"Nice to meet you," I offered.

Becca smiled at me, and we chatted for a few moments while Ava went into the back to get the bundle of hand-me-down baby clothes she was sending to Becca's son. When she left, I headed over to the table of customers that had just come in and sat down.

I had a feeling I was really going to like it here.

3

JORDAN

All around me, there was sound. Explosions. Gunshots. Screams and shouts, both to terrify and out of fear and pain. Engines roared, and metal ground against metal. It was all so loud and intense it felt like it was seeping down into my skin and rattling in my bones. Like I would never be able to get away from it. It was the sound that was becoming a part of me.

I ran. I didn't even know where I was running. Everything was so chaotic, and the dust was so thick in my eyes I didn't know which direction was which. If I looked down, I could barely even see my boots in the sand. But I knew I had to keep running. If I stopped, I'd be dead. Blood ran down my face, stinging my eyes and tasting metallic on my tongue.

I didn't know where the blood was coming from. I didn't even know if it was mine.

I was aware of pain, something burning and deep on my leg, but I didn't pause to find out what happened. There would be enough time for that later. I needed the adrenaline right now. As long as I didn't look, as long as I didn't know what was going on, I could run on sheer will.

Somewhere in the glowing dust and darkness around me, I could hear my name being called. The voice was so distant and muffled by the other sounds closing in around me, I couldn't tell who it was. But there was desperation in it. Terror and agony.

Straining through everything else for the sound, I continued to push myself forward, searching for whoever it was who needed me, whoever it was trying so desperately to get my attention.

Something exploded so close to me I could feel the heat and debris rake across my face. I dropped to the ground and shielded my head. The sand dug into my skin and got into my mouth as I tried to breathe. Finally, I tried to stand, but my feet wouldn't get under me. I couldn't force my legs to support me.

That wouldn't stop me. I could still hear the sound, still hear the screaming. It wasn't as far away now. I knew who it was. The best friend I had out here. The guy I'd been serving alongside for years and had shared experiences with no one but those of us who were out there would ever understand.

Reaching ahead of me, I clawed through the sand to drag myself forward. The heat stung on my skin, and grit mixed with the blood running down my face. But I couldn't stop. I couldn't just give up. Another explosion lifted me up, throwing me forward so I crashed into the ground.

More pain surged through me, and for a moment, I lay there, stunned. When my senses came back to me and I knew I wasn't dead, I forced myself to keep going. I hadn't dragged myself far when I realized I no longer heard my friend screaming. The voice was completely gone.

But ahead of me in the sand was a broken, crumpled body. Seeing it gave me the adrenaline I needed to push harder. I was able to get onto my knees and move forward faster. Dropping down onto the ground beside him, I turned my buddy over onto his back and saw the massive wound down his face and the side of his neck and across his chest.

I tore a bandage out of my pack to try to cover as much of the wound as I could, but there was nothing I could do to stop the bleeding.

I woke up covered in sweat, gasping for breath. They didn't happen very often, but that wasn't the first time I'd had that nightmare. I did my best not to spend a lot of time dwelling on that horrific day or anything else I saw during my time in the military. But sometimes I couldn't help it. Sometimes the nightmares plagued me, and there was nothing I could do to escape reliving the horror and pain I'd experienced.

But I had learned that running right after suffering one of them took away the shaky feeling and made me feel more in the moment again. It was like it cleared my mind and brought me back into the present, rather than those difficult days. Those days were years ago now, but so often, they felt like they had just happened.

Putting on my running gear and tying my shoes, I headed out of the house without any idea how long I was going to run. I would just keep going until I felt like I was finished. That ended up being at a diner across town. It had always been one of my favorite restaurants, serving the best all-day breakfast around. I was a sucker for breakfast food. Always had been.

I convinced myself having a couple of plates full of my favorite breakfast foods would be the best way to fuel up after my long run and headed inside. At first, I walked up to the podium to talk to the young hostess standing there, but then something caught my attention out of the corner of my eye. I looked to the side and saw my brother Matt sitting in a booth by himself.

I pointed him out. "Is he here with anyone?"

She glanced over and shook her head. "No. He came in alone and only got one menu. He's only been here for a few minutes. Just barely got his coffee."

"Great," I said. "I'm just going to join him."

"Perfect," she said, reaching down to the chair beside her to grab a menu from the stack sitting on the seat.

"Thanks."

I took the menu and walked over to the table where Matt sat. He was staring at the mug in his hands like the coffee was going to give him the answers to all the questions of the Universe. The sound of me smacking my menu on the edge of the table made him jump, and his eyes snapped up at me.

"Hey," I said, smiling.

"What the hell, Jordan?" Matt asked.

I laughed and sat down across from him. "Just waking you back up. Looks like last night got the most of you."

"Not really. I'm alright. I was just craving some hash browns with onions and a couple of over-easy eggs, so I came up here. What are you doing here? You look like hell."

"Well, thank you. I appreciate that. I just took a run. But I decided I didn't have the energy to get all the way back because I didn't eat anything before I left, so I'm here to get powered up for the run back home," I said.

"Are you fellas ready to order?" the waitress asked as she set down my cup of coffee. "Or do you need a little more time?"

Each of us ordered our favorite breakfasts and a few extra dishes and handed the menus back to the woman. She smiled and headed off toward the kitchen. I reached for the tiny pitcher of cream near the edge of the table and swirled some into my coffee, then followed up with a couple of packets of sugar.

Matt grimaced. "How do you drink it like that?"

"Because I like it like that," I responded.

"It's supposed to be coffee, not dessert."

"What happened to you? You used to be fun." I looked down in my mug. "I had my fill of terrible instant black coffee when I was in the service. Maybe my taste for drinking it black will come back someday, but for now, I'll have it as sweet and creamy as possible."

Matt shrugged and drank another sip of his own coffee.

"What's on your mind? Anything I can help with?"

Matt tended to be the most dramatic of us brothers, but I never wanted to discount him. There could actually be something bothering him, and I didn't want him to feel like nobody cared. If there was one thing I carried with me out of that desert it was to never turn your back on someone or leave an opportunity to show that they matter to you.

"Not really," he said. "I was just thinking about how everything's changing. Do you realize three of our brothers are married with kids now? Three of them. The grandchildren are catching up with us."

"I know," I said. "It's kind of hard to wrap my head around."

Our food came while Matt and I talked about feeling a little bit left in the dust and bonding over the shared feeling of everything moving forward without us. I left the restaurant feeling better, but also thinking even more about the future and the family I wanted so much.

That night I was training Hannah behind the bar. She was a fantastic cocktail waitress, but it was good to have the people who worked for us be able to do as many things as possible so we could fill in as we needed to depending on how nights went and if there were gaps in the schedule on any given day.

"So, you were saying you just moved to Astoria," I said, picking up a piece of the conversation we'd had on the first day I trained her a couple of weeks before.

"Yep," she said, nodding. "I just moved from New York."

"Wow," I said. "You think you could have made a bigger move? Go a little bit further, maybe?"

Hannah laughed. "It was a little extreme, I guess. But I just can't escape living on the coast. The whole idea of middle America has never appealed to me. Here and New York are about as different as I could possibly imagine, but at least I can still get to the ocean in both of them."

"Fair enough," I said. "Why did you move? Just time for an adventure?"

"I guess you can say that. I wanted to start a new life."

"Nothing left for you in New York?" I asked.

"Other than my best friend, no. And she has a family of her own. A husband and two children. It wasn't like it used to be. I needed to get away and find out where I'm supposed to be and what I'm supposed to be doing."

"I can definitely understand that," I said. "That's part of why I joined the military."

We talked a little bit more, but I quickly found the conversation drifting away from the more personal details of our lives to things like her asking for recommendations for good restaurants around town and what we did for fun. She was trying to settle in and find her way, and I was happy to guide her along.

4

HANNAH

A few weeks after arriving in Astoria, I felt like I had made one of the best decisions of my life. I didn't know exactly what to expect when I'd decided to move to Oregon. As a matter of fact, the most important thing on my mind at the time was just getting out of New York and away from just about everybody who was there. Like I told Jordan, the only people who I really missed were Samantha and her family.

But now that I was here and really starting to settle in, I was enjoying it more than I even could have imagined. It was my night off from the bar, so I decided to walk around the town a bit and get more familiar with it. One of the things I loved about Astoria was how similar it was to New York in that I could walk around and visit shop to shop and restaurant to restaurant.

Of course, that was pretty much where the similarities ended. Astoria was tiny and slumbering compared to New York, but I was also finding that I loved that about it, too. As I was walking down the main street in the village, checking out the shop windows and making note of where things were so I could find them later, I heard someone calling my name.

I stopped and looked around, finally seeing Becca coming toward me. She had a big smile on her face and several shopping bags in each hand. I grinned at her as she approached.

"Hey, Hannah," she said. "How are you doing today?"

"I'm doing great. I see you're doing some shopping."

She looked down at the bags in her hands. "Maybe just a little bit."

We both laughed.

"What are you after today?" I asked.

"Just doing some shopping for my little boy. He's getting so big so fast I feel like I'm always buying him new clothes, and now that he's walking, I'm constantly getting him new shoes. Not that I'm complaining. I have the best time buying him things and dressing him up."

"Where is he? I'd love to meet him," I said.

"Oh, he stayed home with his daddy today. They are having some guys' time," she said with a hint of a laugh. "But I'm sure you'll get a chance to meet him. What are you up to?"

"It's my day off, so I thought I would look around and try to get my bearings more in the area. For the last couple of weeks, I've mainly been going to the bar and to the grocery store, and that's it. Now I think it's about time I figure out where I am."

"Have you had lunch yet?"

"No," I said.

"Come on," Becca invited with a big smile. "I'm going to bring you to my very favorite lunch spot. My treat." We took a few steps, and then she stopped suddenly. "My very favorite lunch spot other than The Hollow. Tyler would kill me if I didn't specify that. He has worked so hard on the menu."

I giggled and nodded. "Understood. I won't let your secret out."

"Oh, good. Come on. I need to put these down, and I am dying for a big glass of iced tea."

I grinned as I fell into step beside her and let her lead me down the street. We got to a small hole-in-the-wall Italian restaurant, and when we stepped inside, the incredible smell of fresh dough, heavy spices, and rich cheese filled my nose.

It was enough to make my stomach rumble, and I realized it had been hours since breakfast. The cook stepped up to the counter from the open kitchen and waved around the restaurant.

"Have a seat," he said. "Anywhere you want."

I followed Becca to the far side of the dining room, and we sat down in a booth. She looked crowded with all the shopping bags in the booth beside her, but her wide smile told me she didn't mind. A waiter came to the table within seconds of us sitting down, and we ordered drinks.

When the waiter left us with menus, Becca leaned slightly across the table toward me.

"How are you liking Astoria so far?"

"I love it here," I said. "I feel like I finally found home."

She smiled and nodded. "It's a pretty wonderful place."

"Have you always lived here?"

"I grew up here, but then I left when I went to college. I was away for about five years before I came back," she said.

"Is that when you met Tyler?"

"No. I've known Tyler just about my whole life. His best friend is my brother, Nick," she said.

My eyes widened. The waiter came by to set our drinks

down in front of us and asked if we were ready to order. We made our orders, and when he walked away, I laughed, taking a sip of my water.

"Your brother's best friend?" I asked. "I bet that went over really well."

Becca shook her head. "It was quite a mess at first. It didn't help that I came back here because my engagement ended, so everybody was scrutinizing when I was starting a relationship again."

"Your engagement ended?" I asked.

I hadn't talked about the awful relationship issues I left behind in New York to anyone, but it made me feel a little better to hear I wasn't the only one who found solace in Astoria.

"Oh, yeah," she said with a laugh. "He all but left me at the altar. It was not pretty. But it got me back here, and I ran into Tyler again. We hadn't seen each other in a long time, and it was really good to see him. My parents were way too protective of me and immediately wanted to lock me away in the tower and keep me from ever going out into the world again. Tyler and I got closer and one thing led to another... Anyway, suffice it to say Nick didn't respond too well at first. He thought it was really weird that his best friend was sleeping with his little sister."

I laughed. "I can only imagine. Do you have a picture of your little boy?" I asked.

"Of course I do."

She pulled out her phone and started showing me pictures of the little boy from the time he was born. He was absolutely adorable, and it was clear both his parents along with his grandparents and aunts and uncles doted on him. I found myself wondering what that felt like, to be a part of a family that was so sprawling and yet so close.

I longed for something like that for myself someday, but it felt so far out of my reach I didn't even know how I would begin to find it.

Even though it was my night off, I decided to go up to the bar that night. It was another of the theme nights, and I wanted to check it out from a customer's perspective. I knew what it was like to work one of the exciting, somewhat chaotic events, but running around waiting tables and tending the bar during them kept me from actually being able to immerse myself in the experience.

That night was a car show night. I heard from Ava the bar had done one of these back early in the days of the theme nights, and it was extremely popular, so they revived it every few months. This event was particularly exciting because it didn't just involve The Hollow.

Two blocks of the street where it sat were shut down and filled with classic cars and car-related vendors. All the restaurants and bars on that stretch were offering specials and combining forces to create an almost carnival atmosphere that would benefit all of them rather than just being purely about competition.

A long line at the front of the event waited to go through a station to purchase an admission ticket and get a wristband, but I was able to go through the employee entrance with a special wristband Ava gave me when she suggested I come check everything out.

I walked out into the event and was blown away. Everywhere people were dressed up to match the eras of their cars, showing them off, eating, drinking, and dancing. I absolutely loved it.

I was waiting in line to get a drink when someone came up beside me. I looked up and saw Jordan smiling at me.

"Hey," I said. "What are you doing out here among the regular people?"

He laughed. "I could ask you the same question. It's my night off. They actually sprung me for the evening because they got all the other guys on deck and a couple of the extra employees that are kept in their back pocket for just such an occasion."

I nodded and smiled as the line moved, and we took a couple of steps forward. "It's my night off, too. I wanted to see what all the hype was about."

"And?"

"And the hype is totally warranted," I said.

"I love coming out here on the rare theme nights I have off. It's a completely different experience than working them, and I love to see the customers having such a good time. They really get into it. What's really fun is seeing the ones who have come to a bunch of the nights interacting with the ones who this is their first one. There's definitely a sense of membership, like they have some sort of inside knowledge because they're seasoned."

"People certainly do like to feel special and like they belong," I agreed.

"That's what Ava said, too. She's thinking about doing something like a beer stein club or something where customers can have their own stein with their name on it that would be on display in the bar and give them special discounts or something," Jordan said.

I nodded. "That's a really good idea. I bet people would love that."

I got up to the booth and ordered my drink. Jordan piped up beside me, ordering his own plus a couple of the food offerings. He whipped out his wallet before I could say anything, and the vendor waved him away. He knew who he was and wasn't going to charge him. According to him, these theme nights were worth four or five regular nights at his place during this time of the year, so he was happy to show his appreciation.

We walked around enjoying our drinks and sampling the food. As we did, we fell into easy conversation. Jordan told me all about his oldest brother buying the bar and how they had to get used to being bar owners.

"I was still in the military then. I remember my brothers trying really hard not to let on how much they needed my help here because I was still on active duty, and they didn't want me to be distracted. But they were having a hard time of it at first. My parents were both sick and needed the support. It was kind of scary times, to be honest," he said.

"It sounds like it. I can't imagine going through something like that," I said. "At least you guys all had each other."

Jordan nodded. "That's the only thing that really got us through. When our father died, I got an early release from the service and came home to be with the family. It was rough, but we did our best to focus on our mother and getting her through not only losing Dad but continuing her own fight."

"She sounds like an amazing woman to have raised all of you and to get through challenges like that," I said.

"She is." Jordan was silent for a few seconds. "How about your parents? What are they like?"

I shook my head slightly, looking down into my drink so I had something to do with my eyes other than looking at him. "I don't talk to them much."

"No?" he asked.

"No." I shrugged and looked ahead as we kept walking. "We've had a lot of conflicts and just don't see eye to eye on life. They send me money every once in a while, but I don't keep it. I donate it all as soon as I get it because I don't want anything to do with them. I don't want to feel obligated or tied to them because of money."

I stopped short of telling him about my ex or the reason I completely separated from my family, but the rest of the conversation was smooth and comfortable. I had always been one to find it easy to talk to people, but there was something different about Jordan and in the very best way.

5

———

JORDAN

My eyes snapped open, and I sat bolt upright in bed, for a moment dazed and not knowing exactly where I was. It had been a few weeks since the last nightmare, but this one was even more intense and left me gasping for breath. The images still flickered across my eyes even when they were open. I struggled to make them disappear, to bring myself back into reality.

When I was finally able to push the thoughts aside enough to get up, I decided I was going to need more than just a run around town and gorging on breakfast food to get my mind clear again. I needed to really force these thoughts away and work off the nightmare.

Snapping up my phone as I made my way to the kitchen for coffee, I called my best friend, Luke.

"What are you doing?" I asked.

"Nothing," he said. "What's up?"

"Want to meet up at the gym for a workout?"

"Absolutely. See you there in an hour?"

"Yep. See you then."

I got off the phone and downed a couple of mugs of

coffee to break through the fog of my late nights and relatively early mornings. It had been a couple of years since I got out of the military and started to adapt myself to the slower pace of life in Astoria, but there were still times when it caught up with me. It was like my body had been so trained and programmed to operate in military hours some of that compulsion was never really going to go away.

When the caffeine started to hit me, I got dressed and made my way to the gym. Luke was already there warming up, and I joined him for a few stretches before we moved on to the cardio machines to do a real warm-up before the weights.

"Tell me more about this new girl at work," he said a while later when we were lifting weights.

"Hannah?" I asked.

"Yeah. The one you said they hired and you were showing the ropes."

"She's the new cocktail waitress, and I've been training her on the bar just to have someone extra. She said she has some experience at bars and restaurants, but I don't really know what or how much. She's good and the customers like her, but I don't know. There's just something about her that doesn't seem like she has actually spent her life bouncing from waitress job to waitress job."

Luke stared at me for a few seconds, then nodded. "Alright. Well, that was a good employee evaluation. Now, actually tell me about her."

"What do you mean?" I asked.

"You know exactly what I mean."

"She's a great girl," I said. "Friendly, funny, smart. It's easy to talk to her, and I like having her around."

"Alright, since you're going to beat around the bush, I'll

just come right out and ask you. Have you slept with her yet?" Luke asked.

I rolled my eyes. "Seriously?"

Luke shrugged and nodded. "Yeah."

"No. I haven't. And I'm not going to. Like I said, she's a great girl, and I like talking to her. She's nice to have around the bar. That's it."

"Is she pretty?"

"Yes," I said, deciding not to elaborate on how gorgeous Hannah actually was. There was no need to fuel him.

"Pretty. Funny. Good to talk to. Sounds like prime hookup material to me. You should go for it. As an added bonus, since she works there, if you can keep it going, you'll have something to do on the slow nights," Luke said, laughing.

"Knock it off," I snapped.

"What?" Luke asked, sounding like he had no idea what he'd said.

I got up from the bench press machine and grabbed my towel from where it was hanging.

"When are you going to grow up?" I asked, stalking toward the locker room.

I was still fuming when I left the gym and got in my car to go home. I would admit I used to not care about talking about girls that way with Luke. In fact, that used to make up a bulk of our conversations. But I was thirty-six years old now. I wasn't some kid with too much libido and arrogance for my own good. I was over all that. Not to mention, hearing him talk about Hanna like she was just some potential hook up pissed me off more than it probably should have. But I decided not to dig too deep into that.

I'd had a lot of one-night stands over the last two years since I got back to Astoria, but I'd had my fill. I was just over that whole thing and ready to put racking up the numbers of hookups behind me. I was ready for something serious.

Later that day, I went into work. Ava was behind the bar, and two of the girls who occasionally came in to waitress were moving around getting the place ready for the late-lunch and early dinner crowd that would come in before we really shifted over to the bar atmosphere.

"Hannah isn't in today?" I asked.

Ava gave me a brief look but didn't acknowledge what was behind it. "No. She has tonight off. Before you get started on anything, Mason wants to talk to you. He's in the office."

"Everything okay?" I asked.

"Tom called earlier today, and I think he just wants to talk to you about that."

I nodded and headed to the back of the bar where Mason set up the office. While all of us were technically equal in running the bar, we figured out early on that we would need some sort of hierarchy to make sure everything got done. Mason fell naturally into place as the manager, and when Ava came along with her business skills and impressive ideas, it just cemented their position.

But to keep up with the sense that we were all in this together, the new location of The Hollow had dispensed with the tiny, cramped office of the last one and replaced it with a room much closer to a conference room. Big enough to accommodate a table where we could all sit, it also featured a computer, files, and everything Mason and Ava needed to do the day-to-day administrative tasks.

Mason was sitting at the table with papers spread out in front of him. He was making notes on a pad of paper to one side and occasionally tapping something out on a calculator.

"Hey," I said when I walked in. "Ava said you wanted to talk to me."

Mason looked up. "Oh, hey, Jordan. Yeah, come in. Sit down."

"Is everything okay?" I asked as I took a seat at the table.

"Everything's fine," Mason said. I relaxed a little, but my shoulders still felt tense. I didn't think they would release until I knew for sure what was going on. "I got a call from Tom today. He's been really pleased with the reports he's getting from the bar and thinks we could do more."

"More?" I asked. "What do you mean?"

"He thinks that since we are doing so well drawing in the crowds, we should start looking into building up even more. Mom's doing well now, and she has everything she needs, but he pointed out that three of us have families now and wants to make sure we can all make a good living for ourselves."

"So, what's he talking about?" I asked. "Does he want to expand?"

"Kind of," Mason said.

"It seems like most of Astoria comes out to the theme nights as it is. I don't know how much more business we could actually get unless we're bringing in people from other towns. Some travel in as it is."

"Well, that's sort of the point. He's not talking about expanding to another location here in Astoria. He had an idea to open another location in Portland."

"Portland? That would be a hell of a commute. Who would run it?" I asked.

"He's leaning toward you and Matt. Neither one of you have families that keep you locked here, and both of you know the ropes of running a bar. Together, you'd be able to build it up and get it running like this one," Mason said.

"Wow," I said, sitting back. I felt a bit dumbstruck and a little blindsided by the whole thing. "That would mean I would have to relocate, wouldn't it?"

Mason nodded. "Yeah. Like you said, it would be too much of a commute. If you were really going to build the place up and get it successful, you would need to be right there, hands-on and involved. That would mean moving to Portland. At least for a while."

"Wow," I said again. It was probably among the worst reactions I could have had. There had to be something more meaningful, but I couldn't come up with any other words.

"What are you thinking?" Mason asked a few seconds later when I had stared silently across the table without looking at him.

"I'm trying to figure that out," I said. "I love it here. Astoria is my hometown, and I've never planned on leaving it after I came back from the service. This was always going to be where I landed. But I understand where Tom is coming from. Getting another location going could mean huge things for the family, and if anyone should relocate to do it, it should be those of us who wouldn't have to uproot entire families to make it happen. It's just hard to really wrap my head around."

"Well, don't let it get to you too much. Nothing is set in stone. It's just an idea. We're trying to figure out all the details and the logistics. It's just something to contemplate."

I nodded and got up to go back out to the bar and start working. It might have just been an idea, but the thought was stuck with me now.

6

HANNAH

I had just finished up washing the dishes from lunch when my phone alerted where I had it sitting on the counter away from the potential disaster of the sink. Wiping my hands on a dish towel, I picked up the phone to check what it was. My first thought was that it might be Ava from the bar sending me a message asking if I could come into work early. Instead, it was an email notification. I knew what it was before I even opened it. My parents had made a deposit into my bank account.

Samantha had asked me why I didn't just close that account and open a new one if I didn't want my parents' money. But I didn't want to go through the hassle of reassigning all my automatic payments and getting all new cards. Plus, if my parents were insistent on sending the money, I would at least put it to good use by way of charitable donations.

Letting out a sigh, I went into the living room and dropped down onto the couch. My laptop was sitting on the coffee table, and I opened it so I could go through my usual habit after getting such a deposit. The website I had book-marked let me scroll through a wide variety of different causes and campaigns so I could choose something meaningful and worthwhile to donate the money to.

I had just settled on the first of a couple of different causes I was going to donate to when my phone rang. Glancing over, I saw Samantha's name on the screen.

"Hey, Samantha," I said as I answered.

Pinning the phone between my shoulder and my ear, I continued the process of making the first donation.

"Hey," she said. "What are you up to?"

"My parents sent another one of their deposits into my bank, so I'm finding places to donate the money."

"Hannah, you've got to be kidding me. That is so ridiculous. You've got to stop."

I was used to that reaction from my best friend. It was how she always reacted when she found out I was just giving away all the money my parents sent to me rather than keeping it for myself. According to her, I should just enjoy it and maybe even have a little bit of fun knowing that they were still sending me money even when I had no intention of doing what they wanted me to do.

But that wasn't something I could bring myself to do.

"Too late. I've already chosen the first of the recipients for the day, and the process has begun," I said.

"So, you haven't given it all the way yet? You can stop now. Keep some of it for yourself. That way you can feel good *and* have money to use."

"I totally hear your suggestion, but I'm going to have to pass. I don't want any reason for them to think I need them or their money to get by. They love thinking I can't possibly survive without them, or that I'm going to crash and burn. I have no intention of failing, and I don't want them to think for a second they made any contribution to me making it on my own," I said.

"And you're sure you don't need it? That you're doing alright on your own?" Samantha asked.

"I don't have the lifestyle I used to. I'm not going to pretend that. But I make really good tips at the bar, and I can afford to live without their money. I don't need to have that life anymore," I said. "I'm comfortable how I am now."

Samantha let out a heavy sigh, and I could almost see her nodding. "I sometimes wish I could be free of that life, too."

"Really?" I asked.

I was a little shocked. I knew Samantha longed for a more carefree life sometimes, and that she felt like she might have missed out a bit by jumping right into marriage and motherhood rather than spending some time by herself when she was younger. But I also knew she enjoyed the money and the luxury that life afforded her. It was surprising to hear her sounding so wistful about not having it.

"Yeah. I'm tired of all the stuffy parties I have to attend all the time. I'm tired of having to limit myself to one glass of wine at those parties because my husband doesn't want me to get out of control," she said.

"Well, maybe he has a point there, Samantha. You know how you can be," I said with a hint of a laugh.

"Sure I do," she said. "And I don't have any intention of getting like that in front of his work people or the society crowd. But I'd like the opportunity to, you know? I'd like to feel that sense of freedom like if I wanted to drink myself silly and do a dance on the copy machine, I could."

"Do copy machines still exist?" I asked.

"Yeah," she said. "I mean... I think they do." We both fell silent as we contemplated the potential extinction of office equipment. Suddenly, she snapped out of it. "Anyway, I just sometimes feel like I'm being slowly crushed. Like those parties and the people and the rules and everything are coming at me from all the different angles and just gradually smooshing me into something totally unrecognizable."

"Are you thinking about leaving him?" I asked.

She let out another sigh.

"I can't. I love my children. And I really love my husband, too. I genuinely do. And the kids need their daddy. We need to be together as a family. It's just a lot sometimes," Samantha said.

I pulled up the next individual campaign I decided to donate to and started inputting my payment information.

Shaking my head, I switched ears to take some of the strain off that side of my neck. "I can't even imagine being married with two children. Of course, I spent a lot of the last five years dating a guy I hated, so that might be coloring that conviction a bit."

Samantha let out a dry puff of laughter. "Maybe. Speaking of which, though. I ran into Ethan the other day."

"You did?" I asked.

Just the thought of him getting anywhere near my best friend made my muscles tighten and my skin crawl. As much as I would like to think Ethan as a human being had some kind of control over himself and wouldn't do anything horrible just to get my attention, that was just my wishful thoughts at play. In reality, I knew he wasn't above going through someone else to get to me, and I worried that was exactly what he was preparing to do.

"Yeah," Samantha said. "It was actually pretty awkward because we were both standing in line at Starbucks and noticed each other. We couldn't just pretend we didn't recognize each other, so we talked a little. He didn't waste any time at all. He immediately asked if I knew where you went and if I knew when you were going to be coming back."

"What did you tell him?" I asked, nervous about what that might mean.

"I told him I hadn't talked to you," she said. "I said you dropped everyone back home and went off the grid."

"Thank you," I said, feeling relieved. "I shouldn't be encouraging you to lie, but that makes feel much better."

"I'm just so glad you got away from that guy. I couldn't stand him from the very beginning," she said.

"I know you couldn't," I said. "You made it pretty obvious. I just didn't see the same thing you did."

"And now?"

"And now I'm really happy I got away from him, too," I admitted.

That evening I went to the bar and was glad to see Jordan was working the shift with me. I smiled at him as I walked through the back door. He smiled back, and my heart fluttered in my chest.

"How are you doing today?" he asked when I got closer.

"Doing pretty good. How about you?" I asked as I tied my apron into place.

"Can't complain."

We spent the rest of the night flirting, our banter sometimes leaving me breathless. It had been a long time since I enjoyed talking to somebody as much as I enjoyed talking to Jordan, or since someone had been able to keep up with me and even best me the way he did. By the middle of the shift,

I wasn't even thinking about the deposit anymore. I was just thinking about this life I was building and how my conversation with Samantha only made me happier and more grateful for what I had.

7

JORDAN

It was almost time to head in to work, but Matt and I had already made plans to grab food somewhere else before the shift. That meant driving to whatever godforsaken place he picked this time. Between the avocado-based sandwiches and kale ice creams, I wasn't entirely sure I could take much more of Matt's food adventures, but I was lucky enough to have been born with an iron stomach. As I drove up to the address Matt had texted me, I was relieved to see it was just a sandwich shop. A hipster sandwich shop, but a sandwich shop that had a big picture of bacon on the front window.

At least it wasn't vegan.

I parked and got out, making sure at least three times that I hadn't left the phone or keys inside the car before locking and shutting it. I was finding myself doing that more and more these days, and I wondered if that was because I'd taken too many shots to the head as a kid or if it was just getting old. Older. Not old yet.

Satisfied that I had everything, I shut the door and went inside, finding Matt already at a table. He looked down at his watch and then to me as if to indicate that I was running well behind schedule, even though I knew I was ten minutes early. I raised my eyebrows and shrugged anyway. He looked upset, and there was no reason to agitate him and make him mad at me. I had a feeling I knew what was bugging him, and it wasn't my imaginary tardiness.

"'Bout time," he said.

"Yeah, yeah," I said. "You order yet?"

"Was just about to. They have amazing sweet potato fries here," he said.

"The buffalo chicken and bacon sandwich looks pretty g—" I began.

"Can you believe it," Matt said, cutting me off, "like our lives don't even matter?"

"Oh," I said. "So, you're upset about the suggestion?"

"It didn't bug you?" I shrugged but my expression gave away a bit more than I intended. "So it did, then."

"I guess, a little, if I'm being honest," I admitted.

"See? I'm not crazy, then," he said as the waitress came up. His ranting paused for a few moments while we made our orders, but as soon as she walked away, he was leaning across the table again, overdramatic fury in his voice. "It's absolutely ridiculous that he thinks he can just tell us we have to pack up and move."

"Well, he didn't," I said. "It's all just talk right now. Besides, I get it."

"What?" Matt asked, his jaw dropping as if I were siding with the literal devil.

"We don't have families, Matt," I said diplomatically. "If we moved to Portland, it would just be the two of us. We could even go in on a place together and save some cash. For us it would be an adventure and a chance to get out in a new town, meet some new people. For them, it would be a whole rigmarole."

"A what?"

"A hassle. A bother. A damn inconvenience. They have kids now, Matt. We don't. We could make something out of that place, you and me, and maybe find people to settle down with ourselves in a city where we don't know every damn body."

"I cannot believe I'm hearing this from you," he said, taking a big gulp of his ice water and looking away while shaking his head. "Judas. I'm sitting with Judas."

"Come on," I said. "You're getting yourself all worked up over nothing anyway. It's all just talk so far."

The food came, and our conversation paused again. Matt seemed to calm a bit in the silence, and when the waitress walked away, we dug into our food without speaking for a few moments.

"Talk or not, it's just rude," he said finally.

"Matt, are you ready to go find somebody and settle down right now?" I asked pointedly. He cocked an eyebrow at me and then laughed mirthlessly.

"No," he said. "I don't think that kind of life is for me. Could you imagine me being a dad?" Matt shuddered in his seat, and I laughed.

"I don't think you'd be too bad at it," I admitted. "Just try to remember not to shake the baby."

"I don't think so," Matt said. "I'm not ready for all that insanity. I can't even stick with one person too long before I get ants in my pants, you know?"

"What about that girl from a few weeks ago?" I asked. "The local girl?"

"Her?" he asked, waving me away as he took a bite of his sandwich. "Soon as it started getting serious, I bailed. She was doing all that clingy shit like making my bed and suggesting we stay in and have dinner 'at home.'"

"You mean, she was being a normal human being who was trying to take care of someone she liked?" I asked. "The gall of her."

Matt snickered. "Shut up," he said.

I'd seen him with the girl several times. Each time I did, he looked like he was head over heels for her, a little lovesick puppy. Then she up and disappeared, and Matt had been surly ever since. Not that I was going to say any of that out loud, at least anywhere he could hear me. But Matt was a whole lot closer to a domesticated man than he thought he was, and probably a whole lot closer than me. At least he had someone to pine over that might actually turn into something.

We finished our lunches and sat there for a few minutes talking about sports before noticing the time. If we got a move on, we could get there a little early, which would make our day easier. That night was a college-heavy night, which meant the more we had everything in place, the less insane things could get. College kids could be rowdy, but they could also be the biggest spenders. To be young, dumb, and full of expendable cash again, I supposed.

Matt left first while I settled the bill. I figured he needed a little pick-me-up and told him he could get our drinks the first night in Portland if we ended up there. He snickered, but it worked. A lunch tab at a sandwich shop was a small price to pay to quell some of his bitching. He was a good kid and a damn fine brother, but the difference in age and experience meant sometimes I had a little less tolerance for his dramatics. Not that I had a whole lot of tolerance for anyone's dramatics, but Matt was around me more often.

By the time I got to work, Matt was already halfway through condiment prep and Mason and Tyler had the rest of the place ready to rock. I grinned, thinking it would be nice to get through a shift where all I had to do was keep the trains running on time and kindly quiet any rebellion among the peanut gallery. It wasn't a job I did proper, but keeping the peace had kind of fallen on my shoulders on nights I was there. We employed bouncers on occasion for the big theme nights, but on a regular weekend, either Mason or I was on the floor, making sure things were going smoothly if we weren't otherwise occupied behind the bar.

The night started off pretty low-key. Mason handled the bar without needing much backup, despite the increasing flow of what looked like overgrown children filing into the bar. It was weird that I saw them that way, I knew, but anyone younger than twenty-five was completely indiscernible to me from a teenager. They all could be college seniors or high school sophomores, and I wouldn't know the difference without seeing some ID.

Then, like clockwork around midnight, two guys started having slurred words and their friends began to take sides. Words were said about girlfriends and mothers and a mixture of the two, and tables got moved unceremoniously. At that point, someone had to step in before the bloodshed, and I made eye contact with Mason and Tyler, who were both busy at that moment. I nodded and walked toward the group.

"Break it up," I said in my best authoritative voice. It seemed to work a bit as most of the crowd around them scattered, but the two would-be fighters were still staring at each other.

"Fuck off, old man," one of them said, and I smirked. *Old man.*

"Shut your face, child," I said. It was enough to get him to turn and look at me. His legs seemed to have trouble with the new distribution of weight, and he stumbled before righting the ship and leaning dangerously close to me for someone who was looking as aggressive as he was. He had one finger out, theoretically to waggle. Also, theoretically as a target for me to break.

"I'm no child," he said.

"You're drunk is what you are," I said. "Which means you are done at my bar, getting into a car that someone else is driving, and going somewhere to sleep it off."

"Give me three seconds and one good punch and I can make him sleep it off right here," the other one said. The chorus of juvenile "ooohs" accompanied as the kid I was talking to turned back to face him.

"I'll beat you the shit," he said, causing a moment of confusion among the entire group.

"Come on, then," the other one said, taking a boxer's stance.

"I said out, both of you," I said, pushing the kid on the shoulder. He seemed to go rather willingly, and both of them shuffled to the door.

"I'll whip your ass, too, Old Man," said the one who had not yet insulted me.

"Hard to whip my ass when you're unconscious, you little prick. Now move," I said, pushing him lightly on the back. He sprawled himself out on the concrete a moment later, unable to get his feet under him to move fast enough to catch up with the reality of gravity. Rolling over to his back, he flipped me the bird, and I shook my head. One of their friends came up and assured me they were getting rides—separate rides—and going home.

When they were all gone and out of the parking lot, I walked back inside. Mason and Tyler were behind the bar, and I walked up to it without saying anything about it. Tyler clapped me on the back, laughing.

"Son of a bitch," he said. "Maybe we ought to just have you be the bouncer from now on."

"Ha," I said without humor.

"It would save us a fortune on theme nights," Mason said. "Plus, you'd get a fancy black shirt out of the deal. Ava could make it glittery, too."

"Very funny," I said. "I don't think that sounds fun at all."

"Who said anything about being fun?" Mason said, and I laughed. After that, the night wasn't so bad.

8

———

HANNAH

The next day I couldn't stop thinking about Jordan and how he'd handled the guys the night before. I tried to focus on going through the list of tasks I made for myself that morning, including washing a couple of loads of laundry and vacuuming the carpets through my house. But no matter how hard I tried not to think about him, my mind kept wandering back over.

I knew he was strong and powerful from the moment I'd met him. Jordan just carried that presence about him. That, though, was a different side of him. He was incredible as he took control and asserted himself in a completely undeniable way without making himself seem like a jerk.

It didn't just impress me. It completely turned me on. My body had woken up and was buzzing with desire the longer I thought about him. Putting away the vacuum, I decided to take a shower, thinking it might cut through the fog.

Almost as soon as I got into the shower, I knew that wasn't going to work out. The hot stream of water rushed down my body, and the arousal only sparked more. I filled my hand with my favorite shower gel and built it into a rich lather that I rubbed across my skin.

I rinsed it off, running my hand through the water to wash the soap away. The thoughts of Jordan took over my mind. He was so sexy, and I couldn't resist the need for him anymore. Letting my hand trail down my belly, I dipped it between my thighs and drew my finger up through the folds of my center. The sensation sent a shiver through me, and I let out a breath.

Turning so I could lean back against the wall of the shower, I spread my feet further and focused the tips of my fingers directly on the taut, sensitive pearl at the apex. My other hand cupped my breast, kneading the flesh and twisting my fingers around my nipple to draw it up to a hard tip.

My hand heated my body up until I was shaking and wet, ready for more. I reached up and took the showerhead down from the holder. Even the sound of the massage setting turned me on more. I was enjoying the fantasies about Jordan rushing through my head and didn't want to rush through it too much. I wanted to savor it and the intense feelings I hadn't had in so long.

Directing the water on my shoulders, I let the rhythmic pulse of the water travel across my chest and down onto my stomach. Sweeping it back and forth across my hips made my body ache. Finally, I slid down onto the floor of the shower and propped my feet up so my thighs spread open. The water touched my clit, and I cried out with the powerful pleasure that surged through me.

Plunging two of my fingers deep inside me and envisioning Jordan filling me, I directed the water. Within seconds, it brought me to a shaking, gasping climax. It took me a few seconds to come down from the peak and let my fingers slide out of me. I sat there for a while longer, running the softer setting of the water over me as I relaxed.

When I finally peeled myself up off the floor, I finished my shower and got out. I felt a little shaky, but relaxed and relieved.

It was my day off from the bar, and I didn't want to just spend the entire day hanging around the house. All that was left on my to-do list was going to the grocery store and doing a bit of meal prep for the rest of the week. I could have headed straight there, but instead I packed up my art supplies and went back to the beach.

I got my easel set up and looked around for what I wanted to be the focus of this new painting. I was drawn to a small boat out in the water and the way the waves moved around it. The process of capturing that image started out slow as I sketched in the spacing, but soon I lost myself in mixing the paints and filling it in.

I didn't know how long I had been there painting when I noticed movement out of the corner of my eye. It wasn't just the people who were also out on the beach taking in the weather. This figure was moving directly toward me. I turned toward it and was surprised to see Jordan heading right for me. He was wearing a pair of baggy athletic shorts and a tank top that highlighted the chiseled muscles of his arms and shoulders and showed off the tattoos on his skin.

Biting into my bottom lip slightly, I turned back to my painting long enough to get myself under control. He was grinning at me when I looked back.

"Hey, Hannah," he said. "Fancy meeting you out here."

I laughed. "Because the beach is such a strange place for people to visit?"

He let out a laugh that sounded just slightly out of breath and combed his fingers back through his damp hair. "I guess you have a point. I just haven't seen you out here before."

"What are you up to?" I looked him up and down like I was trying to analyze the clues.

"Just jogging. I don't work out like I used to in the military, but I still like to keep myself in shape. Jogging out here clears my mind. I like being able to see the water," he said.

"It is beautiful," I agreed. "That's why I like to come out here to paint."

I gestured at the canvas, and Jordan leaned over to the side to get a better look at it.

"That's really good. I didn't realize you did all that," he said. "I mean, I remember you mentioning you did art, but you never said you were this talented."

The blush that came across my cheeks was unexpected, and I didn't know if it was completely because of the compliment or because of what I had just done in my shower. It was a little awkward having Jordan standing right there so close to me while my body was still feeling warm and tingly from the intense orgasm I'd experienced fantasizing about him.

"It's not a big deal," I said. "Painting is just a way for me to get my thoughts out and relax."

"I can understand that," he said. He looked up the beach, then back at me. "Would you want to pack all this up and go for a walk with me?"

I smiled and nodded. "I would like that."

Jordan helped me pack everything up, and we carried it to my car before heading back onto the beach. We walked along at a slow, casual pace for a few quiet seconds before I spoke again.

"Do you ever wish you were still in the service?" I asked.

Jordan shook his head, looking out over the water for a few seconds as he contemplated the question. "No. I was done. For a lot of my life, I thought the military was going to be my whole future. I figured I would go in for my initial term of service, then go career and spend the rest of my life serving. But it didn't work out that way. Not that I regret my time. It was definitely what I was supposed to do for that part of my life. It just didn't turn out to be what I was supposed to do for the rest of it."

"I definitely understand that. Expectations and thinking you know what's ahead of you, then realizing it's something different can be a lot," I said.

"It wasn't just the military that changed," he admitted. "I thought I had my whole life mapped out in front of me down to the detail. I was planning on getting married."

"Oh, wow."

He nodded. "Yeah. I know that's kind of a cliché with military guys. We want to have something good at home, something to look forward to when we got back, and something to keep pushing for when times got hard. I think that was her for me. Not that I realized that at the time. I thought she was perfect. We'd been together a long time, and I was sure we were going to get married, have some kids. The whole thing. Maybe I should have caught on when she never wanted to talk about being a military wife and talked about a future that didn't include the reality of moving around to different bases with me."

"What happened?" I asked, tenting my hand over my eyes to block the sun so I could look at him.

"I got a short leave that let me come home for a little bit. Nobody knew I was coming. It was supposed to be a surprise. And it definitely was that. When I got home, I found her cheating on me with one of my friends," Jordan said.

I cringed. "That's terrible. I'm sorry you went through that."

He nodded. "So am I. But at least it seems like I dodged a bullet in a way. Maybe if I hadn't found out, she would have kept up with it all and I would have ended up marrying her, and it would have been much worse down the line."

"That's a good way of looking at it," I said.

"How about you? Any skeletons in your closet?"

"You could say that. My parents decided they knew what was best for me and that they should have absolute control over my life. That included picking out who they wanted me to be with. They paired me up with this guy I've known basically forever. Ethan. According to them, he was an appropriate match for me and what they thought I should have in a husband. It didn't quite matter to them that I didn't feel the same way," I said.

"So, an arranged marriage situation?"

I laughed. "Not quite, but something like that. I didn't love him. Never. I'll admit I tried. Having couples kind of put together by parents wasn't so unusual in our circles, so I tried to see in him what they did and let the relationship develop. But it never did. Then I started to suspect he was about to propose, and I couldn't handle that. So, I left him."

I left out the big details about my relationship with Ethan. It felt far too soon to get into everything about the mental abuse and the controlling way he treated me. I didn't want to pour too much of that out to Jordan and scare him away. Besides, it wasn't something I talked about with anyone. Even Samantha only knew some of the truth. This just wasn't the time for me to put it all out there.

Instead, I focused on how nice it was to walk down the sand with Jordan and get to know each other better. I hoped the beach would just keep stretching on and we wouldn't have to stop.

9

JORDAN

Work seemed to fly by with Hannah there to talk to. Or more appropriately, to flirt with. I found myself smiling and laughing a lot more than usual when she was nearby and not busy with customers. I also found more and more reasons to get behind the bar and go shoulder to shoulder or hip to hip with her. Occasionally, she would knock one hip into me to move me out of the way for something, and I would do it back. The banter between us was silly and funny, and the customers seemed to like it, which made me happy, but I was enjoying it all too much.

Suddenly, I realized Mason was staring at me from across the bar, a smirk on his face while I was in the middle of another mock argument with Hannah. I could feel my skin get warm as I flushed, and I looked back into her gorgeous eyes. She was making a face at me, her nose and lips all scrunched up because of something I had said that made her fake angry at me. An overwhelming urge to grab her by her face and kiss her soft, supple lips was only held back by the heat from where I could sense Mason watching me.

Instead, I turned on my heel and walked away, shaking my finger above me. She laughed, and so did a few of the patrons, and I went into the back to get some air. I needed to get control of myself before I lost it.

Grabbing an ice water, I passed Tyler in the hallway, who nodded at me.

"Taking your break?" he asked.

"Not a full one," I said. "Just needed a drink of water and some air. It's pretty calm in there now."

"Warm tonight, isn't it?" Tyler asked, pulling at the front of his shirt.

"Yeah," I said, pretending that was the problem. "Maybe check the thermostat."

Tyler saluted with two fingers and walked away. I turned and headed through the door to the outside, taking a deep breath when I got into the fresh air.

I took a deep sip of the cold ice water and closed my eyes as I leaned my head on the bricks behind me. I didn't want to sit. Sitting meant complacency and rest, and I wasn't in the mood for rest. Just a break from the noise and the heat. And Hannah. I needed a break from Hannah before I said or did something really dumb.

My mind kept wandering back to the conversation we had on the beach the day before. She blew me away with how well-rounded she was as a person. At only twenty-eight, she seemed far more my speed than some of the other almost-thirty-year-olds who came into the bar on the regular. She was smart as a whip and creative and talented. She was insanely easy to talk to.

She was also stunning to look at. I couldn't get that part out of my head. People as gorgeous as her shouldn't be so damn interesting and funny and talented, too. It wasn't fair for the rest of humanity. No one should ever have to compare themselves to a knockout with a perfect figure, who was smarter than they were and more talented, too.

I took another sip of my water and sighed, staring into the middle distance. I had to get a grip on myself. She was an employee and a budding friend. Nothing more. I was nearly a decade older than she was and again, one of her bosses. It wasn't something that was feasible. She was new, and she was fun, and she was cool. Leaving it at that was where I needed to settle. A little more time and she'd just be another person I enjoyed hanging out with, like Luke or Ava.

Who was coming through the door. With Mason.

Fuck.

"Hey, guys," I said, "need me back in there?"

"No, no," Mason said, putting his palm up at me. "You're good. We thought we'd take a break for a second, too. Tyler and Hannah can handle the tiny crowd we have in there for a minute."

"Oh, well, I probably should get in there," I said, moving away from the wall.

"Can't stay away from Hannah for too long, eh?" Ava asked, taking a sip from her own water and feigning innocence.

"What? No," I said.

"Right," Mason said, looking at Ava and making some silent married-people connection that I didn't understand.

"What?" I asked.

"We just noticed how you really seemed to like her," Ava said innocently.

"She's nice to talk to," I said, sighing a little. "I enjoy our conversations. That's it. Besides, I know what you two are getting at, but I also know about the policy here about dating employees."

Mason and Ava laughed and looked at each other again. "Uhh," Mason began.

"Hush, you know that's different," I said. "You two are married."

"We weren't always married, remember?" Mason said.

"We started dating again when I came to work here," Ava said. "That policy doesn't matter if you actually are planning on trying to have a relationship."

"I barely know this girl," I said. "I think you two are getting ahead of yourselves. We clicked as friends. I like talking to her. Let's slow the train down."

"You can keep telling yourself that," Ava said, "but one day you'll figure out the truth."

"I just hope it's not too late," Mason said, putting his arm around Ava.

I rolled my eyes and went back into the bar, determined to give Hannah a little space and maybe calm things down for myself a little.

The next day, I got a text from Luke, responding to one I had sent him the night before. I wanted to meet him somewhere other than the gym or our places, so he suggested the same restaurant Matt had me meet him before. Glad I got to eat another plate of sweet potato fries, I headed that way.

"Hey, man, thanks for meeting me," I said as I approached the table. "Before anything else, I just wanted to apologize for how I acted at the gym. I shouldn't have gotten so upset with you, and I am sorry." I held out my hand, and Luke shook it instantly.

"No, stop," he said. "I am sorry for acting the way I was. I was a dick. You obviously really like this new girl, and I was being a frat boy about it. I'm sorry, dude."

I shook my head. "No worries," I said, sitting. "Let's just let it go, yeah?"

"Fine by me," Luke said, sitting down across from me. "So, tell me about this girl. I promise I won't be crude."

"She's just a friend," I said. "But she's really cool and easy to talk to, you know? Like, you know how you can have instant chemistry with someone? Where it's like you've known each other for a long time, but you have all these things to find out about them still? That's what it's like. She's comfortable to be around and to talk to, but she's also interesting and full of stories and life experiences."

"She sounds great," Luke said. "But if I may say so, as your best friend, I can tell you right now that you want more than just being friends. That's why I was making jokes. I didn't mean any disrespect—I was just ribbing you."

I didn't really have a response to that, instead just shaking my head and being thankful for the break in conversation when the waiter came by. I gave my order, and Luke gave his, but before he could walk away, Matt popped his head up behind me.

"Can I join you guys?" he asked.

"Christ, can you not surprise me like that?" I asked.

"My bad." He came around to sit beside Luke. "Hey, Luke, good to see you."

"You too, Matt. You come here often?" Luke asked.

"Came here just a few days back with Jordan," he said. "I had a hankering for their fries."

"So did I," I said. "I ordered a plate for the table."

"Awesome," Matt said, then made a separate sandwich order to the waiter, who was still hanging around. When he left, Matt turned to us. "So, what's shaking, guys?"

"Nothing much," Luke said. "Just chatting about life."

"Women?" Matt asked.

"Not for me," Luke said. "But I was talking with Jordan about this girl he's so hung up on."

"Hannah?" Matt asked.

"Ahh, so you know who it is, too," Luke said.

"Oh, for sure," Matt said. "Jordan's been all googly-eyed since she came to work with us. What did you say?"

"Nothing," I interjected. "It was a misunderstanding. Let's leave that be."

"Fine," Matt said sarcastically. "Best not to anger the beast. Did he tell you about tossing some kids out of the bar the other day?"

"As much as I love hearing these stories, no, he has not graced me with any of them recently," Luke said.

Matt went into a detailed description, with a few extra details I didn't remember happening at all, about the incident at the bar. I laughed at some of his exaggerations but didn't correct him.

"So, what do you think about this whole Portland thing?" Matt asked Luke. "I've had some time to think about it, and I want to know what you two think first."

"I think it would be fun for the both of you," Luke said. "It's only about an hour and a half away. I'm sure we could see each other about as often as we do now anyway. It wouldn't be any worse than when you were in the service."

"True," I said.

"Besides," Luke said, taking a sip of his drink, "more fish in the sea, right?" He grinned as he swallowed, and I rolled my eyes.

"I think he's right," Matt said, surprising me.

"What?" I asked.

"I think Luke's right. More fish in the sea. Adventure. Fun. All that stuff," he said.

"But what about the other day?" I asked. "You were so upset, I thought you were going to blow a gasket."

He waved me off and thanked the waiter as the fries

came to the table. Picking one up and shoving it into his mouth, he took a moment to let the heat out before chewing it and swallowing.

"That was then," he said. "This is now. It could be a lot of fun, and there is a whole town full of women neither one of us has had yet. Imagine the possibilities."

Again, I rolled my eyes and dug into the fries.

"Can we talk about literally anything else?" I asked.

HANNAH

I couldn't seem to get my brain on track a couple of days later. There wasn't anything in particular that was keeping me from focusing, nothing specific bothering me. It was just one of those days when it felt like I was a couple of steps behind myself and couldn't catch up. That left me scrambling to get ready for work.

My phone rang as I was doing my makeup, and my stomach sank a little bit. I worried I was even more behind than I thought I was and was now late for my shift. A glance at the clock sitting on my nightstand confirmed that wasn't the case. That was also when I realized I didn't know where my phone was.

Usually, I kept my phone within arm's reach or at least sitting on the charger. But it wasn't in either place. Just another example of my brain being jostled and out of sorts that morning. I could hear it ringing clearly, so obviously it wasn't too far away.

I could have just ignored it. I could have just let it ring, and Samantha could have left me a message. But there was that little voice in the back of my mind that said this could be the time there was an emergency.

I finally found my phone in the kitchen and snapped it up. It wasn't Samantha. In fact, I didn't recognize the number at all. Talking the phone against my ear, I made my way back to the bathroom attached to my bedroom to keep working on my makeup.

"Hello? This is Hannah."

"I miss you," a somewhat garbled voice said through the line.

It made me go still, an uncomfortable feeling shivering up my spine.

"Excuse me?"

"I miss you," the voice said again. "Hannah, why did you leave me?"

Ethan. I let out a sigh and shook my head as I leaned closer to the mirror so I could put on the last of my makeup. I needed to get this call over with as quickly as possible. Not just because I needed to get to work, but also because I had no interest in talking to him.

Especially considering he sounded drunk. The slurring of his words and the distinct whine in the back of his voice weren't unfamiliar to me. Unfortunately, I knew it all too well. It was in the middle of the afternoon, so Ethan sounding drunk would be about right.

"Hannah," he said again, the whine getting sharper. "Answer me."

Those last words had a bit more force behind them, like the anger was starting to creep into them. That was enough for me. I hung up and set my phone down on the counter to finish getting ready. Within seconds, he called me back. I rejected it, but he called again.

"How did you get my number, Ethan?" I demanded when I snatched the phone up from the counter.

"We're meant to be together, Hannah. You can't think that something like a new phone number is going to keep me away from you," he said.

Again, that was enough. I hung up again, and just as I expected him to, Ethan called me back instantly. I rejected the call and blocked his number. I didn't have time for this nonsense. He might have been able to find my number, but that didn't mean he knew where I was. I had a life here in Astoria now, and I wasn't going to let him mess it up.

After blocking his number, I managed to finish getting ready for work and was just grabbing my purse and keys when my phone alerted that I got a new email. I read it as I headed toward my car. Predictably, it was from Ethan. I could almost hear the slurring in the words as I read them. But it wasn't the same whininess. He was getting angry. The message told me he just wanted to talk, and I needed to stop behaving like a child.

That was far from the first time I'd heard him say that to me. Accusing me of acting like a child and telling me I needed to grow up was a favorite go-to of his. Anytime I didn't go along with what he wanted or tried to demand he show me more respect, he told me I was acting like a child and needed to grow up. As if there was a level of maturity I needed to reach when I would come to the conclusion that being mistreated was acceptable, and that there was no such thing as an actual happy relationship.

I didn't bother to respond. There was nothing for me to say to him, and I didn't want to give him the satisfaction of any more of my attention. Sitting in my car, I blocked his email address, then tossed my phone onto the passenger seat and drove to work. On the way, I wondered if I should change my phone number and email address again.

Going through all that was so much of a hassle, and it made me angry and feel even more out of sorts to think about having to do it all again because of Ethan. I was still fuming when I got to The Hollow and stomped up to the bar. Ava was standing behind it, and she stopped what she was doing to look at me.

"You okay?" she asked.

"It's just one of those days," I told her.

"Don't I know it." She shook her head as she went back to cleaning the glasses. "Our little one is sick, so Mason is home taking care of him. This place was a mess when I got here, and there were all kinds of things wrong, and I had to fire the guy who had been coming in to help behind the bar."

"Let's just blow it all off and run for the border," I suggested.

Ava laughed. "Sounds like a plan. Canada it is." That brought a little bit of a laugh, and she smiled at me. "So, what's going on with you? Did something happen?"

"My ex called me," I said. "I haven't talked to him since I left and moved here. He was drunk and obnoxious, which is kind of him most of the time, but it really got to me. Now I have to change my phone number and email address again. Which seriously pisses me off. I know that sounds ridiculous. But I don't even know how he got them, and I had to go through all that when I moved here.

"It's not even the phone number that bothers me that much. It's not like I hand that out to a lot of people anyway. It's the email address. I'm going to have to go to everything and change it. My bills. My landlord. My bank." I looked at

Ava and saw her staring at me, one eyebrow cocked up. I let out a sigh. "I sound like a crazy person right now, don't I?"

"I mean... a little. But I get it. It's justifiable crazy. It's not so much about the email address. It's about him coming back into your life and causing disruption."

I nodded, but before I could say anything else, the office door opened, and Matt came out. He was shaking his head.

"None of them are available," he said. "I called everybody."

"Damn it," Ava said, shaking her head. "Are you sure?"

"Yep."

"What's going on?" I asked.

"We're short two bartenders tonight, and it's going to be a busy night. We were trying to find one of the people who sometimes comes in to fill in, but there isn't anybody. Mason is home to take care of Robert, and Mom is sick too, so he can't come in. It's just a mess," Ava said.

"What's going on?" Jordan asked, coming through the door, and looking at us with a questioning expression.

Ava explained the situation, and Jordan pointed at me. "What about Hannah? I've been helping her behind the bar. Tonight would be a great chance for her to try everything out."

"I don't know," I said. "It's not like you've taught me everything, and I've definitely never done anything on a night that's going to be busy like tonight. I don't want to mess anything up."

"You can do it," Jordan said. "You've been doing great."

"Please help us out," Ava said. "It will be a disaster here if we are short two bartenders all night. I'll be right here with you, and Jordan is working behind the bar tonight, too."

They were all looking at me hopefully, and I finally

relented. "Alright. I'll try. But I can't promise anything. Honestly, it might be a disaster anyway."

Ava laughed. "It's going to be fine. I know it."

It wasn't fine. At least, it didn't start that way. I was frazzled, distracted, and nervous, and the first several attempts at making drinks were complete failures. But finally, Jordan stepped in and reminded me of everything he'd already taught me. I relaxed and settled into the rhythm of the night, deciding to just let myself enjoy it rather than worrying so much about it.

It turned out to be a really fun shift that let me push Ethan out of my head and get my thoughts back to this life rather than the one I'd left behind. By the end of the night, I had a pocket stuffed with tips that far outweighed even my serving tips, and Ava was already asking me to be backup for the bar more often. I left smiling and felt much better heading back home than I had on the way to work.

JORDAN

Tom was in town again, so that meant dinner at Mom's. I was starting to get a little tired of the "Tom is here, that means everyone has to drop everything" routine, but at the same time it wasn't like I had anything to drop. It was more just jealousy that he had essentially done everything he wanted to do, had a wife and a kid, and was super successful, and I was just a jarhead who worked in the family bar. At least that's how I let myself see it when I was in the process of beating myself up.

Still, seeing Mom and all my brothers was always a good thing, and Tom couldn't help that I chose the military when he chose to go be great at whatever it was he did. I was still unsure of all that. Computers and video games were never really my thing, so when he started talking, I tended to tune out. It wasn't that it wasn't cool, I just wasn't into it.

When I got there, I had to find somewhere to park and noted that it was becoming a bigger hassle to do so. As the family grew, so did the size of the cars and the number of them too. Ava and Mason often drove separately since one of them would be at the bar pretty often. This time around Becca and Tyler had also seemingly come separately. Combined with Tom's minivan that he drove in from his adventures on the coast after he and his wife popped out a kid, and the driveway and street in front of the house were packed.

As I stepped inside, nostalgia hit me in the gut pretty hard. The house always had the same smell to it, a warm, freshly baked food smell. It made my stomach rumble and my heart squeeze at the same time. Instinctively, I looked to the left, where the living room was and where Dad would sit in his easy chair reading a book or watching TV for years and years. That chair was empty now. It looked like it did the last time Dad had sat in it, a book he'd never finished sitting open on the arm. Mom had never had the heart to move it. She only moved the glass of water that he'd mostly finished a few weeks ago. She was a mess all day after cleaning that glass.

It was good to see Mom happy, though. She was bouncing between the kitchen and the dining room, talking in that overly loud way she always did when she got overwhelmed with joy. Seeing all her boys and their partners and kids did that for her. The way her mouth curved up in an ever-rising smile with each son that walked through the door lifted my own heart, and when she saw me and wrapped me in a hug, it was like eating from an endless bowl of love.

"Oh, my boy, how are you today?" she asked while pushing my cheeks together and kissing my head. I had to lean down for her to do it, but I always did.

"I'm fine, Ma," I said. "How are you?"

"Tired," she said, "but good tired. I had a girls' night last night." She pursed her lips, and her eyebrows rose until the creases of her forehead looked like rivers running across her face. She seemed so pleased.

"Really? How was that?" I asked.

"Don't get her started," Mason said from behind me in the dining room.

"No, please, get her started," Ava said. Mason rolled his eyes and let his head fall back in what I assumed was mock frustration. Mom giggled.

"It got a little wild," she said, and I noticed most of my brothers laughing. Tom was in the corner of the room, and I gave him a short wave that he returned.

"Tell him where you went, Mom," Becca asked. Mom turned to her, and her cheeks went red. I knew part of it was her Becca calling her "Mom," but it was also because of whatever she had been up to. I cocked my head to one side.

"Yeah, Mom, where did you go?"

"The Banana Hammock," she said, covering her face with her hands.

"The what?" I asked.

"The male strip club up in Portland," Matt said.

"Oh God," I replied. "I shouldn't have asked."

"See?" Mason said, raising his hands over his head.

"I think it's great," Ava said. "You go, Mom."

"Mom?" I asked, laughing in spite of myself.

"It was all that Carrie's fault," she said, at least having the decency to feign embarrassment. "She drove us out there saying we were going somewhere with dancing. She didn't tell us it would be nearly naked men dancing *at* us!"

The rest of the room laughed heartily, and I sat down, listening to Mom as she tried to desperately explain how chaste and confused she had been inside the club that she had admittedly spent several hours in and had multiple cocktails at.

Considering she had multiple children, I was wary of how confused she actually could have been by it all, but I let her talk because it was hilarious to watch her try to talk her way out of it.

Eventually, she seemed to get to the point where she was too flustered to continue and made her way back into the kitchen. When she came back, she immediately launched into another conversation, signaling that our discussion of her lively night was over. Instead, she eyed both Matt and me with a desperately critical eye.

"So, do either of you have someone coming to join you tonight?" she asked leadingly.

"No, Mom," Matt said.

"Me either," I said.

"What about Hannah?" Ava blurted out, and then her eyes went wide, and she turned to look at Mason, who laughed loudly.

"Hey, yeah, what about Hannah?" Matt asked, turning on me.

"Judas," I said. "You talk about Judas and yet here you are."

"I prefer Brutus, but hey, whichever backstabber you want to go with," he said.

"Who is Hannah?" Mom asked.

I shook my head and looked back to Ava.

"Nicely done," I said quietly.

"Who is Hannah?" Mom repeated.

"She's just a girl we work with," I answered.

"Who you flirt with constantly," Ava added.

"She's adorable," Becca interjected, clearly helping to pile on and get Mom excited over a girl who I hadn't even asked on a date. "Really funny, really smart. I saw some paintings she's done, too. She's super talented."

"Well, how come I haven't heard about her, then?" Mom asked.

"Because he hasn't asked her out yet," Mason said. I wasn't sure whose side he was on, but he was grinning, so my guess was he was enjoying playing both sides and stirring the pot.

"Why not?" Tom asked from the corner of the room.

"Yeah, why not?" Ava asked.

I sighed. "Uh, because she's an employee," I said. There was an uproar in the room, and I held my hands out for silence. "Hold on, hold on! Seriously, she probably wouldn't go for it anyway. She just got out of a really bad relationship that she was deeply unhappy in. She's a friend, and she's fun to talk to, and yes, maybe we flirt some. But that's it."

"Ava," Mom said with the seriousness of a general "*set him up.*"

"That's not a good idea," I said uselessly to a room of cackling hyenas. Mom had spoken. Ava had her orders, and now all I could do was sit back and let it happen.

Dinner talk moved to Tom after that, and when dinner was finished, I decided to go outside for a breath of fresh air. A million thoughts were swirling through my mind, not the least of which was a combination of anxiety and excitement about whatever was going to happen with Hannah. As I got out onto the porch, a new beer in hand, I heard the door behind me. One by one, my brothers followed me out.

"Ahh, time for business talk?" I asked.

"Nothing formal," Tom said. "I just wanted to keep you guys informed. I know it sometimes seems like I make decisions and then expect things to happen, and I don't want you to feel that way."

"Fair," Matt said. He didn't dispute it, which Tom seemed to take in stride, but none of us said anything either.

In reality, we all kind of looked to Mason as the on-the-ground leader of our merry band of brothers. He ran the bar day to day with Ava. Tom owned it all, sure, and made some decisions that were his way or the highway, but after some initial saltiness, we had all pretty well settled on the hierarchy in the bar.

"Well, I wanted to see if three of you could head out to Portland for a week to check some places out. I've got my eye on a couple properties, and I thought Mason, you, Tyler, and Jordan should get out there and see what's going on," Tom said.

There was a momentary pause, and Matt and I exchanged a glance.

"I didn't think it was set in stone yet," I said.

"Well, it isn't," Tom admitted.

"But it is. If you're sending us out there to look at places, it means you are pretty set on doing this expansion."

"Are you against it?" he asked. I could see the wheels turning in his head. I always could. Tom was admittedly smarter than the rest of us. Mason was the kind that could make sure it all happened correctly and the trains ran on time. I was more the type that went along to get along, doing my part to make sure things went well. I did what was asked, and I did it competently until I found something better I wanted to do. If I ever found something better.

"Not against it," I said. "I just wasn't aware that it was an absolute thing. Just an idea was what I was told."

"Yeah, and if we're doing this, why am I not going to Portland to scope places out?" Matt asked.

"Good question," Mason added.

"Because Matt needs more experience running the day to day behind the bar," Tom said. "You both said you'd like him to get more time back there running things. This would be a way for him to do that, plus I don't know anyone else who would know exactly what we need in a location better than you, Mason."

I nodded. "That makes sense, I guess."

"Look, I know it's a big jump, and it feels like I might be pushing it a little," Tom said. "But this seems like a really great opportunity for us to grow from a business standpoint. I know I'm always reaching big, and it can be a little much, but if you guys aren't comfortable, I'll back off. This only works if we're all in this together."

Matt and I exchanged glances once again. I could see the wheels turning in his mind, too. Part of it was Tom's casual cockiness, but another part of it was the adventure. I was stuck here, spinning my wheels, and hadn't found myself something better to do. Not if Hannah wasn't an option.

Why not Portland?

HANNAH

The bar felt strangely empty when I got to work the next day. I already knew it was Jordan's night off. He and I compared schedules, and I had gotten familiar with the pattern of the nights he would be off when I would be working, and also the reverse. I liked knowing when I would see him for a shift and when I wouldn't. It was a bit strange for me to still get those butterflies when I knew I would be seeing him, especially since I was doing my best to think of him only as a friend.

But that night I knew he wasn't going to be there, and yet there was still an emptier feeling when I walked into The Hollow and looked around. The bar wasn't open yet, so there were no customers, and everything felt quiet.

Ava walked out of the kitchen and smiled at me as she took her place behind the bar. I walked over to her as I tied my apron around my waist and gave her a questioning look.

"What's up?" she asked.

"Where is everybody?" I asked. "It feels dead here. The parking lot is basically empty."

"Oh, yeah," she said. "I meant to call you to let you

know I might need you to jump behind the bar tonight, but you'll start with just serving tables. Tonight is Jordan's night off, and Mason and Tyler aren't here. So, we have Jesse in the kitchen with the sous chef, and I'll be behind the bar, but I'll also be acting manager."

"They all have the same night off?"

That sounded a little extreme, even for a non-theme night on a weekday.

"Not exactly," she said. "I mean, yeah, but not."

I laughed and reached over the bar to grab a cup and fill it with water from the soda fountain. "Thanks for clearing that right up for me."

Ava laughed. "Yeah, I'm good at that. What I meant is Jordan just has the night off. Mason and Tyler went with Tom to Portland on a business trip."

I was curious about what that could mean, but I didn't pry. As comfortable as I felt there and as much I was starting to think of these people as good friends, I was still the new girl in a lot of ways. And I was an employee, not a family member. That meant I wasn't privy to everything going on around the bar. If it was something I needed to know, they would tell me.

"That's somewhere I haven't visited yet," I said, transitioning away from what I felt like was becoming an awkward point in the conversation. "I think I need to plan a time to go and see what it's all about."

Ava nodded. "It's a neat city. Definitely growing."

I finished my water and hopped down from the stool to bring the cup into the kitchen to wash it. The sous chef and Jesse were deep in the trenches of preparing for the late-lunch and early dinner customers who would be coming in soon. It was burger night, which meant all the prep surfaces of the kitchen were covered with stacks of vegetables and sliced cheese ready to put on the burgers, as well as containers of the special sauces and condiments they created.

I paused for a minute to watch them and let them tell me about the new burger they were introducing that night. The sous chef let on that it was actually Tyler's recipe they were using, and they agreed he would be bummed to miss seeing the reaction from the customers. But they didn't want to wait to introduce it. The regular customers expected something new that night, and they didn't want to disappoint them.

I was nibbling on the corner of a slice of cheese they handed me when I walked back out to the front and found a woman sitting at the bar. It was confusing for a second considering the bar was still closed and I wasn't sure how she got in.

The way the woman was smiling at me from the bar, however, told me she was perfectly in place. She didn't feel uncomfortable and hadn't wandered in on a whim.

"Hi," she said as I approached. "I'm Amanda."

She extended her hand, and I shook it, nodding as I realized who she was.

"Tom's wife," I said.

She nodded. "That's right. We're in town for just a short time, so I thought I would come by and visit. You must be Hannah."

I was surprised she knew who I was, but I nodded. I expected her to elaborate on that a little, maybe tell me how she knew who I was before I even said anything. But she didn't. I could only assume it was because Ava or one of the brothers had mentioned they'd hired someone new.

Ava came out of the office and got a bright smile on her

face when she noticed Amanda. She waved at her as she headed for the door.

"Hey," she said. "I'll be over in just a second. I just need to open up. Have you ordered something to eat?"

"Not yet," Amanda said.

"Burger night," Ava said over her shoulder.

Amanda nodded. "I know. Anything new since the last time I was here?"

"There's something new tonight," Ava said.

"It sounds really good," I said. "I was just back there, and they were telling me about it. I might have gotten to sample some of the ingredients."

Amanda chuckled. "I noticed that when you came out of the kitchen."

"It was really good cheese," I laughed.

"Alright. You've convinced me. I'll have that."

"I'll go tell the kitchen," Ava said and headed back to tell the guys.

Amanda and I were chatting a little bit about the bar and how things were going since I'd started when Ava came back out. She sat down on the stool next to Amanda.

"I'm just going to sit here for like ten seconds while I still have a chance. Without so many of the guys here, I have a feeling we'll be hopping pretty soon," she said.

"Where's Jordan tonight? I didn't think he was going with the others," Amanda said.

"He didn't," Ava said. "Tonight's just his usual night off. I guess I could have called him in, but I try not to do that. He still really likes to keep to a schedule. There are a lot of times I can't avoid it, and he's really great about coming in for extra shifts and covering them when I need him to. But he likes having some predictability as much as possible. Maybe he'll get through that someday."

Amanda shrugged. "I don't know. I come from a pretty big military family. Some of them bounce back after they get out and can pretty much go back to a completely normal life. Some have little tics and habits pretty much forever after that."

"Well, I guess if he was going to hang on to anything, wanting to stay on the schedule isn't the worst way the military could have stuck with him."

"That's for sure," Amanda said.

I realized I was blushing just hearing them talk about Jordan. I tried to look away so neither of them would notice, but Ava caught my eye and smiled.

"Look at that blush," she said. "You know, Hannah, Jordan has the same kind of reaction when he talks about you."

Amanda grinned and nodded. "He does. I noticed that at dinner at mom's house last night. As soon as he started talking about the new hire here, he started getting all smiley. When he mentioned your name, he smiled even more. I don't think he blushed, but Jordan isn't exactly the blushing kind."

I couldn't help but think through all of my reactions with Jordan and how he made me feel. Now knowing he was reacting to me in the same way I was reacting to him kind of scared me. I needed to get away from the conversation.

Looking across the bar, I noticed a few of the tables had started to fill up. It was the perfect opportunity to slip away.

"I have to get to work," I said. "It was really nice to meet you."

Without waiting for Amanda to respond, I hurried over to the first table and greeted the customers. I recognized them as regulars, and that put me more at ease. For the next couple of hours, I kept my head down and focused on doing my job. It helped me keep my thoughts and fears under control.

During a lull in the night, Ava managed to corner me. I knew she had been trying to get my attention throughout the night, but I had managed to elude her by staying busy. Now I had a few seconds, and she was able to hold me off to the side.

"I'm sorry if I made you uncomfortable earlier, Hannah," she said. "I really didn't mean to. I've just never seen Jordan react to anyone the way he does to you. It makes me happy to see. And I thought that maybe if you were reacting the same way..."

I shook my head to stop her. I didn't even want to hear what she might be thinking after that.

"It's okay. I just got out of a pretty bad relationship right before I moved here. He was really controlling and could be pretty mean. It wasn't a good situation. I'm just not comfortable with the idea of getting into anything right at the moment."

Ava reached out and pulled me into a hug. "I had no idea. I'm sorry you went through that. If you ever need to talk, ever, I'm here for you. I want you to know that. And I'm being totally serious. This isn't just me saying it to sound nice. If you ever just need to vent or have a shoulder to cry on, you can always come to me."

I smiled. "Thank you. That means a lot to me. I am so glad I moved here."

"I am, too," Ava said. She glanced behind me to the bar, then looked at me again. "You know what? It's gotten pretty quiet out there. Why don't we grab something to eat and sit down for a bit? There's actually something I wanted to talk to you about."

I nodded, and we went to the kitchen to put in orders for our own burgers. They served them up to us, and Ava and I carried the plates piled high with golden French fries and the juicy burgers to a table in the back of the restaurant. It was one we usually kept reserved for members of the staff because it was out of the way.

"This looks absolutely delicious," I said. "I got to taste some of the elements of it, but I'm excited to try the whole thing."

We each took a bite, and it was as incredible as I expected it to be. After a few bites and nibbling down some of the fries, Ava took a sip of her drink and swallowed resolutely.

"Okay, so I wanted to see if you could give me some input. We need something really dynamic for the next theme night. The customer expectations are getting higher, and I want to do something that will really blow them out of the water. There are a lot of the themes that they love and are happy to do more than once, like the classic car night, but I don't want to get complacent. I want to make sure we're always surprising them and offering them something that keeps them interested. I usually come up with the themes, but I was hoping some new perspective might come up with something fresh," she said.

I was thrilled she would even consider asking me for my opinion and ideas. The theme nights were a huge part of the appeal of The Hollow. They had become their trademark, and that came with a lot of responsibility. As much attention and draw as a good theme night could have, a bad one could be disastrous. It was flattering she would trust me even so much as to ask for ideas.

We went back and forth for a few minutes talking about

the types of nights they'd had before I started working at the bar and some of the ideas she had been tossing around.

"You know what I absolutely loved in high school?" I asked after giving a couple of suggestions. "Gatsby. We read the book in high school, and I just got totally swept up in it. Then when I was in college, there was a homecoming dance that was themed to that era. Not necessarily the book, but the whole general idea. It wasn't particularly well done, but I remember thinking it could be amazing if it was done the right way."

Ava's eyes widened. "That is such an incredible idea. We've never done anything even close to like that. It would be totally unexpected and something brand-new for us to try. I think people would think it was amazing. I'm going to start looking into that and we'll get planning it."

I couldn't help but smile and feel a bit proud of myself. I couldn't believe something I'd thought of would be turned into one of the special events. It was just another bit of confirmation that I was where I was supposed to be and finally taking control to give myself the life I wanted and thought I might never get to have.

13

JORDAN

At the last minute, Tom changed his mind and decided to keep me in Astoria, which suited me just fine. Sending Mason and Tyler alone meant that only a few extra shifts needed to be covered, and Amanda pitched in for some of them while Matt and I took on the bulk of it. It meant long days and longer nights, but at least it kept me busy enough not to dwell too much on the possibility of the change or what was going on between Hannah and me. Not that there was anything to think about really since she and I were so busy we barely had time to talk the entire time. When we did, though, the sparks were just as bright as always.

As I was heading in for another night of work, though, things had changed. Mason had called me the night before, and things were going to start moving a lot faster. It was a surprise to hear just how confident he was on the phone, but on second thought, I shouldn't have been. Tom was sold on the idea, and while I was a little bitter that we all just went along with whatever he said, I had to admit he was usually spot-on with his assessments. He didn't miss when it came to business opportunities, and he hadn't as far back as when we sold peanuts for Scouts or made lemonade stands in the front yard. He was an entrepreneur at heart, and if he said something would work, he was likely right.

When I got to the bar, I immediately found Matt and pulled him aside with me as we did prep work and got the place ready for open.

"I got a call last night from Mason," I said.

"Oh yeah? Ava didn't say anything," Matt said.

"Yeah, he said he was only telling me. I don't know how much is set in stone yet, but it's enough that I figured I should give you a heads-up."

"What's going on?"

"Well, it looks like they found a place and are headed back today," I said.

"What? That fast?"

"Yeah. Mason loved the place, and Tyler thinks it has even more potential than here. They should be getting back pretty soon. Tom's going to handle all the paperwork from his office in San Francisco."

"Of course he is," Matt said, shaking his head. "Man, I can't believe it." He turned to me, cocking an eyebrow. "Who's going to run it, though?"

"Not me," we said in unison.

"Shit," Matt said.

"Yeah, shit," I said. "We have to figure this out, because it's only right."

"I agree." He sighed.

"What?"

"I dunno," he said, but I knew what he was thinking.

I was about to tell him he didn't have to do anything. He

was an adult, and he could tell Tom to shove it if he wanted to. That his life was his own, and he could stay here and be his own man and a thousand other things I had an inkling to tell Tom myself when my voice stopped in my throat. Hannah had just walked in, and my eyes went right to her like magnets.

She smiled when she saw me, and I felt my throat catch. Then she made her way toward me, and I had to look away so I didn't spend the entire time she was coming staring at the way her hips swayed back and forth. She was mesmerizing.

"Hey," she said casually as she approached us both. "How are you guys doing?"

"Good," I said.

"Great. Busy, though," Matt said. "Matter of fact, I need to get... back... to the back..."

With that, he abruptly turned on his heel and left. It wasn't the smoothest exit in the world, but Hannah didn't seem to notice. Or if she did, she didn't let on.

"Anything you need help with?" she asked.

"Nope, I got it," he said, exchanging a look at me over his shoulder. I could swear there was a smirk on his face.

"So," I said, without any real idea where I was going with it.

"So," she said back, echoing my silence.

"I heard you did some work behind the bar," I said, suddenly remembering talking to Ava.

"Yeah, I did," she said brightly. "It was a lot of fun. Very intimidating, but fun. You guys know so many cocktails."

"They do. I'm mostly the one who just knows about beer. Everything else is a bit fancy for me."

She laughed, and I felt my stomach clench. The sound

of her laughter was enough to drive me wild on its own. I wanted to hear that sound every day for the rest of my life.

"Did you hear about the Great Gatsby theme?" she asked.

"No, I didn't. I tend not to know what the theme is until I walk in and see it, usually."

"Oh, it's going to be awesome," she said. "I'm really excited about it. I think I get to wear a fancy dress, and everything's going to be black and white. It just sounds like so much fun."

"I hope they don't expect me to wear a tux."

She smiled wide, and I caught the faintest hint of her looking me up and down. "You'd look good in a tux," she said. "Or any suit really." Suddenly, she blushed and turned to the side. I had a feeling she was about to find as flimsy an excuse as Matt did to bolt, so I interjected with the first thing that came to mind.

"How's your painting going?" I asked clumsily. I tried to recover by stammering for a second. "I mean, you were saying something about some projects you were in the running for?"

"Oh, I guess I didn't tell you," she said. "The city actually reached out about doing a community mural painting on the side of the library. They're still waiting on final approval, but that should go through in the next couple of days. I'm super excited about that."

"I bet," I said. "Congratulations. That's an awesome opportunity, and I know you'll knock it out of the park."

"Thanks," she said, somewhat bashfully.

"If you need any help, let me know. I don't know if you want me walking around with a paintbrush in my hand, but I can help out in any other ways you might need."

"I'll keep that in mind," she said. "Thank you."

At that moment, Ava and Amanda walked in and took Hannah to the side to discuss the theme night. I listened in for a little bit but eventually kind of zoned out, going back into the prep work. We were apparently going to be raising some money for a local cause with drink specials, which I caught, but I wasn't part of any of that planning usually, so I went back to the tasks at hand.

The more I thought about Portland, the more I seemed to like the idea. Getting away to a new place would give me a chance to take a breath and figure out exactly what it was I wanted out of life. I was getting too old to just hang around like I had been. If I had some clue as to what it was I wanted, maybe I wouldn't be so hung up on a waitress I barely knew.

Then I turned around and we met eyes and I knew that wasn't true. I could be half a world away, back in the desert for that matter, and those eyes would haunt my dreams. She was gorgeous and she was funny, and she was smart. She was out of my league, for a million reasons. And she was just about the only reason I could think of why I would want to stay, and yet, she might just be enough.

I thought I heard my name, and I looked over to Amanda. She had been talking to me. She was looking at me somewhat expectantly, and I realized that while I had been meeting Hannah's gaze, I was being spoken to and missed it.

"Oh, sorry, what was that?" I asked.

Amanda and Ava got knowing grins on their faces and looked at each other. Hannah blushed again and looked straight up at the ceiling.

"I said that you and Hannah will be working that night. If that's alright with you," Ava said. "Then Amanda asked if you could handle the floor with Hannah so I could work behind the bar."

"Oh, yeah," I said. "I'd be okay with that. No problem."

"Good," Amanda said. "Hannah, what about you? Are you ready for a big theme night on the floor?"

"Yeah," she said, looking back at me and smiling. "I think I'd be fine with that, too."

14

HANNAH

I couldn't wait to get started on the mural. I took some time to sketch out some ideas and come up with a few things I might want to do. I wouldn't be able to come up with anything specific or plan out all of the details until I finalized my idea, but having a few basic plans let me start to visualize what I might be able to do.

After a few days of preparing and planning, I packed everything up and headed for the library. Just drawing things out in my sketchbook was a good way to start formulating my ideas. But it didn't compare to being right there where the mural would actually be and visualizing the scope. It was entirely possible I was coming up with ideas that wouldn't properly fill the space, or that wouldn't feel right when it was actually in place. I needed to really see it.

That afternoon found me sitting on a small grassy hill to the side of the library, staring at the wall I would be painting. My sketchbook was in my lap, and I kept flipping back and forth to look at my different ideas and try to figure out which one was the most promising.

Beside me, I had books I borrowed from the library

spread open to images of the town throughout history. I wanted to try to incorporate some distinct local images and make sure the mural was unique and special to Astoria. It wouldn't be as meaningful if it could fit in on any library anywhere in the country.

I was so invested in what I was doing I barely noticed someone calling my name. Finally, it broke through my thoughts, and I looked up to see Becca coming toward me. I was happy to see her and lit up even more when I noticed she was holding her little boy on her hip. Climbing up off the ground, I brushed my pants to get any errant grass off my jeans and smiled at her.

"Hi, Becca," I said. "It's good to see you."

"Hey, Hannah." She looked at her son and bounced him a little bit. "Can you say hi to Miss Hannah?"

The chubby-faced baby smiled and tucked his head into the curve of his mother's neck. I was instantly charmed and couldn't help the happy giggle that bubbled up. Becca turned her head to kiss his cheek and give him a nuzzle.

"He's adorable," I said.

"Thank you. I'm pretty partial to him." She looked at me, and her eyes wandered over to my art supplies and the books splayed out on the ground. "What are you up to?"

"I am actually painting a mural for the library," I said. "I'm here trying to finalize what direction I want to go in and really get the plans going so it can get underway as soon as possible."

"That's awesome. I love this library. I always have. Now that I have my little buddy, I get to spend even more time here. He really enjoys listening to the stories." The little boy started squirming in her arms, and she eventually put him down on his feet. "And playing outside doesn't hurt."

He took off running, and I laughed. "I can see that."

"Tell me more about this mural," she said. "I'm really excited for you. And I'm excited to see something new here at the library. A mural is the perfect idea to liven it up a little bit more. Maybe get more people visiting again. It's not like nobody comes or it's at risk of shutting down or anything. But I know a lot of people nowadays attend to read on their tablets or computers, so they don't spend as much time at libraries. It would be great to revitalize it and get more people interested in spending time here and the community programs and everything."

"I love that idea. It's so nice to think about children having a place to go where they can learn and feel safe. I want the mural to really celebrate the community and the town. I want people to see it and feel proud to be here in Astoria, and want to be a part of it," I said.

"I didn't even realize you were an artist. Have you been doing it professionally for long?" Becca asked.

I shook my head. "Oh, I'm not really a professional. It's just something I love. And I'm not even being paid for this. Not that I care. I'm just really excited they asked me to do it."

"Do you have any plans?"

"I have some sketches. You want to see them?"

Becca nodded enthusiastically. "Absolutely."

We walked back over to where I was sitting and dropped down into the grass. The little boy was still running around like wild. Watching him made me laugh. He had so much energy and enthusiasm, like he was thrilled just to be out and able to run in circles. But he never drifted too far away from his mother. Every now and then, he would look over and check to make sure she was close by.

I picked up my sketchbook and turned to the first of the ideas I sketched out. I held it out to her and pointed out some of the details. She nodded and I moved on to the next one. When I got through all the sketches, I took the book into my lap and grabbed one of my pencils so I could do a very quick mockup of the idea I had that combined some of the features from other ideas.

Becca grinned and nodded. "That looks so good. I love that." She looked at the wall in front of her and waved a hand like she was displaying the whole brick expanse. "I can see it up there. It'll be so amazing."

We talked for a little longer about the mural, and then I set the sketchbook aside and we just talked while her son played and ran in the warm sun. It felt good to be there with her and just feel like we were hanging out. Having genuine friends here meant the world to me, and I was really feeling like that was happening for me with not only these women, but also Jordan.

That got me thinking about the conversation between Ava and Amanda again, and my brain was still churning by the time I got to the bar that afternoon for work. Jordan was already there, and I felt a little ripple in my belly when I saw him.

I put my stuff away and went up to the bar, but before Jordan and I could start talking, Ava came out of the office. She looked relieved to see me.

"Oh, Hannah. Good, you're here. I wanted a chance to talk to you before the night really gets started. Jordan, you're going to want to hear this, too," she said.

My stomach dropped, and a rush of heat tingled up the back of my neck. She couldn't possibly be about to put everything out in the open, could she? Especially not after the talk we had after everything, she wouldn't just lay it all out and force us to talk about the way we were acting about each other.

"Okay," I said, hoping my voice didn't sound anywhere near as nervous as I felt.

"I've been working on the Gatsby-themed night and, like I told you, it's pretty much all finished. But I would really like for you to help with the final details considering it was your idea."

"Oh," I said, the word coming out of me in a rush of breath. "Okay. I can do that."

"Great. Now, here's the thing. I have it set for Saturday night."

"Saturday?" Jordan and I both asked, shocked to find out such an elaborate event was set to go on in less than a week.

Ava nodded, holding up a hand as if to try to stop our reaction so she could explain. "I know. It's soon. I didn't intend for it to be that soon, but I pushed it up earlier because of some other developments. Hannah, I told you about the guys going to Portland for that business trip."

"Yeah," I said, nodding.

"They went because Tom wants to open a new location there. With the success of The Hollow here, he wants to spread out and see if it can grow even more. Everything is happening pretty fast. They were just going on a research trip to see if they thought it was a viable option. But they found a location that was perfect, and Tom just filed the paperwork for it. The Gatsby theme night is going to act as the announcement and a marketing event for the new bar," Ava said.

I was stunned. That really was all happening fast. The idea of putting together the theme night in just a few days was intimidating enough. Now I was also thinking about the new bar in Portland and what that might mean. It was exciting to think about introducing the idea to the customers and watching the new spot grow from the ground up. But it was also a major responsibility.

Now it wasn't just the theme or customers having fun I was thinking about. Pulling off this night would mean a dynamic announcement of the impending second location and building up hype for customers to want to visit.

Ava walked away, and I turned to Jordan to gauge his reaction. He was staring into the middle distance like the thought was totally overwhelming him as well.

"It's a lot," I said. He didn't respond, and I leaned a little closer. "You okay?"

He looked at me. "I have no idea what I'm supposed to wear to something like this."

I laughed. "That is easily fixable. When I was roaming around downtown, I noticed a costume shop. It might be the perfect place to find something that will work for a Gatsby night. I'd love to help you pick out your outfit if you'd like me to."

Jordan grinned, making the butterflies swell again and ticking my heart rate up a bit. "It's a plan."

"Perfect," I said.

"I'll pick you up tomorrow afternoon."

15

JORDAN

Being nervous was stupid, and I knew that. It wasn't a date, it wasn't a sign of some relationship goal being met, it wasn't anything like that. It was simply two friends meeting up, hanging out, and enjoying each other's company. And yet, I felt nervous anyway. Also excited. Extraordinarily excited. The more time I spent with her, the more time I *wanted* to spend with her. She was the only person in my life, sans maybe Luke, who got my wheels moving faster in my brain. It was like she made me smarter just by talking to her. More creative, too. The more I was around her infectious energy, the more I felt like pitching in and helping with the more creative aspects of the job.

Getting to know her was becoming one of my favorite aspects of going to work. Every time we spent any time together, I got to know a little bit more about what made her tick. What her past was like before she showed up in our little bar. Who she was when she went home and took off her waitress shoes and put on her fuzzy slippers. Of course, thinking about what she took off and what she did or did not put on afterward was a thought process that I also enjoyed having, though I felt bad about it. I actively tried to avoid it, in fact, but when I was home, alone, in the dark wasteland between awake and asleep where the nightmares often reared their head, I could think about her and her bare feet slipping into fuzzy slippers and what else she might wear. The nightmares would usually subside then.

I pulled up to the restaurant near her place that she told me to pick her up and got out. I figured she was either grabbing lunch to bring with us or had already eaten, but she was standing by the door when I got there, menu in hand. I smiled wide when we made eye contact and jogged up to her.

"Hey, are you going to order something for the road?" I asked.

"I was actually thinking we could grab lunch here before we left if you hadn't eaten," she said. It was casual, something simple that friends did all the time. But I couldn't shake the significance of it. She was asking me to eat with her. All my arguments about this not being a date were slowly leaking away.

"Sure," I said. "I am starving actually." I found myself surprised to realize I actually was. Knowing the plan for the day, I had somehow not bothered to remember to eat. That was big for me. Years of military life had me eating at the same time every day, like clockwork. Yet, that morning I had my cup of coffee and had just plain forgotten to eat with it. My head was too far in the clouds.

"Cool," she said, grinning and turning back to the door. I reached ahead of it and grabbed it, pulling it open for her. "Thanks." There was a hint of a giggle in her voice, like my chivalry was silly but appreciated.

We walked in and grabbed a booth near the window. Hannah lived just off one of the main roads in Astoria, and the scenery was fun to watch. People were walking by, window-shopping and going about their day. I could see inside some of their bags as they passed, could read some of their names on the sides of the cups of coffee they clutched so desperately, too. I could learn so much about them without them ever even knowing I existed.

But I wasn't interested in them. Not with Hannah sitting across from me in the booth, kicking her legs occasionally as she read through the menu. She made a sound as she contemplated various dishes, and I realized I hadn't looked at my menu at all. Hopefully, it wasn't too obvious.

I picked the first thing that sounded decent and not too heavy, and when the waiter came, we made our orders. Hannah opted for a sandwich that was as impressively named as it was described in the menu. I went with a boring salad. It was like a cliché movie date with the roles reversed.

"The Balrog?" I asked.

"From *Lord of the Rings*," she said, as if that should mean anything.

"I read that in high school. Gandalf and a ring. That's all I remember."

"Didn't you see the movies?"

"I was busy in boot camp by the time the first one came out, I think. I missed the rest of them, too," I said.

"Well, you are going to have to watch them eventually. And read the books, too," she said authoritatively. For some reason I had no problem taking orders on what to read when they came out of her mouth.

"I think I might," I said. "Still, what's a Balrog?"

"Giant, powerful monster. It fits with the amount of bacon on the sandwich. I've only been here a few times, but I challenged myself to get that one day, and I figured with a big strong guy like you around, even if I can't finish it, and I won't, someone else could," she said. "Especially when said someone is getting a salad of all things."

"Fair," I said. "I'm watching my figure."

That got a laugh out of her, and I nearly died at the sound. Lunch went far too fast, and before we knew it, we realized we needed to head to the costume shop, or we wouldn't have any time to try costumes on. She was deadly serious about getting something perfect for the night, and that meant having enough time to try on whatever her heart desired. I had zero issue with being the eyes that evaluated her in various pieces of clothing, but I knew I was going to be terrible at it. I was fairly certain she would look good in anything.

Or nothing.

Especially nothing.

With lunch packed up in a plastic container in a paper bag in the passenger's seat of the car, we made it to the costume shop with a couple of hours left before they closed. It was an old place, having been there for years before I was born. Every high school play and dance studio for miles around routed people to it to get their costumes of various types, and Halloween was made special by some elaborate pieces they loaned out to regulars.

"Okay, so we are going for Great Gatsby, yes?" the lady at the counter said. She wasn't the owner, I knew that, but she had worked there since they opened. The owner was an eccentric older woman who also ran the community theater and was often seen wearing sparkly boas downtown. This lady, however, had a plump and cheerful look that was decidedly less dramatic and more motherly.

"Yes," Hannah said. "We work at the bar that's doing the theming. Ava said you would know about it."

"Oh, Ava," she said sweetly. I saw her name tag read

"Grams" which I assumed was a nickname and not at all something I should blurt out to get her attention. "She's so sweet. She lets me know when you guys do those theme nights and always sends me so much business. I'm surprised you didn't come earlier. Some of the regular costumers have already wiped out most of my flapper costumes."

Hannah looked over her shoulder at me, grinning widely. She was loving this. I was loving watching her love this. As Grams led us deep into rows and rows of costumes, we made it to an area with a million dresses that looked like they were ripped from different eras of glamor. Hannah disappeared into them while I looked on.

"And for you," Grams said, coming up to me, "we will need to find something suitable for a man of grace and class, of course. Thankfully, men's fashion hasn't changed terribly much in the last hundred years, so it should be rather simple."

With that, I was whisked away to an area of the store with tails tuxedos and the like. I noticed a few of the tuxedos had Velcro along the sides to be ripped away and decided not to ask too many questions. Instead, I gathered up a few items that seemed appropriate and a few others I picked solely to make Hannah laugh and went to the changing area.

For the next hour or so, we took turns trying on costumes to increasing hilarity. I was rather fond of a steampunk train conductor outfit I put together but was told that it was wildly inappropriate for the party. Still, it got a smile out of Hannah that made my heart jump up and down in my chest, so it was worth it.

Eventually, Hannah came out in a gold dress that rose high on one side and fell down to her ankles on the other. It was sleek and sexy and showed a little of her ample cleavage, and though she looked a little embarrassed when she walked out, I was floored by her.

"That's it," I said. "That's the one."

"I can't," she said. "It's too much."

"I would argue if anything it's not enough," Grams quipped behind me. "But you look fantastic in it."

Hannah looked like she was on the verge of tears, and I stood up instinctively and went to her.

"What's wrong? Are you okay?"

"I just..." she began, wiping a tear from the corner of her eye. "I feel pretty in this, I do. It's just I could never show this much of myself off before."

"What?" I asked. "I mean, yeah, you look great, but this is nothing compared to some of the stuff the regulars wear in, much less the costumes."

"I know," she said. "Ethan was just so controlling about what I wore. I could never show anything, not even my shoulders. He said I was advertising myself. That it showed I didn't respect him."

"That's ridiculous."

"He was just so... manipulative," she said. "He would tell me I would look like a whore if my shorts were too short, or if I wore a bra too dark that you could see the strap through the shirt or something. But then he would see these women on TV and say I could look like them. If I tried."

I hated hearing her talk about her ex. Not because he was her ex, but because of how he treated her. The way she spoke about him, he seemed like the kind of guy that I would have no time for. The type of guy who would make comments like Luke made but mean them. The kind of guy who didn't say things for shock value or to rib his friend, but because he truly believed them.

"Well, Ethan's not here. And I think you look hot. If you

want that dress, then get it," I said. "If anyone complains they are either blind, stupid, or looking for a fight, which I'll gladly give them." She smiled and wiped another tear from the corner of her eye. "I hate guys like that, and I'm sorry you were treated that way. But that's over. Now you can be you. In all your glory." I motioned to the dress and smiled.

"Thank you," she said. "Now, let's find you something that matches."

"You mean Captain Goggleface won't work?" I teased.

"Is that what you named that character?"

"For now. Unless you have a better name."

"Nope, nothing better than Captain Goggleface. What is he a captain of, exactly?" she asked.

"A train, of course," I said, grinning.

"Ahh, I should have known."

We went back to the dressing rooms, and she helped me pick several pieces together to make a cohesive costume, and we left with our bags and with me feeling a lot closer to her.

16

HANNAH

I found myself looking forward to the Gatsby theme night more than I had any other theme night since I started working at the bar. Maybe it was because the idea for the night had come from me, and I was really looking forward to seeing how everybody responded to such a different approach.

And maybe it was because of how much fun Jordan and I had finding the outfits we were going to wear, and I was really looking forward to seeing him. Either way, the day of the Gatsby night, I spent far longer getting ready for work than I usually did.

This started with several hours of research. As soon as I finished breakfast, I curled up in front of my computer and started going through images from that era, taking notes about how the women looked. I wanted to make sure my look was as authentic as possible. I knew it was just a themed night at a local bar, but I wanted to pay attention to all the details and not miss anything.

That was part of the fun of these theme nights. I really enjoyed taking an idea and running with it, finding as many ways as possible to stay true to the theme in my appearance as much as we did with the food and drinks we offered.

After finally settling on exactly how I wanted to do my hair and makeup to complement the outfit I chose while at the costume shop with Jordan, I took a long shower, then carefully dried my hair. While it was setting in curlers, I went about the feat of recreating the makeup application style of the era.

As I was etching on the line around my lips, my phone rang. I reached over and answered it, putting it on speakerphone when I saw it was Samantha calling.

"Hey, Samantha," I said.

I leaned closer to the mirror to make sure my lip liner didn't end up wiggly on the bottom.

"What are you doing?" she asked. "Why do you sound so weird?"

"I'm getting new appreciation for what the women in the 1920s went through just to get themselves ready. Maybe this is why Daisy never showed up at the party. It took too damn long to get herself presentable," I said.

There was a long pause.

"I have no idea what you're talking about. Is this code? Have you been abducted and you're trying to tell me that I need to help you? Did we come up with this and I forgot?" Samantha asked, her voice getting higher and more anxious with every question she asked.

"No, this isn't code. Thank goodness, because if it were, I would most definitely be dead by now. I'm getting ready for that Gatsby night I was telling you about."

"Oh, yeah, the theme night at the bar," Samantha said. "That makes a lot more sense."

"It does," I said. "It's also complicated as hell. These

women took high-maintenance grooming to a whole new level. Either that, or I'm just not great at trying new things."

"Considering you picked up your entire life and moved all the way across the country, I don't think that's an accurate evaluation of you," she said.

I shrugged even though she couldn't see me. "We'll just go ahead and settle somewhere in the middle. What's going on with you?"

"Nothing, really," she said. "I just thought I would call and check in on things with Jordan."

I let out an exasperated sigh. "There are no things with Jordan. But that was a good effort, trying to slip it in there so I wouldn't notice."

"I've got to keep trying," she said. "But I still want to know why there isn't anything going on with him. You said that he's attractive and sweet, and that you like spending time with him."

"He's gorgeous," I said. "And one of the kindest, funniest people I've ever known. But I technically work for him. And even if I didn't, I don't feel like I'm at a place where I can start anything with anybody. Not after what happened with Ethan. That messed me up too much to even think about a relationship."

"So, you're letting him win?" Samantha asked.

I tossed the phone a disgusted look. "I'm not letting him win. I'm just thinking about myself for once."

"Alright," she said. "If that's how you want to see it. But I still think you deserve to have a little fun."

"I am having fun."

"Not the kind I'm talking about."

"Thank you for your input, Samantha," I said. "But I've got to get going. I've got to get to work."

"Just a little bit. Just one night. It doesn't even have to be the whole night," she said.

"Goodbye, Samantha."

I was laughing as I hung up the phone and put the finishing touches on my makeup before putting on my costume. I wanted to get to the bar early so I could help set up. This was definitely Ava's thing, but I felt a little bit of ownership and pride over it. I was looking forward to seeing the ideas come to life. I had a feeling it was going to be much better than the party that inspired the theme idea.

I pulled into the parking lot behind The Hollow and climbed out just as a familiar truck pulled in beside me. I stepped to the side and paused to wait for Jordan to get out. He smiled at me as he gestured to my dress.

"Nice outfit," he said.

"You too," I said. "Fantastic commitment to the theme."

We looked at each other and laughed. Of course, we knew what the other one was wearing; we'd picked out the outfits together. But I had to admit there was a difference in seeing him put together and polished rather than just throwing the outfit on to make sure it fit.

"You really do look beautiful," he said.

I felt myself blush, and I glanced away in hopes that he wouldn't notice. "Thank you. You look really nice, too."

"Should we go in?" he asked, gesturing to the back door.

If I thought he was genuinely asking, I might have said no. It seemed much more appealing to just stay out here with him. But we had to get inside and help the others get set up and ready for the crowds that would be arriving that evening.

Ava was just coming out from behind the bar carrying centerpieces when we walked in. Her eyes widened slightly when she saw us.

"Wow," she said. "The two of you look great. I love how well your outfits go together."

Jordan and I looked at each other and laughed again. Ava didn't seem to notice, and we both got to work, jumping in to help get everything set up. Throughout the evening as we were decorating at the space and sampling the special food and drinks coming out of the kitchen, he and I kept stealing glances at each other.

At first, I tried to do it subtly so I could feel like he didn't notice. But by the third or fourth glance when I found him openly staring back at me, I decided I didn't need to try it to be sneaky. Instead, I looked over at him and enjoyed the brief moments when our eyes met and held across the room.

It felt like the afternoon and early evening went by far too fast, and we were scrambling to get the final details in place before opening the door. We could already hear the crowd lined up outside, and nervous excitement fluttered around in my stomach.

I was used to being a little bit nervous before the theme nights, not knowing just how crazy it was going to get and if we were going to be able to keep up. That night, I was nervous, but it was because I wanted this night to be wildly successful, and to know people loved it.

I shouldn't have had even a moment of doubt. As soon as the doors opened, the crowd rushed in and the energy in the space became sparkling and exuberant. Everybody looked amazing. While there were a few who had put minimal effort into getting in with the theme, others had gone a much more in-depth route and were wearing elaborate costumes and showy accessories.

Very quickly after opening, it got so busy we couldn't let anyone else in. A line started to form outside, and I knew it was going to be one of those nights when we had to implement the wristband system. One of us would go outside with wristbands for those most likely to gain entrance during the evening.

Half an hour after opening the doors, Ava took a microphone and climbed up on to the bar to make the big announcement. The news went over even better than we had hoped. The customers cheered happily and yelled out their congratulations when they heard about the new bar.

Ava was still speaking when I had several people come up and ask for more details about the new location. Of course, I didn't have a tremendous amount to tell them, but it was encouraging to know how many people were excited to see the new place and willing to travel there to be supportive. I made a note to myself to mention to Ava that she should start an email list of those interested in finding out the grand opening details. Perhaps the most loyal of customers from this location could get a special invite to a grand opening celebration at the new location.

"What are you thinking about?" Jordan asked from directly behind me, making me jump slightly.

I finished dispensing the soda I'd splashed slightly onto the counter when he startled me and put it on the bar in front of me so a customer could grab it.

"Just how people are responding to the news of the new location, and how generous they are being with the fundraiser," I said.

It was a few hours into the evening, and already the donations were flowing in. It was incredible to see just how willing people were to offer their support, and yet again I found myself falling more in love with my new town and the people who surrounded me.

"Feel like taking a break?" Jordan asked.

"Are you taking yours?"

Maybe I should have felt a little awkward or embarrassed at that question popping out of my mouth, but Jordan smiled and nodded.

"Of course I am. Would I ask you if I wasn't? Come on," he said. "Let's get some fresh air."

I thought that meant we would go outside, but a rainstorm had started, so instead we retreated to the back office. It was good to be in the relative quiet and privacy of the small space, and we spent the next several minutes talking. The flirty tone was increasing, and the tension was building between us, but the sound of my phone alerting broke the moment.

I pulled it out of the small purse I had been carrying around and looked at it, letting out a sigh and rolling my eyes when I saw it was a notification of my parents depositing more money into my bank account. But as soon I had that response, I knew what I would do with the money.

Our break over, Jordan and I headed back into the fray. I immediately found Ava.

"Hey," I said. "I want to make a donation."

"You don't have to do that," Ava said. "Everybody around here is being really generous."

"I know I don't have to," I said. "But I want to."

"Okay," Ava said. "How much do you want to donate?"

"Five thousand," I said.

Ava's expression dropped, and she stared at me incredulously.

"Seriously?" she asked.

I nodded. "Yes. I'm serious. Five thousand dollars."

It was by far the biggest donation of the night, and Ava insisted on getting on the microphone and announcing it out to the crowd. It was embarrassing to be the absolute opposite of the anonymous donations I was used to making. But it made everybody cheer with excitement.

It was a great night, and I was so excited to see how much people enjoyed themselves, but it was definitely a relief when the night finally came to an end and the last of the customers left. Tyler let out a heavy sigh as he locked the door behind them, and we settled into the work of cleaning up.

Jordan and I were in the back corner of the bar when he looked over at me. There was something hesitant in his expression.

"What is it?" I asked.

"I was just wondering about that donation," he said.

I felt a little heat and tingle on the back of my neck, the type of discomfort and embarrassment that came from a donation being out in the open like that. But I nodded.

"Yeah," I said. "I wanted to support the cause."

"But why did you donate so much?" he asked. "That really seems like a lot."

I thought about my response for a second, wondering if I should just keep covering the reality up. But I relented.

"I told you that I came from a different world than this, right?"

"You told me a little," Jordan said.

"Well, I come from a very wealthy family and one of the ways my parents like to manipulate me and try to convince me to come home is by depositing money into my bank account. They're trying to control me and make me do what they want me to do because they think I'm completely dependent on them," I said. "I don't want anything to do with that, or for them to ever feel like they have influence over my life anymore. So, I always give the money away as soon as it arrives. Usually, I go to crowdsourcing websites or pick a cause and donate online so I can be anonymous. But this time I decided to donate here."

"Wow." He looked genuinely surprised. "You are truly amazing for doing that."

"Thank you," I said, the fluttering in my stomach now turning to butterflies that swarmed through my belly and around my heart.

Whatever was hanging in the air between us just kept increasing as we cleaned up, and I felt it tingling on my skin when he walked me out to my car.

"This was a great night," he said. "I hope Ava asks for your input more often."

I grinned. "I hope so, too."

I didn't know if it was the night air or the high from how successful the night had been, but I felt a little breathless and even a bit giddy. Jordan placed a hand on my hip and turned me around so my back was against my car. His head dipped and his mouth brushed across mine. Our lips just barely touched, and then he hovered there, letting our breath mingle for a few seconds before the kiss deepened.

It only lasted a few seconds longer than that before Jordan stepped back and wished me good night.

Still breathless, even more now, I got into my car and drove home.

17

JORDAN

It had been days, and I couldn't stop thinking about our kiss.

I was acting like an idiot. I knew that. She was a friend and an employee, and something had been brewing between us since she first showed up, but I knew it wasn't real. It couldn't be real. Not with her history and the need to stay professional. I had to keep myself focused.

I could tell myself that all I wanted, but the tingle on my lips where I kissed her was still there. Inexplicably, days later, I could just about feel her soft red lips against mine. Whispers of her perfume would follow me around, and I would turn suddenly, expecting to see her. She wouldn't be there. Instead, it was if my memory had conjured her smell. She permeated nearly every thought, and I went to bed at night letting my mind wander back to that moment and fantasize about what could have happened next.

Trying to focus on my day, I went about the usual chores and workout routine. I was notorious for keeping things neat, but that didn't mean I didn't religiously pull everything apart and clean it once a month anyway. It was one of the things I hated about the desert. Sand got in everything. Now, if I saw a small bit of dirt, I had to eliminate it with extreme prejudice. They said it was a common aftereffect of coming home from a long time in service, that the edges would smooth over time and I would just end up being an extremely tidy person.

I wasn't there yet.

Once a week there was a deep clean of one of the rooms, and today's happened to be the living room. The cushions of the couch had already been steam cleaned and had dried in the sun of the kitchen. Now it was dark, and I was almost done. The television was on the floor, and I was wiping down the walls when her memory popped up again.

It was just the briefest of thoughts, but it was intense and powerful. It felt like she was right there, her lips on mine as I stood on the stepladder. I closed my eyes and shook my head, trying to make the thoughts go away. I didn't have the time for distractions if I planned on getting things done before bed. It was already late as it was.

"Some people go to a bar on their day off," I muttered to myself. "I stay home and clean. I am a boring, boring human being."

The thoughts of Hannah were too strong, and the realization that shutting myself off from the world to focus on cleaning supplies on my day off was rather sad, I pulled out my phone. It was streaming a podcast that I was only halfway listening to, and I paused it to pull open the contacts. I knew it could continue to stream while I typed out a text to Hannah, but I wanted her to have my full attention, even if it was just words on a screen.

It was the second time I had texted her that day, and

neither got a response. I went back to cleaning and had finished putting the room back together when I glanced at the clock. It was nearly ten, and Hannah never responded. I tried not to let it get to me, but I was bummed. I guessed I thought even in friendship, with one mishap, she would have texted back.

Moving into the kitchen to grab a beer, I heard a knock on my door. Immediately my senses piqued, and my eyes darted to the stand next to the door. It had my keys in a bowl on top, but inside it had a hammer. It wasn't my most sophisticated weapon, but experience I'd rather not dwell on told me that it was extremely useful in a pinch.

I walked to the door and very gently opened the drawer. The wooden handle of the hammer stuck out, and I put one hand on it while I peered through the window. When I saw who it was, I shoved the drawer shut and yanked at the lock. Hannah was on my porch, and she was crying.

I swung the door open, and she fell into my arms, sobbing. I pulled her inside, shutting the door and locking it behind her, guiding her to the couch where I sat her down.

"Hey, hey, it's okay. You're okay. Let me get you some tissues. And water. Do you want water?" I asked. She nodded, and I ran back to the kitchen. When I came back, her tears had slowed, and she blew her nose into the tissues and took a long gulp of the water. "What's going on?" I asked.

"Ethan," she said, and my heart twisted. I knew that name. What could he have done?

"What about Ethan? Did he find you?"

She nodded her head, and a fresh round of sobs came out, though this time they were more controlled. She was shaking, though, and I put the situation together quickly.

Something more than Ethan arriving had happened. A sudden overwhelming sense of protection coursed through me.

"He showed up on my doorstep. I told him he had to leave, but he wouldn't go. He tried to block my path, but I pushed past him. Thank God I locked the door," she said. It all came out almost in one dump of words.

I reached forward and pulled her into me, and she sunk into my chest as we sat back into the couch. I held her, and she clasped my shirt, balling it up in one hand as her tears dried on the fabric. Slowly, her breathing began to return to something resembling normalcy, and she curled her legs up onto the couch, turning her head so she was looking up at me. One teardrop still hung in the corner of her eye, and I used my thumb to wipe it away.

Time froze. For a moment there were infinite possibilities, and I had no idea what I should do next. Leaning into my instincts and the fact that I would never be able to live with myself if I didn't try, I leaned my face down closer to hers. She didn't move away, didn't flinch. Instead, her eyes closed and her lips rose, and I met them with my own.

The kiss was tender and sweet, much like our first. But this time there was a hunger behind it that hadn't been there before. From her. A desire, a need for more. Slowly, she sat up, our lips never parting more than for a second so we could take in a breath. The kiss turned into a passionate embrace, and suddenly our hands were everywhere, ripping at clothes. My shirt was pulled over my head in a hurry and tossed away. Normally it would bother me to have clothes lying around, but for once, I found myself not caring at all.

Her shirt was next, and as it was torn off her body, I broke our embrace for just a moment to marvel at her exquisite body. Heaving, perfect breasts were held aloft by her pink bra, and I reached for the clip in the center of her chest. Our eyes locked as I opened it and it fell away. Her round, heavy breasts tumbled out, and I felt my stomach tighten and my cock harden even more than it already was. The bra slipped off her shoulders, and she held it out to fall off the edge of the couch.

"Where is your bedroom?" she asked.

Silently, I held out my hand, and she took it, and giddily we jumped off the couch, heading down the hall. She went inside before me, and I shut the door behind us. The lights were off except for the bathroom night-light, and it cast the entire room in a dark blue glow that took a moment to adjust to. When my eyes finally did adjust, I could see the outline of Hannah's body sitting on my bed. The skin of her shoulder glowed white from the light behind it, and the outline of her breast was barely visible.

I had only worn running pants to clean in, so there wasn't a lot of wasted motion to remove them as I walked toward her. I reached where she sat and leaned down to kiss her as I pulled my boxers down. Her hand reached up to grab my shaft in one hand and began to stroke me as I pushed her back and onto the bed.

Trailing my lips down her cheek, I let my tongue slide out and trace her collarbone. She stroked my cock against her stomach as I worked my way to her breasts, licking one nipple until it was taut and perky and filling my palms with her soft skin, kneading them. She gasped when my lips touched her stomach, and she let go of me so I could slide my tongue down until I reached the line of her panties.

Hooking my thumbs in the thin fabric around her hips, I peeled them off her and tossed them away. Gently, slowly, I moved my tongue through her folds, brushing her lips and then finding the pearl in the center. I licked at it and she moaned as I worshiped her core. I slid one finger deep inside her, and she cried out, her fingers curling through my hair. Her hips began to rock with my motion, and suddenly she inhaled sharply, and her body bucked underneath me. I pressed my tongue into her clit while she came and then removed my finger, pulling her to the edge of the bed.

Her eyes locked on mine as I positioned myself at her opening. Exploring her with my finger told me she was tight, but as I pressed my head into her, she relaxed into it. Her gasps and cries filled the room as I slowly penetrated deep inside her, my throbbing, hard shaft aching to increase the speed. But I took my time. I wanted her to know how much I wanted her.

I let her adjust to my size, and soon I was rocking slowly back and forth, eliciting cries of passion with each time I thrust deeper into her wet, hot pussy. It didn't take long before her fingers clenched onto my arms as I pounded into her with increased, frantic need. I wanted the release, but even more, I wanted it with her.

Gripping her hips with my hands, I pulled her into me with each thrust, and her hands slid to my chest. My head fell back as I felt the tension building. I knew it wouldn't be long. My mind was wild with passion, and the groans came deep from inside me. I leaned down to kiss her and lost myself in the moment. As our tongues curled around each other and my arm wrapped around her, pulling her down onto me hard with each pump, I felt control slipping away.

Our voices rose together, mixing in one loud cry of ecstasy. I exploded into her, and my body went rigid. I roared until my voice failed me, and she screamed with delight and passion as she came with me. Her pussy pulsed around my throbbing cock, and I emptied myself into her in wave after wave. Our lips found one another again as her body milked me dry, and finally, I crawled onto the bed beside her and we wrapped up in the blankets together. Sleep came easily, my head buried in her neck and her lips occasionally pressing kisses into my chest, and the sleep was blissfully dreamless.

HANNAH

I felt Jordan's arms around me and his warm breath on the side of my neck before I even opened my eyes the next morning. Not wanting to ruin the moment, I snuggled in closer to him and took a deep breath. It felt so peaceful lying there with him, feeling the rise and fall of his chest and stomach against my back as he breathed contentedly in his sleep.

I could have just stayed there all day. I could have pretended the rest of the world didn't exist and I had nothing else to fill my time but enjoy him wrapped around me. For those few moments, I forgot what led me there. I didn't want to think about how I ended up in bed with Jordan or why he was cradling me against him.

But then it hit me. The whole unnerving scene from the night before replayed through my mind, and my heart started racing. I didn't want to think about it. I didn't want to have Ethan's face in my mind or his voice in my head. Leaving my hometown and coming all the way out here to Astoria was about putting him and everything else behind me. That meant never having to deal with him again.

There was a reason I didn't talk with him on the phone or accept his messages. Why I got so angry to find out he knew my number and was able to email me. I wanted nothing to do with him. It took so much strength just to pry myself out of that toxic relationship and reclaim my own life. I had absolutely no intention of going backward.

And yet, there he was. Forcing his way back into my thoughts. Pushing back into my reality.

But it brought me here. It brought me into Jordan's arms, and when he pulled me closer and nuzzled his face into the curve of my neck, I pushed all those thoughts out of my head. I wouldn't let them matter.

We stayed there for a while longer before Jordan rose up on his elbow and kissed my cheek.

"How'd you sleep?" he asked.

I could feel his lips brushing against my ear, and it made a shiver ripple through my body.

"Really well," I said.

"Good. Are you hungry?"

He kissed my cheek again, and I almost giggled. I nodded instead.

"Starving."

"Okay. Let's go get some breakfast."

I would really rather just stay there in bed with him, but my stomach was rumbling, and I realized I hadn't eaten the night before.

We got up, and I dropped Jordan's shirt over my head rather than getting dressed. I wanted to keep feeling surrounded by him, and this felt like a way to do it on the move.

Jordan moved around his kitchen scavenging for ingredients he could turn into breakfast. Eventually, I got up and helped him start organizing what he had spread out on the counter.

"I spend so much time at the bar that I don't end up doing a lot of cooking here," he said.

"I can see that," I teased. "But you've got some good stuff here. We can work with this."

He smiled at me, and we went to work piecing together the ingredients he had and making them into a spread of breakfast dishes. They might not have all been the most cohesive options, but it was something.

We laughed and joked our way through making breakfast, then spread it all out on his table so we could eat. As we ate, we talked about the safe kinds of topics that kept us away from acknowledging what happened the night before. But that couldn't last forever.

As we finished up washing the dishes after breakfast, Jordan looked over at me.

"You can stay with me for a little while if you need to," he said. "If it would make you feel safer to not go back home for a bit until you know he's not in town anymore."

The offer made my heart swell. I smiled at him, so grateful in that moment just to have found all the amazing people I had here in Astoria. Especially him.

"Thank you," I said. "Truthfully, I might have to take you up on that. I'm not sure right now, but I'll let you know."

Jordan reached over and ran his hand down the side of my face, pausing for just a second to look into my eyes in a way that made me melt.

"Anything you need is yours," he said.

I was about to lean in to kiss him when my phone rang in the bedroom. I let out a little groan, and Jordan laughed, kissing me on the tip of my nose before taking the last of the plates from my hand so he could dry it and put it away. I went into the bedroom and searched around on the floor, trying to find where my phone ended up. By the time I found it, it had stopped ringing.

Swiping my finger across the screen, I brought up the missed call log and saw it was from Samantha. Before I was even able to call her back, the phone rang again. I answered it on the first ring.

"Hey, Samantha. I'm sorry I missed your call," I said.

"Are you okay?" she asked before I could even get the words all the way out of my mouth.

"What?"

"Are you okay?"

"I'm fine," I said.

"Good. I need you to keep your eyes open and be ready. I don't mean to scare you, but I just found out that Ethan took off. Nobody knows where he is or where he was going. I'm afraid he's headed there to you."

"He was," I said.

"What?" The word sounded choked in her throat. "Is he there?"

"He's not here right now," I said. "But he showed up at my house last night. It was pretty nasty, but it wasn't as bad as it could have been. Nothing serious happened."

"Oh, my God. I can't believe he came all the way out there just to chase you. What did he say? What did he do? Is he still in town?" Samantha asked.

She was right on the edge of completely freaking out, and it felt like I needed to calm her down. I was safe there with Jordan.

"It's okay," I said. "It was scary at the moment, but I got through it and I'm fine. I'm staying at a friend's house for a while, and he doesn't know I'm here. I'll be okay. I'll just lay low until Ethan gets tired of hanging around here without getting to me and leaves."

"Are you sure?" she asked.

"Absolutely. He won't be able to hold out his patience for long. You know that about him. He'll get tired of not getting what he wants, and hopefully he'll just slink away without incident."

"I hope so," Samantha said. "But be careful. Make sure you're watching out."

"I will be," I said. "I promise. Don't worry about me."

I got off the phone, and Jordan stepped into the room.

"Everything okay?" he asked.

"That was just Samantha," I said. "My best friend from back home. She was calling to let me know that Ethan ran off, and she was worried that he might be headed this way."

That afternoon, Jordan brought me back by my house to get ready for work, and then we drove to The Hollow together. We settled into the routine of getting the bar ready for the evening crowds, and I had all but put the incident of the night before behind me when I looked up and saw Ethan walk through the door.

He looked at me but walked right past and headed for a recently vacated table. I stared at him for a few seconds, wanting to be stunned by his brazenness. But I couldn't be. This was just the way he was. It would probably have been more frightening if he hadn't shown up. Then I would have had to wonder where he was and when he was going to appear.

This way I had the chance to nip this in the bud and move forward.

Finishing the drink I was working on when he came in, I handed it to the customer and walked around from behind the bar to Ethan's table. He looked up at me with a smug smile when I got there.

"Hi, Hannah," he said.

"What are you doing here?"

He looked around, holding up his hands like he was encompassing the bar, and gave me an innocent look. "What do you mean? I just came by to enjoy a beer and check out what I hear is the number one bar in Astoria."

"You need to leave," I said. "Right now."

I thought I would be more afraid when I spoke to him, but my voice didn't even shake. The anger had taken precedence over any wariness or fear.

Ethan shook his head and plucked the beer menu from where it stood on the side of the table.

"No, I don't think so," he said.

"What do you mean you don't think so?" I asked. "Leave. Now."

He shook his head again. "No. I don't think I will. I'm going to just look over this menu and see what this place has to offer."

"Ethan, this is the last time I'm going to tell you. Leave. Now."

The sickening playful note in his voice that had made my skin crawl as he did his sweet and innocent act immediately disappeared. That had been enough to push him over the edge. He leaned threateningly toward me.

"I'm not going anywhere, Hannah. I have the right to be here. Just like everybody else," he said.

"How did you find out where I lived and worked?" I asked.

This earned an arrogant smirk, and he leaned back in his chair, assuming a casual pose.

"It wasn't very hard at all," he said. "My private investigator found you in a matter of days. I was just giving you time to come to your senses before I took matters into my own hands. I told you before there was no point in trying to get away from me. You'll never be able to."

A cold shiver ran down my spine, but before I could say anything, a form appeared at the corner of my eye, and I looked over to see Jordan standing there. He subtly pulled me behind him and faced off against Ethan.

"Get out," he said.

No frills. No elaboration. No room for ambiguity.

"You need to stay out of it," Ethan said back.

"I'm one of the owners of this bar, and I'm telling you right now you need to get out of here," Jordan said.

Ethan scoffed. "I already know who you are. Do you think that impresses me? You're the fractional owner of a neighborhood bar. You might think you can push other people around, but I'm not going anywhere until I get my beer."

Jordan stalked over to the bar and snatched a cup of beer Ava had just filled for a customer. He brought it over to the table and shoved it toward Ethan.

"Here. Enjoy," he said.

Some of the beer sloshed over the lip of the mug and splashed on Ethan. He stood up sharply from the table, nearly knocking it over. His eyes were flashing, his nostrils flaring. And even though he was several inches shorter than Jordan, I knew from experience this was a stance Ethan expected would intimidate anyone who got in his way. He thought people would simply back down when they looked at him that way, too afraid of what was going to happen next to go any further.

Not Jordan. There wasn't even a hint of fear or hesitation in Jordan's eyes. He stood tall and strong, his chest square toward Ethan and threat in his eyes.

"Ethan, you need to go," I said. "Just get out of here."

I was on the brink of begging. It was bad enough when it was just me grappling with what to do with his unwanted appearance. Now I had to deal with the potential clash between him and Jordan. I didn't want to see that happen.

Ethan faced off with Jordan for another few seconds, like he was considering attacking. Finally, he took a step back.

"Fine. But I'll be waiting at your house for you so we can talk," he said. "This isn't over."

Without waiting for a response, he gulped down what was left of the beer in the mug and stalked out of the bar. I watched him in stunned silence, dumbfounded and starting to feel afraid again.

19

JORDAN

S lapping the taste out of Ethan's mouth would certainly do the trick, I thought. Maybe it would just egg him into a larger fight, but that worked, too, since I would enjoy the vicious beatdown I could give him, taking my time roughing up each side of his face equally. Then, maybe, I'd break one of his fingers. A middle one, just to make sure that he couldn't grip anything for a while with it. Break the middle one on both hands. It would be the ultimate "fuck you."

Those were the only ways I could think of for dealing with Ethan. Not that I didn't know there were other ways, it was just that every time I thought of his smug face, those were the only logical outcomes of us being in the same room. Any mention of his name brought up an intense desire to rearrange his face like a six-foot Mr. Potato Head.

I worried about Hannah. She didn't seem to take too well to my personal brand of protection ideas, and I couldn't blame her. She was terrified of what Ethan might try, and the idea that I would resort to preemptive violence made me seem almost as bad as he was. I got that. But it didn't stop the instinctual desire to beat the shit out of anyone who threatened Hannah, much less an ex she was scared of.

She had been staying with me for a few days. While she seemed to be doing well, I knew for a fact that I was doing a million times better. I slept better than I had in ages when she was with me and waking up actually feeling rested was something that I was greatly enjoying. Plus, every night tended to end up with us tumbling into bed with less and less clothing. That was making it even more pleasurable to have her staying with me.

We both had the late shift coming up, so our day was free when we decided to head up to the library. She was working on her mural, and I decided that hanging out there and watching her paint would be nice. I was in the kitchen packing a cooler with sandwiches and drinks when she came up to me and kissed my shoulder.

"You don't have to come," she said. "Not that I'm trying to talk you out of it. I just don't want you to feel obligated."

"No obligation," I said. "I want to come."

"Seriously," she said, her voice dropping a little and making me move my eyes away from the tomato slices I was cutting. "It's a very public place. Ethan might be stupid, but I don't think he's that stupid. I would be fine if you wanted to stay home or something."

I scanned her face, making sure that she wasn't trying to subtly tell me not to go. If that was the case, I wouldn't make a fuss of it, I would just change my mind and offer her the cooler for herself. But the look on her face was not one of someone telling a person they need space or freedom, but one of an almost pleading hope. She really did just not want me to feel obligated to go.

"Well, how about I come, and if I start to bug you, you

just tell me to get the hell out of there and I'll go find something else to do for a while?" I asked.

She smiled. "That's not going to happen," she said as she pulled me down to her for a kiss.

"I just feel better being near you, and I like watching you paint. So, if you don't mind my company, I'd like to be there, but seriously, if you need space, just let me know."

"No, I like the idea of you being there," she said. "I just didn't want you to feel like you had to."

As we drove to the library a little later, I stole glances of her looking out her window. She seemed content, if a little on edge. I could understand why. Ethan was a dumbass and didn't get the hint. It wouldn't surprise me if he showed up at the library, ready for anything. Being there with her made me feel better about her being there, and also it gave me a chance to sit and relax and do nothing.

I was not good at doing nothing.

When I was in the desert, there were wide swaths of time to fill between the chaos. When the chaos hit, there was only survival and orders, but between those moments of pure, unadulterated insanity were huge stretches of boredom. I'd hated it then, too. I learned every card game in existence, picked up parts of several languages, enough to communicate basic needs with a number of points on the globe, and did a lot of push-ups. A metric crap-ton of push-ups. What I never got the hang of that some of my other brothers did was how to relax.

I found relaxing to be agitating. I needed to be moving, needed to be working. When on duty, it was about protection. I needed to be on my guard, just in case. When I was off duty, it was about how I wanted to be prepared to move out at a moment's notice. Since I had been home, it had been about me being kind of a prick who just couldn't sit still. This was going to be a test.

I was going to try to sit down, relax on a blanket in the grass, and literally watch paint dry.

We pulled in, finding a spot just across from the wall where the mural was going, and I helped her unload her large selection of buckets of paint and various brushes and other painting supplies. The building was white cement blocks, and I marveled at the process she had.

First, she set out all her paints in a line with the brushes nearby, a bucket of water, and several old towels. Then, she set up a projector and projected the image onto the wall. An easel stood next to the projector with a smaller version of the mural on it, painted on what looked like a sketch of the building. Then she took a large black pencil, the head of which was nearly the size of my fist and drew the outline of the mural design. Moving her ladder occasionally, I worried she was overexerting herself, but she seemed fine, and the one time I got up to help her, she held up her finger, then pointed back to the blanket. She wanted to do this completely on her own.

The wall had been cleaned and primed the day before, and it sparkled in the sunlight. I could see through the projector image how the final product would look and was in awe of how gorgeous it was. Hannah was incredibly talented, and I wasn't surprised when small crowds gathered to watch her for a few minutes at a time. It was getting close to lunch when the librarian made her way out to check on her.

"Oh my, Hannah, this is looking incredible," she said. Hannah was working on the mural in six sections, completing them before moving on to the next, and the first section was nearly finished.

"Thanks," she said, wiping her forehead with the back of her hand and putting a yellow streak of paint across it. "I think it's going to come together really nicely."

"I am sure it will," the librarian said, stepping closer. Their voices lowered and their conversation turned to artistic mumble, and I didn't really catch most of it, but I got the gist. The librarian was extremely impressed, both with the concept and design, but also with her execution as it was thus far. The sparkle in her eyes as she talked about her look was uplifting, and I found myself grinning from ear to ear along with her.

Happiness looked good on her.

After the librarian stopped, we took a break and ate. The sandwiches I made were seemingly a big hit, even though I silently smacked myself for forgetting the bacon. It was still at home, on a plate next to the stove. I was in such a good mood that I guess I got forgetful as we walked out. We had just finished eating, and Hannah had returned to the mural while I picked up and tossed our trash when Becca showed up.

"Hey!" she said as she approached Hannah. There was a weird dance where Becca made to do the friend hug and then thought better of it.

"Hey, sorry," she said, indicating her shirt. "I'd hug you, but I don't think you want this paint all over you."

"You would be correct," Becca said jokingly. "This is looking great, though. You are amazing."

"Thanks," Hannah said.

"Hey, Jordan," Becca said, turning to me and dropping her voice in a weirdly conspiratorial way.

"Hi," I said awkwardly. "Dropping off some books?"

"Oh," Becca said, looking down as if just noticing she was carrying a stack of four or five books in her arms. "Yes, actually. I had some ideas, and I wanted to do some research for the bar expansion."

I grimaced. "Cool," I stuttered out.

"So I heard what happened the other day with your ex," Becca said. "How horrible of him to just drop in where you work."

"It wasn't fun," Hannah admitted. "He's like that, though. Rude, demanding, and no sense of propriety at all."

"Sounds like he was a blast to date," Becca said sarcastically. "Seriously, though, I am glad you got out of that relationship. Guys like that aren't worth your time."

"Thank you," Hannah said, a streak of red crossing her cheeks. It was adorable when someone complimented her for any reason and that blush would fill her face.

"It's a good thing you had Jordan there with you," Becca said, turning a glance at me. "I heard you were rather insistent on him leaving, weren't you?" she asked me.

A pained smile came across my face, matched by a sunny "what, me?" smile on Becca's. She was going to try talking me up, I could feel it. I didn't need a matchmaker when we were already sleeping together—not that she knew that. *Yet*, I thought.

"He's been very helpful," Hannah said, and I turned to her. She was smiling at me in a somewhat devious way, and this time it was my turn to feel a rush of color cross my cheeks.

"I'm just glad you have someone watching over you. But anyway, I have to get going. Jordan, would you do me a favor and carry these books in for me? I hurt my wrist yesterday, and these things are heavy," Becca said.

"Sure," I said, taking them. They were light, even for Becca. "I'll be right back, Hannah."

As soon as we were out of earshot, Becca held out her hand, and I gave her back the books.

"Well, that healed quickly," I said.

"Should I tell Mom?" Becca giggle-whispered.

"Tell her what?"

"About you and Hannah," she said, and never more so in that moment did I feel the kinship of an annoying little sister with Becca.

"Stop," I said. "Don't get ahead of yourself. We're just enjoying the moment for right now. No labels. It's hard enough navigating the whole dating while working together thing." One of Becca's eyebrows curled up, and I immediately jumped back in. "*If* you would consider this dating." I sighed. "No labels," I said defeatedly.

Becca put one hand on my shoulder and stuck out her bottom lip. "Poor boy. You have it bad, don't you? Well, regardless, I am happy for you. For whatever that is. No labels."

Laughing, she walked away to the front desk, and I turned to go back to where Hannah was standing near the top of the ladder, looking for all the world like she was one wobble away from destroying every adorable bone in her body.

20

HANNAH

It was one of those rare quiet days at the bar when it seemed like maybe we would all get a chance to breathe a little bit during our shifts. Those days were getting fewer and further between. Even since the time I had been working at The Hollow, I'd noticed it getting busier and more popular.

While it had never been a place I would consider slow, there were plenty of days that were less overwhelming than others. Particularly during longer stretches between the theme nights, the crowds thinned out a little bit and we might be able to get a breather. That wasn't so much the case recently.

Even on days when it had been a few weeks since a special themed night, the customers packed in and kept us going basically nonstop from the time the doors opened until we had to lock them behind the last customers. I definitely preferred it that way. As much as my feet hurt and I was exhausted sometimes, I would much rather it be busy and have way more than enough to do than to get bored or have to worry about the bar not doing enough business.

The doors were already open, and a few customers had trickled in for dinner, but things were still quiet. With Tom back in San Francisco, all the other brothers were in the bar. They were taking advantage of the quieter night and using it as an opportunity to have a meeting. I had just brought one of Tyler's famous burgers to a table when Jordan came out of the office.

He did not look happy. The other men trailing behind him didn't look particularly thrilled about whatever was going on, either. Not acknowledging them or saying anything else to them, Jordan walked away from his brothers and came over to me.

"Do you have a second?" he asked.

I nodded. "I've taken care of my customers. I can probably snag a second for you."

I offered him a playful smile, but the upset expression on his face didn't lessen any. We walked to the back of the bar and the small area with a view table we usually reserved for our own use.

"What's going on?" I asked. "Is something wrong?"

Jordan paced back and forth for a couple of intense seconds, then looked into my eyes.

"We just got off a call with Tom," he said. "He has made the final decision and will be sending Matt and me to Portland to start getting the new place ready."

"That's exciting, isn't it?" I asked. "You get to be a part of opening the brand-new location and starting to build it up. It's an honor that he asked you."

"Do you really feel that way?"

"I mean, I think that you'll be a part of something pretty amazing. It's not my favorite thing in the world to think about you going away."

He let out a sigh and nodded. "Exactly. That's what I'm upset about. I don't want to leave you here."

I smiled at him and reached for his hands, giving them an encouraging squeeze. "Jordan, I'll be fine. Really, I will. Honestly, I should really be getting back to my own house, anyway. It's been more than a week, and I would think by now you would be tired of our little extended sleepover."

Jordan smiled and kissed both of my hands. "Never. It's been fun having you stay there with me."

I nodded, but the moment between us was shattered by the sound of Ava shouting to us that she needed some help.

"We better go see what's going on," he said.

There was heat in his voice, but I had to ignore it. Now wasn't the time to give in to the draw I felt to him. Especially not after what he just told me.

After Ethan showed up at the bar and announced he would be waiting at my house for me, I knew there was no going back there. Not until I knew Ethan wasn't in town anymore. Jordan brought me right back to his place after work that night, and he and Tyler went over to my place the next day to grab some clothes and other necessities. They said they didn't see Ethan, but I wouldn't put it past him to be hiding somewhere out of sight.

At least the guys were smart enough not to drive right from my place to his or back. That way even if Ethan was trying to track me down by following them, he wouldn't have a direct path. Now I knew I wasn't going to be able to rely on that anymore. Even more, I wasn't going to be able to be with Jordan all the time.

And as disappointed as I was feeling about Jordan moving away, I needed to move past that. This was never intended to be permanent, and it seemed it was time to go back to the real world. I reminded myself that I was in no place for a relationship. No matter what my heart was trying to convince me of.

We walked together back to the front of the bar and saw a huge crowd of customers had come in. We dove back into work and didn't have another chance to talk to each other for a couple of hours. Finally, there was enough of a break in the influx of customers for Jordan and me to take a meal break. Tyler had already put together plates of food for us, and Jordan brought them into the office so we could eat in some semblance of quiet.

"So, when I leave for Portland, I should really only be there for a couple of weeks. And I've already spoken to my mother," he said.

I gave him a quizzical look. "Your mother?"

"Yes. I would really like you to stay with her while I'm gone."

I was immediately hesitant and pulled back a little, shaking my head.

"I am really not sure about that idea," I said.

"Why not?" he asked. "You can't just go back to your place. At my mother's house, you would be safe. He wouldn't be able to find you."

"I don't want to involve your mother in my drama. That's unfair to her. Plus, we don't even know one another," I protested.

"Well then, lets fix that," Jordan said. "I want to take you over there tomorrow so the two of you can meet. I've told her a lot about you and she's excited to get to know you."

A surge of nervousness rushed up inside me all of a sudden

thinking about how Jordan's mother would react to me, especially knowing I was having issues with my ex. Hopefully, Jordan had been relatively discreet, but I doubted that. I figured by now, his mother knew the entire story. I wasn't relishing the thought of hearing all about that while I was there.

"I'll tell you what," Jordan said. "If you really don't want to stay with my mother, that's fine. But until we know that asshole is gone for good, I don't feel comfortable leaving you alone. He told you he was going to be waiting at your house to talk to you about what you did. "Will you at least stay with Ava and Mason?" he asked.

After a few moments' thought, I finally agreed to the compromise.

"If it's alright with them, I will stay with Ava and Mason," I agreed. "But only because I have no idea where Ethan is right now or when he might resurface."

I hadn't seen Ethan since the night he came to the bar. Though he threatened to wait for me at my place, I hadn't heard a single word from him, and the one time I was able to go back by to grab a few extra things, there was no sign of him.

That didn't necessarily mean he was gone. I knew him well enough to know he could be doing this on purpose. It could mean he was either messing with me so I would be as anxious and on edge as possible, or he was lulling me into complacency so he could pounce. Either way, it would make the moment he did come back even more fun for him.

Because of that, I couldn't be certain he had actually left. Until I got confirmation of where he was, I needed to stay cautious.

21

JORDAN

I was not excited about leaving the next day and bringing Hannah to meet my mother was an added level of stress that made my stomach hurt. I could swear I could take live rounds with less stress than that forty-eight-hour window was giving me. There were so many tightropes to walk, so many ways things could go terribly, horribly wrong, but I held out hope it would all be fine. If I just kept my cool, stuck to the plan, and put one foot in front of the other, I could have it all.

The last thing I wanted was for Hannah to make any indication that we were together any more seriously than potential dating. I knew my mom, and if we put any labels on what we were, she would be off to the races planning our wedding and naming our children after long-distant relatives I wasn't aware we had. Her imagination and enthusiasm were legendary.

Hannah and I were clearly in some form of relationship, but we hadn't given any labels to it or talked about it. There eventually would be a conversation, I knew, but I wasn't sure when we would have it. I knew I had no plans on sleeping with anyone else, and I was more than ready to be exclusive, and I had a feeling she was, too. But the fact remained, I didn't want my mother planning what dishes she was going to give as a wedding gift before Hannah and I had a chance to even discuss what this new relationship meant and to figure out what we would do about my impending Portland move.

On our way to Mom's house, I turned the radio down, and Hannah turned to me.

"So, before we get there, I just wanted to warn you, Mom is rather excitable and is excited to meet you specifically. She might say something about us dating. Just ignore her," I said.

Hannah laughed, putting her hand on mine on the center console.

"Why? What's so exciting about me?" she asked.

"She's just the type of person that will go to the extremes when it comes to her boys. She's watched all of my brothers but Matt and I get married and start having kids, and she really wants us too as well," I said. "I just don't want her to run you off, you know?"

"She won't," Hannah laughed. "I'm excited to meet her. Nervous, too. But I won't be offended if she says something about us being together. It's nice she cares so much about you that she wants you to be happy."

There was a note of sadness in those words, and I felt for her. Her own parents didn't care if she was happy or not, as long as she did what they wanted her to do. In that way, she was right. It was nice that Mom cared so much about us. That she wanted us all to have a partner and a family. But I was still very aware that what Hannah and I had was very new, and Mom had been a bit much for girls in the past that my brothers brought home, resulting in promising relationships fizzling out quickly.

When we arrived, I opened the door to the shuffling feet of my mother, who was on her way to open the door. I smiled and opened my arms, and Mom fell in for a big bear hug. She kissed me on the cheek and nearly pushed me out of the way to get her first look at Hannah.

"You must be Hannah," she said. "I am so pleased to meet you. We're huggers here."

Giving Hannah no other option, she threw herself around her, and Hannah laughed as she patted Mom on the back with arms that were pinned to her sides.

"It's nice to meet you, too," she said. "Thank you for having me over."

"Oh, that's no big deal at all," Mom said, leaving the hug long enough to stare at her for a second. "My goodness, Jordan was right, you are absolutely beautiful."

"Jordan," Hannah said teasingly. "Thank you, Mrs. Anderson."

"Come on in, you two. Dinner's ready," Mom said, taking Hannah by the hand and leading her inside.

I chuckled and shook my head as she showed her the bottom floor of the house. Dad's chair was still the eyesore of the room, but it was my favorite place in the house now. Sitting there reminded me of him, and had dinner not been ready already, I likely would have taken the opportunity to sit and relax in it for a few minutes.

As I got into the dining room, I could see Mom had been busy. There were dishes all over the table, including some of Mom's regular hits. It was enough food to feed the whole family, most likely, but it was just the three of us. Which meant she was fully intending on sending most of it home with us. Already I was trying to figure out how in the world I was going to fit it all inside my refrigerator.

We sat, and Mom immediately launched into stories about our childhood. Thankfully, she kept away from some of the more embarrassing things in our past and seemed to be a bit more reserved due to my requests from immediately assuming we were planning a wedding date. When dinner was over and Mom brought out her infamous tiramisu, I indulged as I always did in a slice that could be better described as "half a cake."

"This was my specialty," Mom said. "Ever since I married Jordan's father, I have made homemade tiramisu every Sunday night. This week I didn't feel like eating any, and none of the other boys have come by. So, you two are getting the spoils."

"It looks delicious," Hannah said.

"It is," I said. "It's my favorite thing she makes."

"He asked for it for his birthday three years in a row," Mom said, her voice trailing off as she slipped into her memories. "So did his father. Peas in a pod they were."

"He used to sneak down in the middle of the night and get a slice," I said. "When I was eleven, I caught him doing it, and it became a weekly tradition for the two of us. Sneaking down and eating a bit of Mom's delicious dessert before going back to bed."

"Is it an old family recipe?" Hannah asked.

"Sort of," Mom said. "My mother wasn't much of a cook. Just made the basic stuff for us kids to eat, but my father's mother was brilliant. She left him a book of recipes, which I still have. It's all handwritten, and some of them are almost a hundred years old."

Mom had separated some small plates and had just carved off a few pieces for us. I was already diving into my slice when Hannah took her first bite. Her eyes widened, and she looked over to me. Her mouth hung open.

"I know," I said.

"But," she began.

"I know," I said again.

Mom smiled, and we ate our dessert quietly for a few minutes before Mom cleared her throat.

"Now," Mom began, making my ears perk up. "Jordan told me that you might need a place to stay for a little while to avoid an ex-boyfriend?"

Hannah glanced at me before going into it. I knew it was a touchy subject for her, as it would be for anyone, but since I was asking Mom to make space for her for a little while, I had to tell her why.

"Yes, I might," she said. "It's a whole situation, but Jordan is just trying to look out for me."

"He's like that," Mom said, smiling at me. "He's a good boy." She turned back to Hannah. "Well, I have a lot of room now that none of my boys live here. I went ahead and got the old guest room ready anyway, just so you wouldn't have to stay in one of the boys' old rooms. No pressure, but if you want to stay here with a doddering old woman, you have a place."

"That is very sweet of you, thank you," Hannah said. "I'm honestly not sure what I'm going to do, really. And you don't seem doddering to me."

"Aren't you sweet?" Mom asked, then turned to me. "I can see why you like her so much."

"Mom," I began.

Hannah put her hand on mine, and our eyes met. She smiled. I decided to let it go for now, since Mom was being on pretty good behavior otherwise.

"Well, that was delicious," Mom said. "I'll be in the

kitchen cleaning up. You two make yourself comfortable."

"I think we're going to get going actually," I said.

"But we should help with the dishes," Hannah said, standing. She didn't look at me, but I got the feeling she was intentionally offering to help for multiple reasons, one of which was to make Mom feel like we weren't rushing off.

"Oh, I can handle it," Mom said.

"Please," Hannah said. "You cooked all this wonderful food, let me help you. Jordan and I can handle dishes. You should get a chance to relax."

"Thank you, dear," Mom said, stunning me. As she walked away, I turned to Hannah, who shrugged, and we made our way into the kitchen.

A half-hour later, we hugged Mom goodbye and got back in the car. As we got on the road, I cleared my throat. It had dawned on me that I had been pushing Hannah a bit.

"Hey, so, you don't have to make a decision tomorrow if you don't want to. But I would feel a lot better if you made sure all your doors were locked," I said.

Hannah smiled and nodded but stayed quiet for a few minutes. When she did speak, it broke the comfortable silence.

"I really like your mom," she said.

"She really likes you."

"Really?"

"Yeah," I said. "She's a bit pushy about the whole kids thing usually, but I've never seen her abdicate household duties to a girl one of us brought over, no matter how tired she was. She trusts you with her kitchen. That's big."

"That makes me feel good," Hannah said. "I adore her. She's funny and sweet. How I imagine a mother should be, you know?"

I nodded, grimacing a little. It hurt to hear how she felt like she missed out on the family experience.

"Well, if you let her, she will mother you to death. So be wary."

"I'll keep an eye out for it," she said. "I really don't know how I feel. I might want to stay there. I don't think I can make a decision right this second."

"That's fine," I said.

"I just don't want to be a burden. Yet, I don't want you to worry about me so much."

I turned to look at her. A burden. How in the world could she think she was a burden?

"I don't feel like you're a burden at all," I said. "I just don't want to pressure you into something you don't want to do."

"I appreciate the sentiment, but I am an adult. I am independent. I can take care of myself."

I picked up her delicate hand and pressed my lips to it. We were pulling into my driveway, and I was looking forward to getting inside and starting the evening that tended to end the same way. A very desirable way.

"I know," I said. "I didn't mean to imply you were incapable of taking care of yourself. I just want to make sure you're okay. If there is anything I can do to make sure of that, I want to do it."

She smiled and raised my hand to place a kiss on it.

"Thank you," she said. "Now, what are we going to do with all these leftovers?"

22

HANNAH

I tried to hold off waking up for as long as possible the next morning. I knew as soon as we were up, Jordan would have to get ready and leave for Portland. The reality of him actually leaving wasn't something I had let myself think about since he told me he had to go.

In truth, it still felt strange to even consider being stressed about him not being there. Whatever was going on between us, we hadn't talked about it. There were no commitments or definitions. We were what we were, whatever that was, and all I could really do was keep figuring it out one step at a time as it came.

Part of that meant realizing I really would miss him. I hadn't just gotten used to having him around. He wasn't just a nice guy or somebody fun to talk to. He was a part of my daily life, somebody I thought about several times a day, every day, and somebody I relied on seeing.

It wasn't something I'd expected when I came here, and definitely not something I was looking for. I'd moved to Astoria to escape other people trying to control my life and tell me who to be and what to do. Finding somebody wasn't even close to being on my agenda. In fact, I didn't want anything to do with it.

But then Jordan came along. People always said you find the perfect one when you stop looking. It seemed that might be true for me. I didn't know if I was ready to really consider Jordan perfect, or get anywhere near the possibility of referring to him as the one. But I couldn't deny what was happening between us. I couldn't pretend I didn't feel the closeness forming, or the feelings growing inside me.

I couldn't pretend he didn't make me feel safe and appreciated for who I was, rather than what he might want me to be. I didn't know what it all meant, but I did know I didn't want him climbing out of the bed and getting in that car.

But he did get out of bed. I couldn't really stop him. In fact, I asked, just to be sure.

"Do you think I could write you a note saying you don't have to go because you need to stay here with me and it would work?" I asked as I watched him get dressed.

Jordan smiled and turned around to face me. He leaned over for a kiss.

"If I thought it would, I would have you do it. Unfortunately, I don't Tom would see it that way," he said. He dropped his shirt over his head and came to sit down on the edge of the bed and put his shoes on. "But you are more than welcome to stay here while I'm gone. If you feel safe and comfortable here, you can make yourself at home."

There was something strained in his voice.

"Why don't you sound like you're actually offering?" I asked.

He shook his head. "No, I don't mean to sound like that. I'm actually offering. If you are comfortable here and want to stay, you are more than welcome to. Really. It's just that I don't trust Ethan. His private investigator was able to find you here in Astoria without any trouble, including where you live. We haven't seen Ethan around here and don't think he followed us, but I really don't put it past him to find out where I live and find you here. I would just rather you be with other people, so I know you're safe. Especially while I'm not in town to do it myself."

I smiled and squeezed his hand. "Thank you for caring so much. It means a lot to me. Right now, I don't really know what I'm going to do. But I will be sure to lock up before I leave for work tonight."

"And after that?" Jordan asked.

"I guess I'll just figure out my game plan later. But I'll let you know what I decide."

"Sounds good," he said. "Just take care of yourself. I guess I should get going."

I let out a sigh and nodded. Walking him to the front door, I hugged him tight, wanting to delay him being gone for a few more seconds. He pulled back from the hug and kissed me.

"Let me know when you get there," I said.

He nodded. "I will."

We shared one more kiss, and he left, his suitcase and duffel in hand. I watched him put the bags in the back of the truck, and then he walked to the driver's door and opened it. Before he got in, he waved at me and blew me a kiss. I laughed and blew one back, waving until he was in the truck and had driven out of sight.

When he was gone and I was sure this wasn't going to be a rom-com situation where he would turn around and rush back to me, I closed the door and locked it. Turning around to lean my back against the door, I looked around. It already felt weird being alone in his house.

He said I was welcome to stay, but I didn't feel right being there without him. I got dressed and packed everything that had migrated over to his house aside from some bathroom stuff that I wanted to leave just because it made me feel good to know I had a toothbrush there. Making sure all the doors and windows were locked, I put my bags into the car. It wasn't until I was sitting behind the wheel that a creepy feeling went up the back of my neck. I slammed my hand down on the lock and looked around, waiting to see Ethan coming out from between the houses or popping out of one of the cars on the street.

Pushing the thoughts out of my mind, I pulled away from the house and started toward my own place. I hated that Ethan was getting to me like this. Even just being able to make me nervous felt like he was controlling me all over again. I picked up my phone and called Samantha.

"Hey, Hannah," she said. "Everything okay?"

She didn't sound as panicked or on edge as she did the first time we spoke after Ethan came to Astoria, but the tension was there.

"Everything's okay. I just wanted to be on the phone right now."

"You just wanted to be on the phone?" she asked, sounding confused.

"I'm going back to my house," I explained.

"I thought you said you were staying with a friend."

"It was Jordan," I admitted. She gasped a little, but I pushed right past it. "It's been great, and I felt really safe there, but he had to leave for a business trip to Portland. He isn't going to be in town for a bit. He said I could stay at his place, but it just didn't feel right to be there without him.

So, I'm going back to my house. That's why I wanted to be on the phone. I know it sounds silly, but I don't exactly want to go in for the first time completely alone. I wanted to be talking to you."

"That's not silly at all. After what you've been through, it is completely understandable," she said.

"Well, thank you for talking to me. I really appreciate it."

"Of course. I just wish I could be there with you. Have you seen or heard from Ethan again?" she asked.

"No. Not since the night he showed up at the bar. Have you?"

"No. No one around here has. Nobody knows where he is. It's actually really strange," she said.

That definitely didn't make me feel any better. I pulled into my driveway and sat for a couple of seconds just like I did outside of Jordan's house. As much as I wouldn't want to think that Ethan would actually just hover around waiting for me all this time, I couldn't honestly put it past him. He would do anything to get his way. Anything to scare me and make me feel under his control.

But he didn't show up.

"Alright, I'm here," I said. "I'm going to grab my bags and go inside."

"I'm right here," she said. "If you see anything strange at all, you tell me, then get off the phone and call the police."

I didn't like the way she said that. It made even more heaviness press down on me. I climbed out of the car and got my luggage, then headed for the door. With every step, I paid as much attention to everything around me as I could, waiting for even the slightest movement or indication of anything being off.

When I got to the door, I unlocked it and pushed it

open hard so it swung all the way and hit the wall on the other side. If he had somehow gotten in and was lurking there waiting for me to come through the door, that would have been a rude awakening for him.

I took a step inside and tried to sense anything different.

"Everything okay?" Samantha asked.

"It seems like it."

"I want to stay with you until you walk through all the rooms. Just to be sure."

"Talk to me while I do it," I said. "It doesn't matter about what."

As I toured through the house, checking each room and closet, and hating Ethan a little bit more each step, I listened to Samantha tell me about her children and what they were up to that week. When I finished, I walked back to the living room to get my bags.

"All clear?" Samantha asked.

"Yes," I said.

"Doors locked?"

"Double-checked," I said. "Thank you for talking to me."

"Anytime. I really don't like that you're alone. Isn't there somewhere else you can go?" she asked.

"I don't want to keep changing my life to suit him. This is my home. Until there's a reason to leave, I'm going to be here."

We got off the phone, and I hauled my luggage to the laundry room to wash what I hadn't gotten to at Jordan's house. A little while later, my phone rang, and I smiled when I saw Jordan's name appear on the screen.

"I got here," he said. "Lovely Portland."

I laughed. "I'm glad you're safe."

"I'm glad you are, too."

I wanted to tell him I missed him, but I stopped myself.

"You go and get settled in. I have a refrigerator I haven't touched in far too long to wrangle back from disaster before I go to work," I said.

Jordan laughed. "Good luck with that. I'll call you later. I miss you already."

My heart swelled, and I held back a sigh.

As soon as I walked into work that night, Ava came up to me.

"Are you doing okay?" she asked.

"Yeah. Jordan said I can stay at his house while he's gone, but I just can't get comfortable there without him. So, I went home. But everything's okay."

"Alright, so where are you going after work? Are you staying with Susan or me? My house is totally open to you. It's full of toys, but it's comfortable," she said.

I laughed. "Thank you. Toys sound like fun right about now. I really appreciate you welcoming me, but I think I'll just stay home. I'll be fine. There's no sign of him. I'm not worried."

"Are you sure about that?"

"Yes. I'll admit, it freaked me out having him here, and I was a little scared leaving Jordan's place and getting home for the first time. But nothing happened. I'm okay now," I said.

It might not have been one hundred percent true, but I was working on convincing myself of it as well.

"Alright. Well, if there's an issue, don't hesitate to call me. Not for an instant. I already talked to Mason, and he's all for having you with us for as long as you need to be. No worries," she said.

"Thank you."

It felt good knowing I was surrounded by people who

cared about me and were willing to go so far out of their way to help me. The rest of the night at work was uneventful, and I went home to my quiet, empty house. Even though nothing happened, and everything was exactly as it always was, I couldn't shake the feeling I was being watched.

23

JORDAN

I snapped awake covered in sweat. I couldn't place where I was; everything was different. It was a room, with a bathroom across from me and a little kitchenette. Other than that, I had no clue. I reached for my gun and realized it wasn't there. I was naked. What the hell was going on?

Slamming my hand on the nightstand produced a crashing sound as the alarm clock was swiped away and a glass with some sort of liquid spilled, but eventually I found a lamp. I crawled my fingers up it until I found a switch and clicked it on. The room filled with a white-yellow light.

In the corner of the room was a coatrack. My coat hung from it as well as an apron. It had The Hollow's logo on it. Suddenly, it all came rushing back to me, and I fell back into the pillows.

I was in Portland. And I hated it.

The nightmares had returned and were mixing with my current reality. Sometimes I woke up, like just then, thinking I was still in the desert. Other times I woke up thinking I was in Astoria and horrible things were happening. When I did sleep, it was fitful, and rest wasn't happening. I hoped that I would sleep better during the morning hours when the sun was up. In the dark, the shadows came.

Hannah was on my mind often. I worried about her and hated being away from her like I was. We hadn't talked since I got in and told her I was there safe, aside from text messages simply saying good night. My mind raced as I tried to think of a way around all this. I couldn't just ask her to move with me. Uprooting her life again, right after she had just started to settle down, to move with me, a person who she was barely just getting to know, seemed like an insane proposition.

That left finding out if a long-distance thing could work. It would be stressful, and I would hate not seeing her in person as much as I had been, but at least we could video chat and I could see her on my days off. If we scheduled the same days off, one of us could come to the other and spend our time there. While I would most certainly do that, considering how recently she had gotten out of her relation-ship with Ethan and the drama that still surrounded that, I felt like a long-distance relationship might be too much for her.

A few hours later, I was in the new restaurant with Matt. The building was really interesting and looked clean and new on the outside, but inside needed a lot of work. It had previously been another bar that had been very successful for some time, but the inside of the building came into disrepair and the owner retired. With no family and all his business partners uninterested in running a bar, he just sold it to Tom as it was. It had closed its doors for the last time under its old name only a week ago, and we had a lot of work to get it ready for us.

Matt was pissed and stomping around with two by fours and hammers in various areas of the building as we found new things that needed to be fixed. I ducked into another room to get away from him, presumably the office, though it was junked up with ancient barstools and glassware. Sitting gingerly on a stool I wasn't sure would hold my weight, I called Mom to check up on Hannah.

Apparently, Hannah had decided to stay at her own place. Mom was still keeping a room open for her in case she changed her mind, but as it was, she hadn't seen her since we left dinner. After promising I would call her again soon, I hung up with Mom and dialed Hannah, relieved when she answered on the second ring.

"Hey, you," she said.

"Hi, Hannah," I said. "I was just calling to check in."

"I'm fine. I decided to spend a little time at my place. I've got all the doors locked and the windows barred, just so you know," she said. There was a hint of teasing in her voice, but I didn't feel very humorous.

"Good," I said. "I don't want to push you, but if you feel like you might not be safe for any reason, Mom's keeping the room open for you."

"That's very sweet," she said. "Ava and Mason also offered to put me up if I need it. But I haven't seen any sign of Ethan, and I think he probably went home. I think I'm okay here."

"If you say so," I said. I loved that Hannah was so independent, but I was worried.

"It's okay," Hannah said sweetly. "I'm safe."

Matt's mood didn't improve throughout the day. In fact, the entire drive up there the day before he had been a bear, and it hadn't gotten any better with a night's sleep. He was apparently handling being told to leave Astoria even worse than I was, and as I stood at the bar, wondering why in the world board game pieces were glued underneath the taps, he kicked a cardboard box across the room.

"Hey, Matt, chill," I said. "That box didn't do anything to you."

It was meant as a joke, but Matt seemed to miss it.

"Fuck that box," he said. "And fuck Portland."

"Well, that's certainly a take," I said, giving up on the figures on the taps and moving to more pressing issues. Like the wood coming up from the floor.

"It's bullshit," Matt continued. "We shouldn't be the ones having to do this. If Tom wants a second bar so bad, he should be out here with us."

"I know you're frustrated," I said. "I am, too. But we don't have families. And both Tyler and Mason thought this was a good idea, too. So, suck it up, Buttercup. Besides, Portland won't be too bad. It's Portland."

"It's Portland," Matt repeated mockingly. "Like you give a crap."

"Hey." I put down the tools I had picked up and coming around the bar toward him. "I left Hannah back in Astoria. It's not exactly easy for me either."

"So you finally gave in, eh?" he mumbled.

"Yeah, well, we're seeing each other. And it's been really great. She'd been over at my house for the night multiple times, and something was starting to happen for us," I said, realizing that emotion was starting to take over. I paused and took a deep breath. "But that had to get put on pause. I came here because we're brothers, and we're doing this together. I had to pack up and leave an extraordinarily rare chance for me to find someone and come here to be with you and open this bar. So shut up and help me do that."

"Your fault for getting involved," Matt mumbled and

then walked away. It was a good thing, too. I was liable to grab his head and put it through the extremely cheap glass windows that let in all the cold and let out all the heat.

Choosing to ignore Matt for the rest of the day, I went to work on back of house. The kitchen was in pretty decent shape, and aside from restocking food in the pantries and doing some general cleanup, there wasn't much that needed to be done. The office, on the other hand, that was going to need some work.

We had rented a large dumpster for anything we didn't think we could sell and a pod storage unit for the stuff we did. I began emptying the office and finding all sorts of trash and treasures hidden inside. A map of Portland from the early 1900s was rolled up in a corner, and I immediately envisioned it behind the bar in a frame. Several old flags from both the state and nation were kept reverently in a cabinet in the corner, along with a plaque that had the very first owner's first dollar bill in a glass case on it. At that time it had been called "Maddow's Pub."

Slowly, an idea for how to decorate the bar came into shape. Something that would acknowledge the history of the space while giving way for evolution. Putting up the Maddow's Pub plaque behind the bar would serve as a good-luck charm in a way. I felt good about the sudden idea, and if I wasn't annoyed with Matt, I would have pulled him inside to pick his brain.

As I was bringing some stools out to the dumpster that I was pretty sure were used in a riot at some point, my phone rang. I tossed the stools in and opened it up, seeing the call was coming from Tom.

"Yo," I said. He hated when I did that, which was precisely why I did it.

"Jordan," he said, completely ignoring my greeting, "how are things? Any updates on the space?"

"Well, things are moving along," I said. "I have a decent idea for what I want to do for décor. I found some really neat old stuff from when the bar had other names, and I was going to go for a whole nostalgia thing, while freshening it up and making it modern. Kind of like *Cheers* meets home-brew CBD hippie beer."

"Please don't serve home-brew CBD hippie beer in our bar," Tom said wearily.

"It was an example," I said. "For the mental image."

"Good," Tom said. "Did all the furniture arrive?"

"It did. All at once."

"Good. I was hoping they wouldn't send them in two blocks. I asked for one but wasn't sure they would do it."

"Well, it's a mess in the front left room of the bar. Just chairs and tables and stools everywhere while we figure out where it all goes," I said.

"That's fine."

"You might want to talk to Matt, though."

"What's going on with Matt?"

"He's being a real dick." "What's he being a dick about?"

"Just being here in general, I think," I said. "He's pitching a fit and kicking boxes and muttering to himself. If I didn't know any better, I'd think he didn't like it here."

"Very funny," Tom said. "Tell him he needs to shape up and deal with it. You guys have another six months in there before I'll be able to hire a manager to run it, and then he can come home. You too if you wanted."

"You think we could get someone in that fast?"

"I believe so. The bar was pretty much fully equipped

when we bought it, and most of that stuff is salvageable, isn't it?" he asked.

"Almost all of it," I said.

"Well, then. All we need to do is hire a competent manager, work them long enough that we feel comfortable with them having the responsibility and know they won't bolt on us, and then you guys can come back to Astoria. Why you would want to do that is beside me, but you could."

"I'll tell him," I said.

Hanging up, I felt a lot better. Six months wasn't a year. A year was what I guessed when I moved out to Portland. Maybe Hannah would be okay with only two days of spending time together if it was only for six months. Maybe.

HANNAH

It seemed like forever when I finally got the phone call from Jordan I'd been waiting for since he walked out of his house and got in the car to head to Portland.

"Hey," he said when I answered it. "I'm on my way home."

I couldn't help but grin. "Really?"

"I've hit the highway, which means I was being totally accurate. The car is gassed up, and I am officially en route to Astoria."

"I'm so glad to hear that," I said.

"Where are you?"

I dried my hands on a dish towel and draped it over the faucet. "In my kitchen. I just finished up doing the dishes. Nothing but excitement and revelry going on over here. I did, however, make a mean apple crumble today. It was the highlight of my week, so I probably shouldn't go bragging about it."

"I like that it was the highlight of your week. That means nothing else happened," he said. "Have you been at your house this entire time?"

I chuckled as I dished out what might have been my third bowl of crumble and put it in the microwave. "Is that your less than subtle way of asking me if I took your mother or Ava up on their offers to stay at either of their houses while you were in Portland?"

"You caught me," he said. "I was really hoping they would be able to convince you to stay with one of them. Or both of them. You could have done a rotation."

Taking the crumble out of the microwave, I added a dollop of ice cream and leaned against the counter to eat it.

"Well, as much as I will admit that knowing I had the options was nice, I've been fine here. But I've spent too much of my life with people trying to control me and force my life into being what they want it to be. When I left, I told myself I wasn't going to let that happen anymore. Besides, there's been no sign of Ethan," I said.

"None at all?" he asked. "You haven't seen him; he hasn't called you? No emails? Nobody at the bar has mentioned seeing him?"

"I haven't put out an all-points bulletin to the regulars so they would call him out if they saw him, but no. No calls, no visits, no appearances at the bar, no emails. After the encounter with you that night, he seems to have just faded away," I said.

"I'm glad to hear that. I've been worried about you."

"I appreciate you worrying. But I told you I would call if anything happened."

"I know. Didn't stop me."

I laughed. "Alright. Well, you should be paying attention to the road. I'll see you soon."

"Absolutely."

We got off the phone, and I washed the now-empty bowl.

I was ironing my clothes for work a little while later when my phone rang. Without looking at the screen, I grabbed it and tucked it between my shoulder and ear.

"Are you home already? How fast were you driving?" I asked in a teasing voice.

"I never speed," Ava replied.

"Oh, Ava," I said. "Well, that was embarrassing as hell. I didn't realize it was you."

"Thought it was Jordan?"

"Maybe."

"Uh-huh. I know he's on his way back home. And I'm sure you're excited to see him, but I have to ask you a massive favor," she said.

"What do you need?" I asked, still feeling the heat on my cheeks.

My plan of not making a big deal out of what might be happening between Jordan and me didn't seem to be working out too well.

"There's a new girl training tonight. We're mostly bringing her in as a kitchen back so people get their food faster, but I'd like to have her prepared to do full wait duties so there's someone else for the busy nights or when we are shorthanded. If you could come in an hour or so earlier than usual to show her the ropes, it would be great," Ava said.

"Sure. Not a problem," I said.

"Great. I appreciate it. See you soon."

I covered my face with my hand, shaking my head as she hung up laughing.

I got to the bar a couple of hours earlier, and the new girl was already there. She was sitting at the bar, looking nervous, but like she was trying to already fit in. Since the bar had gotten so popular, snagging a waitress or bartender job there was a coveted position. I have already had my fair share of people mention to me that they wanted to work there so they can show off to their friends and get into all the theme nights.

Unfortunately for those just looking for a chance to jump the lines at the events and to hand out drinks to their friends, Ava had strict standards. They had gotten more intense even since I started working at the bar. That meant this girl must have some experience and a personality Ava thought would fit in with the rest of us.

It didn't guarantee she would last. There had already been a few who had come and gone because they couldn't handle the pressure. But at least it was a good start.

I walked up to her and held out my hand. "You must be the new girl. Hi, I'm Hannah. I'm going to be showing you around."

She smiled and nodded. "I'm Sarah. I'm really excited to get started."

"Then let's go ahead and jump in."

I started the same way Jordan started with me, touring her around the space and introducing her to the others as I encountered them. It brought up memories of my first day there. It seemed funny to be so nostalgic about something, but it only happened a short time before in the greater scheme of things, but I had gotten so comfortable at the bar and with the Anderson family it made me a little emotional to remember.

It was obvious Sarah had done this type of job before. She caught on quickly and seemed confident. I had a feeling that she would quickly move her way up to the main waitstaff.

The crowd was manageable that night, so we spent most of it with Sarah shadowing me and learning all aspects of waiting the tables. Some of my favorite regulars were there, and they slipped me extra tips to share with Sarah. It brought a grin to her face and she tucked them away eagerly. I had a feeling there was a story there, something that I didn't know about her yet.

I had just collected a bill and split the money tucked inside with Sarah and was turning to check on the next table when the door opened. The guys at the table looked up and waved.

"Hey, Jordan. Where've you been?" one of them called.

I looked over and saw Jordan coming toward me with a big smile on his face. My heart leapt, and I had to use all my self-control not to run toward him and jump into his arms. As it was, he gathered me up in a hug as soon as he got close.

"I thought you were just going to go home and crash," I said.

"Not without seeing you first," he said. "Do you have a break coming up?"

Glancing over at the bar, I met eyes with Ava. She offered a hint of a smile and nodded, then called for Sarah to come over to the bar to fill her in on what she had learned that evening. It was nothing short of a diversionary tactic, but I appreciated it.

I finished up checking on the tables, and though some of the guys did their best to tease us by delaying me, soon Jordan and I were headed toward the back of the bar. As soon as we were in the back room away from prying eyes, he wrapped me up in his arms again. I closed my eyes and nuzzled my face into his shoulder, just enjoying having him close to me again.

He pulled back and kissed me. It seemed like it was meant to be a gentle kiss and nothing more, but as soon as our lips touched, it deepened. I could feel myself heating up and had to step back from him to stop myself from turning this into a literal not-safe-for-work situation.

I was beyond happy to see him and relieved he was back. He held my hands as he told me a little bit about his trip, but he couldn't go into all the details because I only had a few minutes before I had to go back to work.

"Let me follow you home tonight," he said as he walked me back toward the front of the bar.

"No, you don't have to do that," I said.

"I can just hang out here until your shift is over."

I shook my head. "I still have hours to go. I'm sure you're tired and just want to get home and relax for a bit. Don't worry about me. I promise I'll call you when I get there."

He finally agreed and squeezed my hand before walking toward the kitchen so he could say hello to the guys in the back before leaving. I went to the bar to collect Sarah, and we got back to work moving through the tables.

The rest of the night was smooth, and I had a nicely lined pocket by the time the shift was over. Sarah and I sat down with Ava for a late dinner to talk about her first day, and then Ava cut us loose rather than having me stay to help clean up. It was a perk of training and getting there early, and I didn't argue.

I was feeling good right up until I pulled into my driveway. As I sat there staring at the house, something started twisting in my stomach. I felt off as I got out of the car and started up the sidewalk toward the door. Climbing the steps onto the porch, I lifted the key toward the lock but stopped. Something deep down was telling me not to go inside.

Tossing my key back into my bag, I hurried back to the car, got inside, and locked the doors. I got out my phone and called Jordan.

"You got home okay?" he asked.

"Yeah, but…" I said, hesitating.

"But what?" his tone was instantly on alert.

"I don't know. Something's weird. I don't know what it is, but I just feel off."

"Don't go inside," he said firmly. "Are you in your car?"

"Yes."

"Good. Stay there. Don't get out. Is the door open or anything? Any broken windows?" he asked.

"No. The door's closed, and I don't see anything else strange," I said. "It doesn't look like anything's wrong. I just feel weird."

"You need to trust your gut. Come over to my place," he said.

"Alright. I'm on my way."

Jordan was waiting for me at the door when I got to his house. He pulled me in for a tight embrace.

"Are you okay?" he asked.

"I'm fine. I'm sorry for all this," I said. "I can't explain why. I just felt like something was telling me not to go inside."

He shook his head as he guided me inside and shut the door behind me. "There's nothing to apologize for. Instinct is important. You'll stay here with me tonight, and I'll go over in the morning to check it out."

"Thank you," I said, still feeling a little shaken.

25

JORDAN

The next morning, she seemed in good spirits and less stressed, so I was happy to take her back to her place. Even if she was going to stay at her place, it would be good for me to see that it was safe. When we pulled up, everything seemed normal, and the doors were still locked. All her shades were drawn shut, so we couldn't see inside, but there were no marks on the doors or windows.

But as soon as the door opened, all that changed. The house was ransacked. Clothes, books, furniture was all torn up and thrown around the house. I pulled her behind me as she screamed in horror at how utterly destroyed it all was.

"Go get in the car. Lock the door. Call the cops," I said. I used my drill sergeant voice, and she, like everyone else who heard it, got moving before their brains caught up with why. She was in the car with the phone out when I turned back to the house. There was a broken piece of a wooden chair on the floor by the door, and I grabbed it. He must have smashed it against something repeatedly because it was a sturdy-looking piece of wood. Using it as a protective weapon, I slipped inside.

The living room was hit the hardest from what I could see. Some of her underwear was on the floor, cuts going through them as if they had been sliced with scissors or a knife. The walls had messages on them in crude script and red spray paint. I walked through the kitchen, which seemed relatively untouched, and got to the room at the end of the hall, what I assumed was her bedroom.

I swung the door open, hard. If he was in there, I wanted as much of the element of surprise as I could have. I held the wooden leg of the chair above my head, ready to strike, but the room was empty. Trashed, but empty. More messages were spray-painted on the walls. These were cruder, viler. The living room had been more "why me" with messages like "how could you do this to me?" and "I hope you're happy." The ones in the bedroom just filled me with disgust. How a person could say things like that about someone they supposedly loved.

But that was just it. He didn't love her. He thought he owned her. This wasn't about winning back the affections of a person. This was about acquiring something that he believed was stolen from him. A piece of property.

I checked the rest of the house, clearing each room with the preparation that he could be there. Her bed was messed up, and I could just see him lying in it. He had been. How long before we got there I didn't know, but he had been there. Waiting.

When I got outside, Hannah flung the door of the car open and ran to me. I held her as she sobbed. She wanted to go inside and see it, but I held her tight, shaking my head.

"You don't want to do that right now."

"Why not?"

"You just don't," I said, then thinking of a reason that might not scare her so much, I added, "Remember, the police might need to dust for fingerprints. The less contaminated they can have it, the better."

That seemed to work, and she nodded, then curled it into my chest. The sobbing had stopped, but now she just looked vacant. There was immeasurable sadness and fear in her expression, but all I could do was hold her and kiss the top of her head.

The cops arrived shortly thereafter, and I gave them a statement as to what I saw when I went in. I remembered each surface I touched so I could tell them where to expect my prints. The other officer was a veteran too, and he nodded grimly as Hannah explained the story. He took some notes before going inside with two other officers. The other two carried their phones out as cameras and had bags to collect evidence in.

"I need to go sit down," Hannah said.

"Come on," I said, guiding her back to my truck. I opened the door for her, and she sat in the passenger's seat, staring blankly ahead at the house.

"He was there when I came home, wasn't he?" she asked. Her voice was monotone, and the tears seemed to have dried on her face.

"I don't know," I said. "I think so." I reached behind the driver's seat and pulled the cooler out. I had some water bottles in there from my trip to Portland. I pulled one out for her and broke the seal on top. "Here, drink this. It will help with the shock."

She took the bottle from me without looking and took a big sip. I turned in my seat to watch the door of the house and wait for the officers to come out. After a while, she had leaned back in her seat and closed her eyes. I didn't think she had dozed off, but she was trying to remain calm. The officer made his way out and came to her side of the truck, and I rolled the window down. Hannah turned her head and opened her eyes.

"Ma'am," the officer said. "I would suggest, if possible, sleeping somewhere else for the night. We have a few resources if you need. We will likely be processing the house for quite some time anyway. But if you wanted to go in and get a few things, now would be a good time."

"I can do it," I said. "If that's alright with you."

She nodded slowly and turned to me. "It would be. But I can do it. You can come with me, though."

She sounded distant and distraught, like she was on the edge of completely breaking down but was holding herself up. I got out of the truck and went inside with her. For a long time, she stared at the messages on the walls without blinking. Then, she sighed heavily and went into her room, grabbing a duffel bag and stuffing it with clothes.

"I already have most of my toiletries at your place," she said as she brushed by me into the bathroom. "I just need a few things."

Despite the terrible situation, a part of me was happy to hear how casually she decided she was coming home with me. It wasn't even a question.

After she had what she felt like she needed, she removed the key from her keychain and handed it to the officers. She apparently had a backup in her car, which was locked. The officer made sure she opened her car and verified it was still there. Then, we headed back to my place. We got inside, and I brought her bag to the bedroom.

"Thank you for letting me stay here again," she said. "I'll find a new place soon."

"You could just live here," I said automatically and went stock-still.

I turned to look at Hannah, expecting her to react

poorly to it. I was shocked it slipped out of my mouth. Instead, she smiled. It was a genuine smile, even if there was a lot of stress and hurt etched on her face.

"I don't know if that's such a good idea right now," she said. "It's just a little soon, you know?"

"I understand, seriously," I said. "The idea just kind of slipped out."

"It's okay," she said. "Part of me wants to. I just think that maybe it's a little early for that."

I nodded and kissed her head. "As long as you feel safe and secure. I have a call I have to make. I'll be on the back porch if you need me."

She nodded, and I walked into the kitchen and opened the glass door. Stepping outside, I pulled open my phone and hit Mason's name. He needed to know what was going on.

"Hey, Bubba," Mason said. It was his usual greeting for me and had been since we were kids.

"Hey, Mason," I said.

"Uh-oh, that voice doesn't sound good," he said.

"It's Hannah," I said. "Her ex broke into her place last night and tore it up pretty good. Wrote some really heinous shit on the walls."

"Oh God," Mason said. "Is she okay?"

"Physically, yes. She was with me," I admitted. "But she's going to stay with me for a bit, and I don't think it's a good idea for her to try to come in to work or for me to leave her alone tonight."

"Hell no," Mason said. "You are both taking the day off. That's an order from the boss."

"Ava said so?" I teased. It felt good to make a joke. Mason laughed on the other end.

"She would if I told her," he said. "Just tell Hannah that

she can take all the time she needs. The new girl should be able to handle herself without shadowing anyone. She's been waiting tables for a couple of years."

"Will do," I said. "Thanks, Mason."

I went back inside to tell Hannah what Mason said. She nodded and continued folding clothes. She was setting them in neat piles on my bed, and I suddenly realized she needed a drawer to put things in.

"Thank you, Jordan," she said. "And tell Mason I said thank you, too."

"I will when I see him. I'm staying home tonight, too," I said.

"Really?" she asked, her eyes floating back up to mine. Tears pooled at the edges. I walked to her and pulled her in for a deep hug.

"Of course. I wouldn't leave you home alone tonight. Now, let's clear out some of these drawers for you and order a pizza," I said.

We ordered from my favorite Italian place nearby and launched up my streaming service. I let her pick what movies she wanted to watch, which turned out to be a couple of really funny romantic comedies. They were decidedly not the types of movies I usually watched, but the ones she picked were pretty good.

I tried to keep the conversation light and distracting. A bottle of wine I had put away got cracked open. I wasn't much of a wine guy either, but for her I would avoid beer for the night. I tried talking about everything except for the house and Ethan. Eventually, she started to come out of her funk, and talk turned to the only other subject I wanted to avoid. Portland.

"So, about that," I said after she mentioned when I was

planning on leaving again. "I found something out about my expectations there."

"What's that?" she asked.

"Well, I found out that I'll only need to be there for about six months," I said.

"Really?" The happy note in her voice made me look up at her, and I noticed for the first time in the evening a smile crossed her face.

"Really," I confirmed.

HANNAH

Another week passed and there still wasn't another sign of Ethan. He didn't show up again, and I hadn't gotten any phone calls or messages from him. I almost wished I had. That way, at least I wouldn't have to wonder so much. As it was, I wasn't sure how to feel about him just disappearing again.

On one hand, it was good to not have to deal with him. I didn't want to see him or hear his voice. After what he did, I was so angry I couldn't see straight. But I was also unnerved. Ethan hadn't just threatened me. He had gone into my home and destroyed my belongings. He was in my personal space, a place where I should feel safe. It felt like a violation.

Wondering where he could be, if he was watching me, and when he might turn up next were all pushing me to the edge. The anxiety was creeping up, and I felt like I was becoming paranoid.

I wanted him found. I wanted him held accountable for what he did. More than that, I wanted him out of my life. I needed to know he wouldn't be able to keep doing this to me.

Sitting on the couch in Jordan's living room, I called Samantha. I ran my fingers back through my hair as I waited for her to answer. In the kitchen Jordan was making something that smelled spicy and delicious. I wanted to just be able to relax and enjoy the time with him, but I couldn't.

"How are you doing? Is everything alright?" Samantha asked by way of answering the phone.

"I remember a time when those weren't the most common things people said to me," I said. "Those were the good days."

"I'm sorry. I'm just on edge when it comes to you."

"I'm on edge when it comes to me, too," I said with a sigh. "Have you heard anything about him?"

"No," Samantha said. "I'm sorry. I've been trying to find out anything I can. I've asked everybody I can think of, but no one has heard from him or anything about him."

"So, once again, no one knows where he is," I said. "That worked out really well for me last time."

Jordan had a meeting with his brothers about the new bar that afternoon, and I didn't want to sit around at the house by myself. Instead, I headed for the library to continue working on the mural. It was taking longer than I expected it to, but the library didn't mind. I didn't want to rush and not have it turn out the way I envisioned it, and they agreed.

Part of me felt like I was taking extra time just so I had something to do. It filled my mind and made me feel better, especially when I couldn't be with Jordan. This was something that was mine. Something I did because I was not only good at it but enjoyed it.

Art was one of the things that was largely kept from me

when I was at home. My parents encouraged me to paint, but only if it was classical art, and only if it didn't take my time and focus away from events, networking, and being there for Ethan.

Now, I got to do whatever I wanted. I could create whatever came to mind and take as much time as I wanted to with it. It was a luxury and an indulgence, and one that I was leaning into more and more.

I stepped back from the wall and looked at the new section I was adding on to the picture. It wasn't quite as seamless as I wanted it to be, almost as if my thoughts and emotions from the different days I painted were showing up in the painting.

"You did a much better job on the one in New York."

The voice behind me startled me. I didn't have to turn around to know who it was, but I didn't want my back to him. I whipped around to face him.

"Ethan," I said.

He stepped up closer to the wall and pointed out a section of the mural. "You see right here? Your lines are weak here. They don't live up to the rest of the piece, like you gave up on this area."

Of course he was there to criticize me. That was what he did best. While we were together, he could have listed it as his hobby on a resume.

"What are you doing here, Ethan?"

My heart was starting to beat harder in my chest, but I didn't let my expression show my fear even as I looked around to make sure there were other people who could see us. I didn't want to give him the satisfaction of knowing he was getting to me. Seeing me upset and frightened was always one of his favorite things. I gave into it for far too long. I wasn't going to do it anymore.

I noticed a group of mothers with their young children heading for the field nearby to play. It gave me comfort to know we weren't alone. There were too many witnesses, which gave me confidence he wouldn't do anything.

"I'm looking at your mural," he answered. "Isn't that why you're painting it? So people will look at it?"

The reply made my teeth grit and my jaw twitch. That was just like him. A sarcastic, nasty comment wrapped up in something innocent. It was why so many people trusted him when he didn't deserve it. Why so many were charmed by him and convinced he was so perfect. They didn't want to see beyond the veneer he put up. But I could see past it and it made my skin crawl.

"How could you do that?" I asked.

He looked at me like he just didn't understand what I was saying. "How can I look at your mural?"

"Don't act dumb, Ethan. It's not going to impress me. Why did you do that to my house last week?" I asked.

He shook his head. "Do what to your house?"

"You know what," I said, getting angrier with every word that came out of my mouth.

"No, I don't. I have no idea what you're talking about," he said. "I didn't do anything to your house. I couldn't have. I was in California for the last couple of weeks."

"Don't try that. I know you're lying."

I waited for him to argue, to try to defend himself again. But he didn't. Instead, the faux innocence melted away from his expression and his eyes narrowed.

"Why are you with that guy?" he asked.

"He has a name," I said. "And I know you know what it is."

"I don't give a shit what it is. I want to know why you're with him."

The anger had shown up in his voice, and the words were coming through his teeth with greater force. Somehow that felt more comfortable. He was more predictable this way. I would rather be on edge because his aggression was ticking up than dangling, waiting for the next thing to happen.

"I'm with Jordan because he treats me with respect. And that's all you need to know. It's more than you *deserve* to know. Now, go back to New York and let me get on with my life," I said.

I took a step back toward my paints, hoping he would just walk away. Ethan immediately took a step toward me, lessening the space between us again.

"We aren't finished, Hannah. I'm going to prove to you who the better man is. Mark my words, you'll be running back to me soon. You just better hope that when you do it isn't too late," he said.

There was an ominous threat in those words, but I didn't back down. I looked Ethan directly in the eyes and spoke clearly and calmly to make sure he understood every word I said.

"Get the fuck away from me, Ethan."

He started to move toward me, but the squeal of tires stopped him. We both looked to see Jordan getting out of the truck he had just parked haphazardly in the closest spot to us. Ethan looked back at me with an arrogant smirk on his face and gave a little half shrug.

"That's my cue," he said.

He was gone before Jordan got to us, heading across the front of the library toward the parking lot. Jordan started after him, but I put my hand in the middle of his chest to stop him.

"What was that all about?" Jordan demanded.

"He was just being an asshole, then he said he couldn't have been the one in my house because he was in California the last couple of weeks," I said.

"That's bullshit."

"I know. He asked why I was with you and said he was going to prove he's the better man and I would go running back to him." I took a breath and let it out slowly.

"I'm going to kill him," Jordan said through gritted teeth.

The sound of a car flying out of the lot made us turn, and we saw Ethan speeding away.

"You can't go after him," I said.

"Why not?"

"Because he isn't worth going to prison for. I just have to try to ignore him and not give him any indication he's getting to me at all. Eventually he will get bored and go away," I said.

"It's that 'eventually' I don't like," he said.

"I know. I don't, either."

"You're probably right, but I want to make sure that really does happen. From now on, I don't want you to be alone."

As the words sank in, I didn't know how to feel about Jordan's assertion.

27

JORDAN

Ethan was really starting to piss me off. The fact that he would have the gall to even get anywhere close to her after what he did to her house was incredible, and if I could have gotten my hands on him, I would have ripped him to pieces. Hannah stopping me was probably exactly what she said, good because it kept me out of prison.

Apparently, his prints were nowhere to be found in the house. As far as the cops were concerned, it was a break and enter and vandalism, but they couldn't go after Ethan without evidence. It frustrated the hell out of me, but Hannah just wanted to let it go. She thought that him doing that to her place "got it out of his system" somehow, and that he would disappear eventually.

I wasn't so sure.

It had been a pretty quiet few days since the mural run-in, but that didn't mean he was gone. I didn't trust him not to be watching us from somewhere and ready to strike at the worst possible time. I didn't want to be paranoid, but my instincts were kicking in, and I was extremely frustrated not to be able to go scan every car in every parking lot and make sure.

Driving by all the hotels and motels in town was a slow crawl, but I did it anyway. Hannah thought I was out with Luke usually, and most of the time I was. But we were both on reconnaissance. I scanned every parking lot for his car and found nothing. I knew there were a few houses in Astoria that were rented as vacation homes, but I had no idea where they were and online searches came up with nothing. Wherever he was staying, he was keeping out of sight. Even Luke thought he might just be gone, but I couldn't buy that. Not yet.

It was about time to leave for work, and I was putting on my shoes when Hannah came into the living room dressed to go.

"Umm," I began.

"I'm coming to work, Jordan," she said.

"I don't know if that's such a good idea."

"It is," she insisted. "I can't just keep hiding out. It's giving him way too much power over my life to never go anywhere or do anything. I have to be able to go to work and get back on track with my life."

"I understand that," I said. "I do. But I don't trust that he isn't hanging around here somewhere. What if he attacks you?"

"Well, you'll be there, won't you?"

"Yeah," I admitted.

"Then I am much more worried about how he will survive than me."

She grinned, and I returned the expression. Hannah was right. By the time he got within touching range of Hannah, I would have already ripped out his eyes and used them for dice.

"Okay," I said. "You're right. I'll drive."

We headed out to the truck and drove through the early evening darkness to get to the bar. When we arrived, the place was already rocking. Getting inside, we went to the back, put on our aprons, and kissed before opening the door and disappearing into the din of The Hollow.

The money was flowing in off some really decent tips, and when I felt like I couldn't take the people anymore, I would switch with Mason and go behind the bar and make drinks for table orders. It helped give me a little break from one-on-one interactions while also giving me the best view of the clientele. From behind the bar, I could see the entire floor, and if Ethan walked in, I would know.

My eyes were peeled for him the whole night, and as closing time got closer, I began to relax. If he had planned on coming in, he would have done so before then. And I would have ripped him into little, tiny pieces, stuck them on skewers, and had a barbeque.

As the night got closer to being over, I was on the floor and noticed Mason had taken a call in the hallway. I didn't think much of it, but when he got off, he headed over to me. The look on his face told me that the news he was going to tell me wasn't something I particularly wanted to hear.

"Hey, can we talk for a minute?" he asked.

"I have three tables. Can someone take care of them?"

"Yeah, let me get her," he said.

Mason walked back to the bar, said something to Ava, and pointed to the three tables that were still sitting. They were regulars, and we usually let them hang out a bit later than others, provided they were drinking water or soda and their drinks were done by lights up. Ava came over, and I handed her my book with their orders so she knew what they would want if they wanted refills.

"Come with me," Mason said. I followed him down the hall and to the door outside. As I passed the kitchen, Hannah came out carrying a plate of mozzarella sticks. We maintained eye contact as I backed through the door, and when it closed, she was standing in the hallway, sadness in her eyes.

"I guess I know what's coming," I said. "It was Tom, wasn't it?"

"It was," Mason said. "He said the licenses are all in order, and we're clear to open the bar now. He wants Matt and me back there next week to finish up the setup and get it going."

"When's the grand opening?"

"Tom's thinking a couple weeks. He wants to spend some time working out the ad campaign. We might lose a little bit having a bar we could open that's still closed, but if we build enough buzz it might see us through the lean period that usually comes after a place opens and then the novelty wears off," Mason said. "So, maybe first of next month?"

"It would be a Friday night," I said.

"It would," Mason said. "Ava has already gotten busy working out a big theme party for it. She's playing on the décor idea you had. From what I understand, she already had internet fliers and a mailing list ready, so he cleared her to release those earlier today. The wheels are officially moving."

"Ah." Knowing that the plans were already in motion before I was even told when I was heading back there was irritating. I got out of the military once already, I wasn't particularly enjoying the rest of my life taking orders, too.

But it was part of the business. Mason and Tom were the business guys, and Ava was probably better at it than both of them. If the three of them had cooked up a plan for getting the Portland bar off the ground, I had no doubt it would work like gangbusters. It was just terrible timing for Hannah and me.

"Look, I know the situation with you and Hannah is... complicated," Mason said.

"That's one way of saying it."

"I just want you to know we are going to be looking after her. If she wants to come stay with us, she is more than welcome," he said. "I know Mom has a spot for her, too, but I can completely understand why staying with Mom would be a little much for her. If she stays with us, she would have a ride to work every shift, and we would make sure she was safe. I just wanted you to know that option was out there."

"I appreciate that," I said. "Seriously, that's very cool of you."

"So, where are you with this thing?" Mason asked. "How serious is it?"

I tried waving him off, but Mason was probably the one brother who could see through me, and he had zero problems calling me on my shit. He always had. It's one of the things I respected most about it.

"Let's just leave it at she's been staying at my place with me, and I am not thrilled with leaving Astoria," I said.

"Fair enough," Mason said. "She will be okay, Jordan. She's a smart woman, and she has resources. We will look out for her. And Portland, for you, will be temporary."

"I know," I said. "Come on, let's get in there and finish up. I feel like having a beer after the shift."

When we finally got back to the house in the wee hours of the morning, I was physically exhausted, but my mind was still rolling. I told Hannah what Mason said before our shift was even over. I wanted her to have time to process it before car ride back. It turned out that during the ride back we were engaged in a conversation about one of her customers, and it never came up. But the second the door shut behind us and she started getting changed for the night, I knew it wasn't going to stay that way.

"Are you ready for bed?" she asked. "I'm weirdly awake."

"Want to put on some TV and hang out on the couch a little while?" I asked.

"Grab the popcorn," she said.

As I was making the popcorn, Hannah made her way into the kitchen, grabbing a couple of glasses and filling them with sweet tea before pinching my butt and walking into the living room. I was going to miss that. The little couple things that we did that I didn't even think about. We had fallen into such a comfortable routine that we didn't even talk about where we were.

But I knew. I was falling for her, hard. And I needed to address it sooner rather than later.

I sat down next to her, and we put on a cooking game show. When the popcorn was mostly gone and sitting on the coffee table, I lay back on the couch, and she curled up next to me. We kept watching until a commercial, and then I leaned down to kiss her on the nose. She moved at the last second, and I kissed her lips and laughed.

"Gotcha," she said.

"You sure did," I said. "Speaking of. I kind of wanted to talk to you about that."

"I thought we weren't going to talk about anything serious."

"Is that the way you want to keep it?"

"I didn't say that," she responded.

"Well, it's not how I feel," I said. "I know we wanted to

take it slow, especially in light of... everything. But I needed you to know something, especially before I went back to Portland."

I took a deep breath. Staring into her eyes was like looking into the sun. She sparkled, even when she was sad or upset. I just wanted to hold her up and let her light the world with those eyes.

"I just needed to tell you I have never felt the way I feel with you before. Never. I know I have been protective and everything with you, and I never want you to feel like I am controlling you. But I care about you so much. Like I said, I've never felt this way before. I don't know how to handle it sometimes."

I expected her to say that it was too early, like she did when I suggested she live with me, or for her get upset. Instead, she smiled and rested her head against my chest.

"Me too," she said.

28

HANNAH

I couldn't believe it was already the night before Jordan had to leave to go back to Portland. But instead of it being a romantic night for us to spend together and savor before we were going to be apart again, it was quickly and getting tense.

The dinner he had delivered and then served in candlelight was sweet right up until he reached across the table to take my hand.

"I want you to come with me to Portland," he said.

It was by far not the first time he'd said the same thing over the last few days. He had been trying hard to convince me to go with him. But it wasn't because he didn't want to be away from me again so he wouldn't have to miss me. Instead, he insisted I had to go with him so he could keep me safe.

"Jordan, we've talked about this," I said.

I really wanted that to be the end of it. This had the potential of being such a nice night, and I didn't want him to leave on a negative note. But I also wasn't going to just give in.

"I know we have. But I wanted to ask again. Come with me. Get out of Astoria for a little while. Come see Portland. You even said yourself that you thought it was pretty impressive I got to watch the bar grow from the very beginning. So, why don't you come watch it, too?" he asked.

"It is impressive. But it's not my bar. And I can't just pick up and leave so that you can babysit me. I have responsibilities here," I said. "I can't just throw those away and leave everybody at The Hollow in a lurch because you've decided I should never be out of your sight."

"You don't have to think about it like that. Just think of it as a vacation. You've been working really hard at the bar; anybody will tell you that. You deserve some time off, and I think you've earned a vacation where you can relax a bit."

"You really expect me to buy that? I'm supposed to think that going to Portland with my bosses while they oversee the building of a second location is a relaxing vacation?" I asked incredulously.

"Is that how you think of me?" Jordan asked, seeming taken aback. "Your boss?"

"You do own the bar where I work."

"Wow. Good to know."

"Don't get so defensive. Of course I don't think of you as my boss all the time. But in this circumstance, yeah. That's kind of what it looks like. Either that, or you are putting me in a fishbowl so you can watch every one of my movements and decide if they're acceptable to you," I said.

"I'm not putting you in a fishbowl. I'm trying to protect you."

I was starting to get irritated. "You're babying me. And I really hate being babied."

"I don't understand why you're being so difficult about this," Jordan said. "You're the one who has been so freaked-out by this guy. You're the one who called me when you didn't want to go in your house because you thought he was there."

"And now you're going to hold that against me?" I asked, shocked by the way he was acting. "I called you because I was scared, and I thought I could trust you."

"You can trust me, Hannah. That's the point of all this. I want to make sure you're safe, and I can't do that if I'm all the way in Portland and you're here. Either that, or let's get you packed and bring you to my mother's house. She can keep an eye on you until I get back into town."

That was it. I was officially done with this. I got up from the table.

"Stop. Seriously. That is enough. I can't believe you're acting like this. Did me telling you about how Ethan acted when we were together mean absolutely nothing about you?" I asked.

"What's that supposed to mean?" Jordan asked.

"I've told you how controlling he was and that he tried to dictate every moment of my life. And what he didn't dictate, my parents did."

"Are you seriously comparing me to him? Because I want you to be safe, I'm acting like a controlling prick?" he asked, scoffing in disbelief.

"It's not because you want me to be safe. It's because you want me to be safe on your terms. You don't think that I am capable of living my life." I forced myself to stop and close my eyes, taking a breath. "Look, I don't want this to turn into anything. I'm going to go home."

"Hannah, you don't have to—"

"Yes, I do," I said, avoiding him as he came toward me. "Have a good trip, Jordan."

I grabbed my keys and left, hopping in the car and

driving off before he could say anything else. For the next half an hour, I just drove around town. The truth was, I didn't want to go back to my house. I hadn't been there in weeks.

Finally, though, I decided all that time away from the house was probably all the more reason I should go back. It would need some serious cleaning, and now that I was thinking about it, I couldn't get it off my mind.

I got to the house and sat in the driveway for a few moments, gauging how I felt. I didn't feel completely comfortable, but I also didn't have the instinctive hesitation I had before. I went inside and made sure all the doors were firmly locked before going through each room and closet carefully. When I was done with that, I checked the doors and windows again.

Satisfied the house was empty and I was secure, I went to work cleaning. Music blaring, I cleaned the entire house, chipping away at the hours of the evening and into the night. By the time I was finished, it was late, but I felt wired.

After pacing around for a little while, I grabbed my phone and called Samantha.

"Was there a fire?" she said when she picked up.

At least, I was pretty sure that was what she said. It was more mumbling and sleep snuffles than words. That was when I remembered there was a three-hour time difference and it was already late there.

"I'm so sorry," I said. "I didn't mean to wake you up. Go back to sleep."

"It's okay. It's fine," she said, groaning.

"No, no. It's okay. Go to sleep." I hummed a little bit of a lullaby. "Good night."

"Hannah, you are the worst lullaby singer ever. I'm awake. What's going on?"

I told her about the fight with Jordan and that I was back at my house.

"I just don't know what to do. Getting away from New York was about breaking out of that box they were trying to keep me in. Since leaving, I've realized I'm far too independent to deal with this nonsense. I can't let him insist on babysitting me," I said.

"Okay, I'm going to go ahead and stop you right there. You need to let that go. Right now. You're being stalked by your ex. Stalked. Do you understand that Hannah? This isn't just some guy being annoying, and it's not Jordan controlling you. This could be a really dangerous situation, and Jordan is just trying to protect you. I know you're sensitive to it because of everything you went through, but you need to stop judging everybody based on what other people have done. See him for what he's really doing for you.

"Jordan cares about you. A lot. He might have gone off the deep end a little in the way he's showing it, but wouldn't you rather him take wanting to protect you a little too far rather than not caring if you were safe?"

It was really good advice, and I knew I couldn't just let things hang with Jordan. I needed to talk to him before he left town.

"Thank you, Samantha."

I ended the call and called Jordan as I headed for the door so I could head back to his house. As I stepped toward it, I heard a phone ringing on the other side. I opened it and found Jordan standing on the porch. He answered the phone and held it up to his ear while he looked me in the eyes.

"Can I call you back? I'm kind of busy right now. I'm trying to say I'm sorry for being an ass." He held up a bottle. "I brought wine."

I reached out and grabbed Jordan by the front of the shirt, pulling him into the house. He tossed his phone onto the couch as I wrapped myself around him, catching his mouth with mine. Our tongues tangling and our hands starting to pull at each other's clothes, we made our way to my room.

We kissed the entire way to the bedroom, and he lifted me off my feet to carry me when we got to the hall. I giggled as we made it into the room, and he shut the door behind him. Grabbing his shirt, I pulled him over to the bed, and he sat down on the edge of it. I dipped my head again to kiss him and grabbed the hem of my shirt to pull it up. It was a tight tank top that I wore often when I cleaned, and there was no need for a bra. So, when it came up and off my head, my breasts spilled out, and Jordan dove his face between them.

His tongue swirled over my nipples, bringing them taut while I untied the sweatpants cord and dropped them to the ground. His fingers wrapped around the fabric of my white cotton panties and yanked them down, too, and I kicked my clothes away. Before my leg could make it all the way back down, Jordan grabbed it and sat it beside him on the bed. I leaned my head back as he began to move his lips down my stomach and to my core.

A sharp breath escaped my lips as his strong, talented tongue made its way through my folds and to my clit. I let my head rock back and my eyes close as he teased it and slid one thick finger inside my pussy. His other hand rose up to grasp my breast, and I grabbed one finger to stick in my mouth. I sucked on his finger as he licked me, and I could feel the climax building. Suddenly, like a wave, it crashed over me, and I bucked into his mouth as my body convulsed.

When my legs stopped shaking, I let the one on the bed

drop back to the floor and knelt in front of him. He stood up to get his pants off, and I pulled his boxers away greedily. Immediately, I wrapped my lips around his cock and sucked him. One hand went to his balls and massaged them while the other stroked him into my mouth. He groaned deeply, and I felt one of his hands reach behind my head to guide me in slow, deep motions.

I felt his head brush the back of my throat and tried to relax. His cock was massive and filling, and I relished in pleasing him. But I needed more. I needed him inside me. I stood and pulled off his shirt so that he was as naked as I was. Pressing onto his chest, I gently pushed him and he dropped back onto the bed, his cock standing straight and long. I crawled up him, sinking my mouth over him one last time before continuing to make my way up and letting his staff slide between my breasts as well.

Finally, I was straddling him, and he pulled me with him until his back was against the wall, sitting up. I settled over his cock and gasped as he filled me. He stretched my walls until I accommodated him, and I began a slow, rocking motion. Jordan grasped my ass and squeezed each time I rocked forward, and he took my nipples into his mouth one at a time to tease them with his tongue.

I placed my hands on the wall for leverage and rode him hard, bouncing on him until I screamed in pleasure. Without a word, he tossed me onto my back and then flipped me back over. Positioning me so that my hands were in the same place on the wall as they had been, he got behind me. His cock penetrated deep inside me, and I groaned heavily. Each thrust only seemed to make me want him more.

"Harder," I cried as he pounded into me. He needed little encouragement. One hand tangled in my hair and tugged hard enough to create the sensation of pain but not enough to actually hurt. It sent a thrill down my spine, and I leaned into the overwhelming pleasure of the moment. His other hand wrapped hard around my hip and pulled me back into him with each thrust.

I could hear my voice spilling out of my lips, one long continuous stream of sound, punctuated by each thrust. His grip got tighter, and I knew he was about to come. Just knowing that made me slicker, and the tension built in me as well. The wave crashed over me in a moment of intense, passionate, and explosive climax, and I screamed out his name. He roared in response and exploded into me, pulling me as fully over him as possible so he penetrated me so deep he pressed against my back wall. He filled me until he was empty, and then we collapsed into the bed together, kissing the sweat from each other's chest and trying to catch our breath.

JORDAN

I was back in Portland, and Matt was exactly how he was last time. Bitching and moaning and kicking boxes, he was in rare form. I didn't particularly care, though. Nothing was going to get my mind off Hannah. She permeated every single thought I had. Every time I closed my eyes, I could see her face. Every time I took a deep breath, I could smell her perfume. Sometimes I could feel the tingling sensation of her lips having just been pressed to mine. It was distracting, but in the best of ways.

Matt cursed as he dropped a box with a blender in it and began to complain loudly that it was a sign of his situation. He tried making some sort of complicated analogy, but I only paid attention to part of it before giving up and focusing on retubing the taps. It was one of the last bits we needed to do behind the bar, and the guys were coming later in the day to pressurize them.

I wished Hannah had come with me, but I understood why she didn't. Still, we were opening that weekend, and on top of the joy of just having her in my arms every night, we could have used an extra experienced hand on the floor and someone to train the new staff. As it was, that job was going to fall on me, since Matt was next to useless with other people at the moment.

There was still a lot of work to do before opening, including training the new hires that Matt had approved of. I could only imagine the interview process. He had come up a day before me to take care of them, and I shuddered to think what they must have thought being introduced to surly, bitchy Matt. At least I would train them, and they would get to see not everyone here was a man-child.

Still, with so much to do, I needed to get Hannah off my mind long enough to get things done. But every time I would get into any rhythm like wiping circles on a table or using a screwdriver on one of the chairs to tighten up the legs, my mind would wander in the monotony and end up back with Hannah. Hannah in bed. Hannah painting the mural. Hannah waiting tables. Just Hannah, everywhere, at every time, with no break.

Finally, I decided to end the madness and just call her. Taking a break from Matt and being in his negative presence, I walked into the office and sat down. It was mostly ready back there, all the neat stuff kept and organized, junk tossed. I'd asked Tom to get a new desk in there with a new chair, and he went all out, getting a really nice mahogany desk with a state-of-the-art desktop placed on it. It was going to make doing all the paperwork easier, as well as anything else we needed to do.

I opened my phone and hit her contact info. There was a click on the first ring.

"Hello?"

"Hey, you," I said.

"Hey," she repeated.

"I got a bit of a break, and I thought I'd call you. How is your day?"

"It's been fine." There was something off in her voice, but I didn't want to push it. If it was important, I was sure she would tell me eventually. She liked to have a little time to work things out.

"Well, good," I said. "I didn't have a bunch of time, but I wanted you to know that Matt and I are going to go do some research on the other bars in the area tonight. We might be a little late getting back, but I'll text you."

"Okay," she said. "Have fun. I've to go."

"Okay. Bye."

"Bye." The line clicked, and I sat there looking at my phone for a moment in confusion.

"That was weird," I said to myself. Shrugging, I slid the phone back in my pocket and went back to work.

"The Jail Cell," I said, reading the sign.

"Yup," Matt said. "It used to be an old jail. The upper floors are apartments now."

"Old jail cells?" I asked. "As apartments?"

"No, only the bottom floor were jails. The upper floors were offices," he said. "Now they're apartments. Come on, let's get something to drink."

We stepped inside, and the darkness consumed us. The bar was one of those newer places that thought that keeping everything so dark you tripped into one another was good for meeting new people. The bar itself was in the back of the room, and we made it there through what I could only assume was sheer dumb luck.

"Two... somethings. I don't care. Alcohols," Matt said. The bartender smirked.

"Liquor or beer?" he asked.

"Liquor. Something that tastes good and isn't mostly water," he said.

It was an old trick for scouting bars, but it held up. Go in and ask the bartender for something but not specify what. See what the bartender served you, how expensive it was, and how much alcohol it contained. You could learn a lot about a bar by what the motives of the bartender was when they first met you.

A tall martini glass came back with some yellow liquid in it. I assumed it was pineapple juice. Matt immediately downed about half of it.

"Damn, that's good," he said. "I'll have another one of those. Jordan?"

"Sam's, please," I said.

"Another one of these and a Sammy for my brother," Matt said to the bartender. As he ducked behind the bar to get the glass for my beer, two girls sauntered over our way. They were very pretty, but one of them looked like she'd had about twenty drinks too many and was swaying wildly. She was also having a tremendous amount of trouble keeping one of the straps of her dress on, and it kept falling and exposing enough of her breast that I had to look away.

"We don't recognize you two," the sober one said. Her voice was nasally and had an accent I couldn't quite place. I figured it was Canadian.

"That's because we're new here," Matt said, eagerly finishing his first drink before the second arrived.

"You're hot," the somewhat coherent one said, then stumbled ever so slightly into the person behind her. She didn't seem to notice.

"Thank you," I said. "But I'm taken. Matt, on the other hand, is wildly single."

Both women descended on Matt like vultures, and I

scooted a little out of the way so he could bask in their atten-tion. He ended up ordering two drinks for the ladies, a real one for the sober one and a "special" one for the other. I made eye contact with the bartender, and the shared glance told me he was already on top of it. When he handed her the mostly cranberry-flavored water drink, I pulled out an extra bit of cash for his tip.

Dropping the cash on the bar, I began to walk away, but Matt grabbed me. He was deep in conversation with the sober one, and the drunker one was just hanging on every word the both of them said.

"I was just telling these girls here that we're opening a new bar," he said excitedly.

"Is that The Hollow one?" the sober girl asked. "I saw some fliers and got an email about it. I heard you guys do theme nights!"

"We do," Matt said, matching her enthusiasm and raising the stakes even higher. It was like his entire attitude was shifting. It made me chuckle.

"Yup, and karaoke if we can get the machine installed in time," I said.

"Oh, I love to sing!" the drunk one said. The short snippet of whatever cursed song she broke into for the next few seconds told me that while she might love to sing, not many people loved to hear it.

Before long, it was time to hit another of the bars, and Matt got both of their numbers. As we were walking out of the bar, he was grinning from ear to ear, and I noticed he had lipstick marks on both cheeks. I shook my head.

"I love this town," he mumbled.

I decided not to call him on it and instead headed to the truck where I could drive the two of us to the next place. I only drank a quarter of the beer in each of the three bars we had been to already. I figured by the time the night was done, I might have two whole beers in me. Matt, on the other hand, was well on his way to happy town.

All of this was making me miss Hannah even more. By the time we got back to the hotel we were staying at until we found a cheap apartment to rent close by, I decided to give her a call. She was used to late nights anyway, and a text just didn't seem like enough. I called, but it went right to voicemail.

I shrugged. Maybe she had an early night. Bidding my brother farewell and sending him into his room, I went into mine and tucked in for a few hours' rest.

30

HANNAH

Morning wasn't particularly my favorite time of day, but that morning took it to another level. I didn't just wake up feeling like I wished I could sleep longer. Even before my eyes opened, my stomach was turning. It was that kind of nausea that simultaneously made me afraid to move because I never did make it worse, and also afraid I wasn't going to make it to the bathroom in time.

I was feeling a little odd the night before, but nothing too serious. Now, I felt like my stomach was right on the verge of revolt.

I tried to talk myself out of it. Throwing up was definitely on my list of most hated things.

Within a few moments of waking up, I was scrambling out of bed and rushing for the bathroom. I made it, but not by much of a margin. When the waves of nausea finally ended and I was able to pull myself up from the floor, I leaned over the sink and rinsed my mouth with handful after handful of water from the faucet.

I was feeling less shaky, and I drew in a long breath to further settle my stomach. My body was shaking as I brushed my teeth and tried to figure out what the hell was going on. Nobody I knew was sick. I took an extra couple of seconds to go through all the brothers and their respective wives, then the rest of the staff again just to be sure.

None of them had been sick as far as I knew.

Maybe it was something I ate. I thought back on everything I had eaten the day before but couldn't think of anything that would cause food poisoning. But it had to be something.

Even though I'd brushed my teeth, my mouth still tasted sour. I got the mouthwash out of the medicine cabinet and swished it around. As I opened the cabinet to put the bottle away, I saw something that stopped me still mid-swish. The mouthwash burst out of my mouth into the sink, and I snatched the box of tampons out of the cabinet.

The unopened box of tampons. Unopened because I didn't use them when I should have gotten my period... a month ago.

Holy shit.

I rushed back into my bedroom and grabbed my phone, pulling up the calendar.

I scrolled back through the last few months and found the little star I'd scribbled with my stylus in the corner of the target date. And beside it, a little check mark.

And there they were for the four months I scrolled through. Star and check. Star and check. Star and check. Star and check. But then I got to last month. Star. No check.

I couldn't believe it. I had been so preoccupied by Ethan sneaking around I stopped paying attention. I hadn't even noticed my period didn't come.

Maybe it was stress. That could be it. I was definitely experiencing more than my fair share of stress because of the whole situation with Ethan. I could have stressed myself into not having a period for the month.

That thought brought a little bit of comfort, but there was only one way to know for sure. I got dressed as quickly as I could and ran out to the nearest drugstore. The array of pregnancy tests available was nothing short of mind-boggling, and I grabbed several different ones just to cover my bases. When I got home, I took a few of them and waited in the bathroom for the results while I guzzled a few bottles of water.

Twenty minutes after my first round of tests, I took a few more. They all told me the exact same thing, but that didn't stop me from going for one more round to use up the selection I bought. By the time I was done, the entire bathroom counter was lined with tests, and they all had the same result glaring back at me.

I was pregnant.

It took me a while to leave the bathroom. It felt like stepping over that threshold was the moment my life changed. As soon as I stepped out of the bathroom and back into my bedroom, I was really going into a whole new chapter of my existence. I walked into that bathroom with a question mark over my head. I walked out of it with a big plus sign.

"I'm pregnant."

The silence on the other end of the line didn't really surprise me. By this point Samantha was probably getting used to getting phone calls from me that seemed to forego the beginning of the conversation in favor of dropping right down into the middle. But up until this point, most of those conversations had been about Ethan and the anxiety he was bringing into my life.

This conversation was admittedly a curveball.

"I'm sorry, you're what now?" she finally asked.

"Pregnant. I'm pregnant."

"Yeah, that's what I thought you said." She let out a breath. "Wow. That's... that's a lot."

"I know," I said. "I woke up this morning thinking I had food poisoning, but it turns out it was morning sickness. So, I was hoping maybe you could give me a couple of pointers for how I can handle that."

Maybe it wasn't really the main issue I should have been thinking about right at that moment, but it was keeping my mind adequately distracted so I didn't have to think about anything else. Samantha obliged, rattling off tips for how to deal with morning sickness and other symptoms I was going to start having.

"Thanks," I said after almost an hour. "I feel more prepared now."

"That's good," she said. "But tell me something, Hannah. Why did you call me first and not Jordan?"

"Because you're my best friend," I said.

"And?"

I let out a sigh. She knew me too well.

"And I'm terrified to tell him. He has so much going on with the new bar and everything. I'm afraid it's all going to be too much for him," I said. "When I tell him, I don't want it to be more stressful."

"So you're thinking about his well-being before your own," she said.

"I guess so."

"You're in love with him," she stated plainly.

There was no point in trying to deny it. "I think I am."

When I got off the phone with Samantha, I briefly considered calling Jordan. Maybe I shouldn't delay it. But I stopped myself. He needed to get through the grand opening first. Then I could tell him. It would also give me time to process it for myself.

I had to do something. I couldn't just stay there in my house by myself thinking about it. It was still a couple of hours before I needed to be at work, but I got dressed and headed for the bar anyway. Just as I walked in, I felt like I was interfering with a family moment. Tyler and Mason were gathered at the bar with Becca and Ava. The guys were cheering, and Becca threw her arms around Ava in a close hug.

"Congratulations," Tyler said happily.

"Congratulations," Becca echoed. "This is really amazing."

I stepped in cautiously. "I'm sorry. Am I interrupting?"

Ava looked over at me and shook her head, grinning widely.

"No, no. Not at all. Come in," she said.

I went over to the bar and looked at each of the faces there. They were all smiling.

"What's going on?" I asked.

"I'm pregnant," Ava said.

My mouth fell open slightly. "You are?"

She nodded. "I found out a few weeks ago."

I gathered myself and forced a smile past the shock. "Congratulations. That's wonderful."

I hugged Ava as she thanked me. Fortunately, the little gathering broke up after that, and we all went our separate ways to get the bar ready for the night. I didn't think I'd be able to keep it together if we were all standing there for much longer.

I threw myself into work that night, trying to keep busy so I didn't drive myself crazy. It was almost closing time when I went into the storeroom for napkins and ran into

Ava. She smiled at me and started out of the room, and I knew I had to tell her.

"Ava, can I talk to you for a second?" I asked.

She paused and looked at me with a bit of concern in her eyes. "Sure. Is everything okay? You didn't see Ethan again, did you?"

"I am really looking forward to the days when that isn't a question anymore," I said. "But no. It's not about him."

"Good. Then what's going on?"

"I wasn't planning on saying anything quite yet, but after your announcement today, I feel like I have to. I don't want it to look like I was trying to steal your thunder or anything," I said.

"What do you mean?"

"I'm pregnant," I said.

At some point saying it would feel more natural, but I was still getting used to it. Ava's eyes widened.

"You're..." she started, and I nodded. "And it's..."

"Jordan's," I said to finish her thought.

She squealed and threw her arms around me in a tight hug just as Becca came into the room. She gave us a playfully quizzical look.

"There sure is a lot of hugging happening around here tonight. What, Hannah, are you pregnant, too?"

She asked it as a joke, but I nodded, and her eyes went round as she gasped. Hers was my next hug, and she was still holding my hands when I looked at both of them seriously.

"I haven't told Jordan yet," I said.

"Why not?" Ava asked.

"I'm scared to," I said. They exchanged glances, and I looked back and forth between them questioningly. "What was that?"

"Both of us have some experience with what you're going through," Ava said.

I listened to both women tell the stories of finding out they were pregnant and being hesitant to tell their partners. It made me feel better to hear that I wasn't alone, and they had gotten through to the other side even better than before.

"So, you're going to tell him?" Becca asked.

"Yes. I promise I will tell him tomorrow. Well, maybe not. I'll tell him Sunday. I don't want to ruin the grand opening," I said.

"It's not going to ruin anything," Becca said.

"If I know Jordan like I think I do, this will make everything better," Ava said, causing a sense of relief to wash over me.

31

JORDAN

The soft opening had been incredibly packed and gone off well. That should have been a good indication that the grand opening was going to be insane. I should have prepared for a night of pure unadulterated craziness, but I didn't. I only saw ahead enough to get a bouncer, just in case, but I had done that for the soft opening too. Very quickly, on the night of the grand opening, I realized we were going to need more than one of them and asked the guy we hired for the night to see if his company had anyone they could send as backup.

The two extra bouncers that arrived were two more new faces in a crowd of people I didn't recognize. Matt was running the kitchen with the new cook and two expo staff who could also cook in a pinch. The floor was being run by a girl we hired who had just returned to town and had been employed in top restaurants in LA, where she had been at school. As floor manager, she was holding down the fort effortlessly, and no matter how busy it got, she seemed unflappable and kept the other waitstaff in line.

I had two other bartenders with me, and by the middle

of the night found myself completely outclassed by them. Slowly, I sunk behind them and watched them take over, keeping the crowd entertained and always with a drink in their hand. It was incredible to watch how the seasoned bartenders took to the opening like it was just another day, and it afforded me a chance to leave the bar to go check out the other elements of the place. One of the bartenders was a guy named Lamont, but the more experienced and authoritative one was Cris, a short-haired firebrand of a bartender who had an adorable smile to go along with her sassy conversational tone.

"I'm going to head out to the floor," I told her. "Let Lamont know."

"You're good," she said in the midst of making a cocktail for one of her customers. "If we shit the bed, I'll let you know. But we won't. Will we, Lamont?"

"Hell no, sis," Lamont said between pours from the tap.

"Go on," Cris said, shooing me away from the bar. I grinned as I walked down the steps to the floor.

I took a quick walk around the floor and saw that I was, at least temporarily, unneeded. Seeing my chance, I made my way to the back and slipped into the empty office. Taking a deep breath and shaking my head, I pulled open my phone. There were no messages from Hannah, but I figured she probably didn't want to bother me. Considering I had a minute, I went ahead and called her.

"Hello?" she answered. Her voice had a downtrodden tone to it, and I worried that something had happened.

"Hey," I said. "Are you okay?"

"I'm fine," she said. "Just had a sick day. A couple of them, actually."

"You're not pregnant, are you?" I joked. I expected a big laugh from the other end. None came.

And then the silence stretched out for way too long.

Way, way too long.

Before I could say anything else, the door burst open and Matt's frantic face was there.

"Jordan," he called out.

"What?"

"There's a fight. You need to come take care of it!" he exclaimed.

"I hired bouncers for that," I said. "Where are they?"

"Also handling the fight," Matt said. "Come on, you have to get out there. I have stuff burning in the kitchen!"

"Fine, I'm coming," I said, then pulled the phone back to my ear. "Hey, sorry, Matt's going nuts because of a fight. I'll have to call you back."

"Okay," she said.

I didn't wait for her to say goodbye or for the words to come out of my mouth. I just hit the end button and ran toward the front door, where Matt was pointing. A thousand thoughts were going on inside my head, but I had to push them away as I neared the group of frat boys who had been served just to the point of too much. The bouncers were struggling with one of them, and another was on the ground, nursing a bloody nose. Two more were outside screaming and being handled by the other bouncer.

"They just came in fighting," the waitress said. I didn't recognize her at first but then placed her as one of the girls who'd come over from a neighboring bar on a temporary basis. Her nametag read "Blythe," though I had no memory of hiring a girl with that name, so it must be something she went by when working with customers at the bar. She seemed like she had a few years of annoying kids hitting on her under her belt already.

"You didn't serve them?" I asked.

"No, they were already like this and bust through the doors," she said. "Security has been fighting them the entire time."

"Alright," I said, rolling up my sleeves. "Go see your other tables."

Blythe ran off, and I jumped into the fray, holding the flailing one down long enough that the security guard could get a few moments to breathe. Tossing his hat away, he jumped back in and helped me get the kid to his feet and forcibly exit him through the door. The bloody nose one stood up but had his hands in the air. I was about to toss him, too, when Blythe showed back up behind him.

"Don't," she said. "This is my brother. They came in and just hit him out of nowhere."

"Do you know them?" I asked.

"I know one of them," he said through a tissue Blythe had brought him for his nose. "He has a problem with me for dating his ex. He's a douche."

"Well, he's a douche who is banned from this bar. You okay?"

"I'll be fine," he said. "He got me by surprise, otherwise..."

"He's a boxer," Blythe said.

"Ah. Well," I said. "Maybe I'll hire you for extra security next time so you can see them coming."

Blythe's brother laughed mirthlessly. I turned back to the door and went outside where two guards were sumo-pushing two frat kids away from the door. I stepped up and was immediately pushed by one of them. He didn't get a chance to get his feet settled before I decked him back. He went down like a felled tree, and his buddy stood in shock.

"You hit him!" he screamed.

"You're next if you don't get the fuck out of here," I snarled.

"Yo, your boy hit him first, I saw it," one of the security guys said.

"Me too," the other agreed.

"Me three," some hopeful waiting in line by the door chimed in.

"Get out," I said. "Take your buddy and any of your friends and never come back here again."

"Man, fuck you," the snot-nosed brat said, but only as he was walking away. I noticed a girl join him in the classic outfit of a blouse that was more akin to a bathing suit top and leggings that she might have had to paint on. Another guy joined them, and they walked off toward the cars, getting into two of them and driving away.

"Let that guy in," I said as I turned and pointed at the extra witness in line. "Good job, fellas."

"Yes, sir," one of the guards said as he opened the door and I walked through. The other witness came in behind me and went right to the bar, as if attracted by a magnet.

With that behind me, I looked down to see my knuckle was all scratched up from decking the kid, and I went to the back to wash it off. As I stood in the bathroom with the door open, Matt came by and ducked his head in.

"All good?" he asked.

Suddenly, the conversation I had with Hannah jumped back to the forefront of my mind, and I tried to shake it off.

"Yeah, fine. Just drunk kids who had a bone to pick."

"Gone?"

"Like the wind," I said. "The waitress Blythe, she either knows them or knows how to find out their names. Remind me to get that so I can post their info in case they try to get back."

"Will do," Matt said. Then he stopped and looked at my reflection in the mirror as I shook my hands dry. "You alright?"

"Yeah," I lied. "Going to go finish my break now, though. I'll come let you know when I'm headed back out to the floor."

Matt nodded and tapped the doorframe with his hand before heading back into the kitchen. I dried my hands on a paper towel and tossed it before heading back to the office. Once inside, I took a seat at the fancy office chair I bought for the desk. I pulled out my phone and hesitated before I dialed Hannah.

She had taken way too long on that pause. Maybe she was having a scare? Maybe she had a medical thing and couldn't have kids and my saying that was like a cruel joke? I tried to come up with every possible scenario except the one that seemed the most likely.

I dialed the number and waited, but the line never answered. I called again, and suddenly my phone died and I realized I had forgotten my charger. It was still plugged in behind the lamp at the hotel room. I had been on the phone all damn day with my brothers, vendors, and eventually security people that I had run the battery all the way down. Just making sure everything arrived on time was exhausting and required so much more coordination than I figured it would beforehand. Especially with Matt being more preoccupied with making the right food and making sure the big-picture things were being taken care of.

Sitting my phone down on the desk, I propped my elbows and dropped my head into my hands. What was I supposed to do? First off, I was extremely frustrated with myself for forgetting the charger. Also, I was upset that I had left Hannah so quickly without getting an explanation.

I should have made Matt go deal with it, burning food be damned. But instead, I left and now I had this question ringing through my head.

Was I about to be a father?

It was a real possibility, and until I heard back from Hannah, I had to operate under the idea that it might be true. At thirty-six, I almost thought that chance had passed me by years ago. Being a father was what my brothers did, not me. I was the military brat who might get itchy feet and run away again, not one who suddenly settled down and became a dad.

And yet...

There was an appeal. There was an appeal to being a father, and to being that close to Hannah. I was falling for her, deeper every single day, and having a kid, while not the greatest timing, wasn't something I opposed. If it was with her, then it would be worth it. She made everything seem worth it.

I slammed my hands on the desk. How could I be so stupid as to leave the charger at the hotel? Now I was stuck in the bar, with hours left on the clock, with no ability to communicate to the outside. To communicate with Hannah.

What if she was calling me back? Leaving me because I reacted that way to the news? I had to figure this all out. And I had to figure it out at the expense of anything going on around me. My brothers would just have to understand.

HANNAH

I could hear my phone ringing in the other room, but there was no getting out of the bathroom. The floor and I were having a serious love-hate relationship as of late. I loved that it was the perfect amount of space for me to throw down a pillow and blanket when I had to camp out for a couple of hours at a time. And that was where the hate came in. Maybe I would get accustomed to these bouts of sickness, but I was really not having a good time with them at that point.

My stomach had given me a dire warning that there would be no moving around for a while when the phone started ringing. I had a feeling it was Jordan calling me back, and I wanted to talk to him, but there was no way I was going to be able to get to the other room and answer.

Finally, the sick feeling dissipated, and I was able to climb shakily to my feet. Like I always did, I paused for a couple of seconds to feel out how I was doing. When I confirmed it was over, I rinsed my mouth, brushed my teeth, and headed into the bedroom for my phone.

Checking the missed calls confirmed it was Jordan who

had called, and I called him back. It didn't even ring. I hung up and tried again, thinking there was a chance he was calling me at the same time, and we were managing to block each other. It went straight to voicemail again, telling me the phone was off.

I sat on the edge of the bed, looking at the phone for a few long seconds. I didn't know what to make of him turning his phone off after I missed one call from him. Was he angry at me?

He was obviously joking when he asked if I was pregnant. Which made two people who'd made that joke within the last couple of days and had it turn around and bite them in the ass.

And then there was that pause. I knew he caught it. He noticed my hesitation. Which probably meant he had put it all together and knew I was pregnant. He said he would call me back, so he wanted to talk about it. And he did call me back. But then he turned his phone off immediately. That had to mean something.

I hated the way my thoughts were starting to spiral, so I swallowed them down and got dressed. Even though the rest of Samantha's recommendations hadn't done any good for me, I tried one more of them by chewing on some candied ginger as I got into my pajamas and curled up in bed.

It was earlier than I usually went to bed on my nights off. Staying up late helped to make it less of a shock to my system when I had to work until the wee hours. But Sam had already warned me the next few weeks would bring on a whole new kind of tired, so I figured I might as well start stockpiling sleep now.

Besides, if I was asleep, I wouldn't have to worry about Jordan and what he was thinking. At least for a little while.

The next day, I headed back to the library to keep working on the mural. I wanted to get it finished sooner rather than later, and now that I was making progress on it, I could really see it coming together. That motivated me even more and highlighted areas where I could add design elements I hadn't even thought of before.

I stepped back from the wall and admired the new section I'd just finished. Putting all my focus and energy into it was making my creativity flow, and I was making great progress. It was exactly what I needed. I'd been trying to keep my mind preoccupied from everything. I still hadn't heard from Jordan by the time I left that morning, and I decided to leave my phone at home. Not having it with me would allow me to just focus on the painting rather than wondering when my phone was going to ring or I would get a text.

By early in the afternoon, I felt finished with my work for the day, and I needed some rest, so I headed home. I took a quick shower and went to the kitchen for a snack, then got my phone from where it was plugged in on the bedside table. Scrolling through the notifications on the screen, I noticed I'd missed several calls from Jordan.

The subsequent text messages he sent were increasingly worried. I immediately called him back.

"Hannah!" he said, sounding like he was in a semi-panic. "I've been trying to reach you all day."

"I know," I said. "I just noticed that. I'm sorry."

"Why were you ignoring my calls and messages?"

"I wasn't," I said. "I went to the library to work on the mural and left my phone at home so I wouldn't think about it. But speaking of ignoring people, what happened last night? You said you would call me back and you did, but I was sick, so I couldn't answer it. I called you back just a couple of minutes later, but you had turned your phone off."

"No," he said. "I hadn't turned my phone off. I forgot to put it on the charger and it died. I didn't have another charger at the bar with me. I didn't mean to leave you hanging. I really want to talk to you."

"I really want to talk to you, too," I said.

"Good. So, I'll see you soon."

"What do you mean? I thought you had to be in Portland."

"I do," he said. "But I need to be with you, too. After the fourth call you didn't answer, I decided to drive home. I'm almost there. I can come right to you so we can talk if you don't mind."

"I don't mind at all," I said. "I'll be waiting."

As soon as I got off the phone, I felt nervous fluttering in my stomach. I paused for a couple of seconds to determine if it really was just nerves, or if it was another bout of sickness. The concept of morning sickness was definitely a misnomer. I was getting sudden waves of nausea at all times during the day. Fortunately, I'd been feeling fairly well that day, and I soon came to the conclusion I was just nervous and not about to get sick again.

I changed my clothes out of the sweatsuit I put on when I got back from the mural and went to the kitchen to make a pot of tea. About fifteen minutes after I got off the phone with Jordan, I heard a knock on the door.

Even though I was expecting Jordan, there was still a spike of fear. I went to the door and peered out of the peephole to make sure it wasn't Ethan on the other side. Seeing Jordan's face both made me both relax and increased my nervousness. Taking a deep breath, I opened the door and let him in.

I wasn't sure what to expect when he stepped inside. As soon as I closed the door behind me, he turned around and pulled me into him.

"I'm so sorry about last night," he said. "I didn't mean to make you feel like I was ignoring you or that I was upset at you. My phone died when I was at the bar, then when I got back to the hotel, I plugged it in, but I was so exhausted from the opening that I passed out before it had enough juice to call you."

"It's alright," I said. "I understand. I know the opening has been really hard on you, and from what I heard on the phone last night, it sounded like it was pretty rowdy."

"It was definitely that," he said.

Jordan suddenly grabbed me by my upper arms and guided me back from him so he could look into my eyes. I could see emotion in them, but I didn't know exactly what that emotion was. He searched my face for only a second before asking the question I knew had been burning in him since that pause the night before.

"Are you pregnant?"

I nodded. "Yes."

I didn't know how he would react, but it didn't take long for me to find out. He pulled me into his arms again, cradling me close. I was surprised at first, then wrapped my arms around him and held him equally as tight.

"Did you think I was going to be angry?" he asked.

I drew in a breath and nodded, pulling back to look at him. "I worried that you might be. I didn't know how you would react. It's so soon. We've never talked about..."

"I'm okay with it," he said. "Really, I am."

I opened my mouth to respond, then closed it so I could think over my words carefully.

"You're okay with it?"

He shook his head. "That's probably not the best way to put it. I... I'm not mad, Hannah. I'm not upset." He rested his hand on my stomach. "I'm happy."

Relief washed over me, and I smiled, but a second later, that smile faded.

"We have to be really careful who we tell. It's not that I want to keep it a secret, I just don't want Ethan to somehow find out. With the way he was talking, I have no idea what kind of rage it might send him into," I said.

Jordan shook his head. "You don't need to be afraid. I will protect you and our baby from Ethan. No matter what. Neither of you will get hurt. Not on my watch."

For the first time in a while, I felt all the fear and worry disappear. With Jordan, I knew I was safe.

We spent the rest of the day cuddled up together, talking and enjoying being near each other again. But he couldn't stay. Far too soon, he had to get back on the road to Portland so he could be at the bar that night.

I didn't want to let him go, especially not now. But I understood. He couldn't just drop his responsibilities at the bar. They needed him there. I walked him to the door, and we stood in a soft, slow kiss for a long time, stretching every second until the very last possible one before he had to leave.

When the door closed behind him and I knew he was on his way, a heavy, deep sense of loneliness settled over me. I'd missed him while he was away before, but now it was different. I felt absolutely lonely, and it made me wonder how I was going to get through this pregnancy with him gone like this.

33

———————

JORDAN

Driving back to Portland was absolute torture. I kept wanting to pick up the phone and call someone, but there was no one to call. I could call Hannah, but it felt like we needed to let the dust settle between us a little. Things were changing in a big way, and we both needed the time to understand what it meant for us individually as well as together. I knew I needed the chance to do that for myself. But that didn't mean I didn't instinctively want to go to my brothers or friends for advice and to share in the excitement.

Being stuck in Portland was going to be terrible. I knew that. There had to be some way out of it. If I could talk to Tom and tell him what was going on, maybe we could find a way, but we both were wary of telling people just yet. We needed to plan how we were going to do it. I agreed with that, it just didn't make it easier.

When I pulled into the bar, right from the road, I took a second to try and calm my nerves before I went in. Matt was pretty intuitive, and if I looked off, he would know. I grabbed one of my bottles of water and downed it while trying to steady my nerves and focus on the work ahead.

It was still wild to me that we'd opened already. Things had moved so quickly, I hadn't even really had time to process it.

I sighed and got out of the car, walking in just before five. The bar would be open at seven, but Matt and some of the other crew were already inside. Matt had called to ask where I had gone when I left work, so he knew I wasn't coming in too early, and I expected him to be surly again. Instead, as I closed the door behind me and locked it, he popped his head up over the counter of the bar with a wide smile.

"Hey, brother," he said. "Everything okay?"

"Yeah," I said, keeping my eyes down so I didn't make eye contact, "just had some stuff to take care of. Sorry I'm late."

"It's all good," he said, shockingly cheery. "The place wasn't in too bad a shape when we closed up last night, and I couldn't sleep anyway, so I came in early and tidied up. Last night was great, wasn't it?"

"It was," I said, making my way back down the hall toward the office. I swung the door open and hung my jacket before heading back to the floor. "So, same plan as last night?"

"I think so," Matt said. "Though I don't think you will need to be behind the bar at all. Cris and Lamont don't seem to need any help. Maybe you could help get the food out of the kitchen? We got a little behind a couple times last night."

"Sounds good," I said. "You going to make it all night on no sleep?"

"If something smells funny, just come check and make sure I didn't fall asleep on the stove," Matt said.

I laughed. At least his mood seemed to have done a one-eighty, which was good. I didn't know if I would be able to handle a full night of Cranky Matt.

"Will do," I said.

"Alright, well, I have some prep work in the kitchen. Want to help me?" he asked.

"As long as you make me one of those buffalo sandwiches. I'm starving."

"Deal," Matt said, and I followed him into the kitchen to prepare for the night.

The night went really well for the most part. Only occasionally did someone seem like they might have had one too many drinks before coming in or needed to be cut off at the bar, but they were generally amiable about it. The bouncers had much less to do, and the business was packed but not as hectic as opening night. The customers seemed to be in a good mood, and the waitstaff was excited by how well they were being tipped, so they were doing great.

I found it difficult not to blurt out to Matt what was spinning through my head, but I was able to make it. Part of the ability to make it through was that Matt seemed to be enjoying himself quite a bit. Multiple times he left the kitchen and ambled around the floor, greeting customers, and generally having a good time. Portland seemed to have rubbed off on him, all thanks to one night out, and I felt like it would actually be difficult to get him to go back to Astoria. At least as long as things kept going well.

I needed to talk to someone, and Matt probably wasn't it. As I wiped down a table and turned it over, I thought about how Hannah was probably at home, alone, with my baby inside her and no one to help her or protect her. It drove me mad, and I could feel futile urges of protective rage fill up inside me with no outlet. I couldn't be angry or mean or sad. I had to just get on with the job and try not to screw up the new bar with my attitude.

When the night finally ended and we closed up shop with little fuss, I turned to Matt, who was talking animatedly with Cris. I walked over to them, putting on my jacket and checking for my keys. Matt looked over at me, seeing me in my jacket, and looked at me curiously.

"You heading out?" he asked.

"Yeah," I said. "Long day going back and forth. Need some sleep. You should get some rest, too, you know."

"I know," Matt said. "Can't pour from an empty cup. I'll get out of here soon."

"Alright," I said. "I'm out."

"Hey, make sure you get up earlyish tomorrow. I have something we need to go do," Matt said as I walked away. Rather than ask what it was, I simply pointed my finger up in the air and kept walking away, acknowledging I heard him without turning around.

I got into my car and drove to the hotel, thoughts of Hannah and my baby swirling. I hadn't been able to get them off my mind all night, and I had come to the decision that something needed to change. I wasn't going to be able to leave Hannah alone during her pregnancy for so long. It just wouldn't happen. There was only one person to talk to about that, and I needed to just find the confidence and make the call. When I woke up in the morning, I was going to give Tom a ring and sort this whole thing out.

I fell into my bed just after four and slept like a rock until my alarm went off at noon. Not thirty seconds later, there was a knock on my door.

"Hang on," I said, getting up and sliding into my shirt. I opened the door to the grinning face of Matt, a coffee in hand.

"I said earlyish," he said. "Noon is not earlyish. Why are you still asleep?"

"I'm not asleep. I'm standing here," I said, taking the coffee.

"That was mine, but fine," he said, coming in and going directly to my coffee maker to make a replacement. "I've been thinking."

"That's dangerous," I quipped. I was proud of myself for that one, considering I was still mostly asleep until half the coffee was in me.

"Funny," he said. "I've been thinking we need to go apartment hunting today."

"Eh," I said. He was right, and I knew it, but I just didn't want to face it. I didn't want to find an apartment in Portland. That seemed too concrete, too final. "I suppose so."

"You sound thrilled," Matt said.

"Yeah, well, I just woke up."

"So, you were asleep."

"Can we just not?" I asked.

"Get your clothes on. I'll be back in twenty minutes and we can head out."

I grimaced into my coffee but kept drinking. It was terrible stuff, but it did the job. Eventually, I downed it and got up, stretching for a few minutes and doing a two-minute workout. It wasn't going to be enough for the day, but I had to do something or else I'd feel off all day. After that, I hopped in for a five-minute shower, got dressed, and was ready to go when Matt knocked again.

"I am genuinely impressed," he said as I opened the door and walked out. "I had it at about eighty percent chance you lay back down to go to sleep."

"Can't," I said. "Marines. Once you're up, you're up."

"Ahh, yes, *the desert*," he said. Matt was probably the only person in the world who could poke fun at that and I wouldn't get offended. I knew he respected my choice to go, but he also liked to rib me for being dramatic. It was how he dealt with being uncomfortable. We had never talked about my time there, and he had never asked. The others had, but never Matt. He just poked fun at me, and I laughed. It was understood.

The first place we visited was awful, but the next few weren't so bad. One, just a couple blocks from the bar, bowled Matt over, and I could see he was about thirty seconds from saying yes when I took him aside.

"Hey," I said. "I don't want you to get offended, but I think we should have separate places."

"Oh?" Matt asked. "Planning on having a string of ladies over you don't want your little brother screwing up? I get it."

"No, it's not that," I said, smiling. "I just... I don't know if Hannah is going to want to come up and spend some time up here, and I have nightmares, and neither one of us do well living with other people. You almost threw your last roommate off the roof, remember?"

"Well, he was on the roof playing a bagpipe at three in the morning. No jury would have convicted me."

"That might be true, but you and I both know we'd be at each other's throats if we lived together *and* worked together all the time."

"Yeah," Matt said. "But I'm getting a place here. My only rule is you can't be more than five miles from here. That way we can coordinate easily even if there's bad weather."

"Deal," I said. "Now go get your keys."

Matt walked away and finished up with the agent, taking an apartment on the top floor.

It took three other places before I gave up and accepted an apartment just a few blocks away from Matt and a little further down from the bar. It gave me a better walk in the morning, which I liked, and it kept Matt and me from being on top of each other. I hated hurting his feelings, but he knew it was true. I was never good living with anyone.

Hannah was the only exception.

Settling on an apartment felt like betrayal. The only time I ever felt okay was when Hannah was wrapped up in my arms. Signing a lease in Portland felt like I was giving up on that being my reality anytime soon.

34

HANNAH

I was hoping that I would get used to Jordan being gone. Maybe it would be one of those things where it was really difficult at first, but if I could just get through the first day or two, it would be easier. Then I would get used to it and it wouldn't be anywhere near as hard.

Then when those first couple of days passed and it wasn't any easier, I told myself that I was going to give myself permission to pull the pregnancy card for the first time. I was missing Jordan for two. That meant I just had to get through a couple of more days, and then things would settle down.

As it turned out, that logic didn't work, either. I got through those next couple of days, and it wasn't any easier. If anything, it was actually harder. The longer he was away, the more I missed him. That didn't bode well. Especially considering we were looking at a six-month separation. And that was *if* they got someone to run the place that they trusted to leave there in that time.

I didn't want to be that woman. The kind of woman who absolutely had to have a man close by every second or expected him to change his life to fit mine. After all, I hadn't been willing to change mine for him yet. I couldn't expect anything different from him.

No matter how much I wanted to.

A week after he left again, it was my day off. My plan was to go to the library to put some finishing touches on the mural, but when I woke up, it was pouring. The rain didn't let up through my daily communion with the bathroom floor, shower, or breakfast of tea and dry toast. By the time I'd gotten through two terrifying true crime documentaries I probably shouldn't be watching, I figured the trip to the library was officially out.

That meant I got to resort to plan B for my day off: comfortable clothes, my favorite blanket, and some time curled up on the couch with a stack of books and the remote in close reach. Usually by the afternoon my appetite was back, and I had a few hours without waves of nausea, so I put together lunch and brought it into the living room with me.

It didn't take long before I was missing Jordan too much not to call him. He sounded tired when he answered the phone.

"You doing okay?" I asked.

"Yeah," he said, sounding like he was trying to swallow down a yawn. "I knew this was going to be a lot of work, but it's been harder than I was expecting. I don't remember it being like this when we opened the first place."

"You're trying to change the reputation," I said. "You have something that was already so popular to live up to, and the name traveled."

"That's true," he said. "It's a lot to live up to. I couldn't believe how many people showed up for the grand opening from Astoria. They drove all the way to Portland to stand in line just to be there for the opening because they like the first location so much.”

“That’s pretty amazing, though, when you think about it. These people enjoy The Hollow so much they went ninety minutes out of their way to support the new location. They want to feel like a part of it.”

“It is. I just hope we’re living up to their expectations.”

“I’m sure you are,” I said.

“I’m sorry. I’m sitting here going on about what I’m doing, and I didn’t even ask how you are,” he said.

“It’s okay.”

“No, it’s not. How are you feeling? How’s everything going?” he asked.

“Pretty much the same. Still dealing with being sick throughout the day, but I probably have a few weeks of that ahead of me still. I’m just trying to get through it and find ways to deal with it. I made an appointment with the doctor, but it’s not until next week.”

“It will be exciting to find out everything.”

That wasn’t exactly the response I was hoping for. It made a heavy feeling start forming in my stomach.

“Do you think you’re going to be home for it?” I asked.

He hesitated. “I’m not sure. Actually, there’s something I should tell you. I got an apartment here in Portland.”

My heart sank. “You did?”

“Tom arranged for it. He said we couldn’t just keep staying at the hotel when we were down here. That I needed to have a place to settle in so I could really focus on the bar,” Jordan said.

So many emotions went through my mind, I didn’t know where my thoughts were going to land. I couldn’t really say I was surprised at the development. After all, Tom had been insisting on him moving down to Portland.

Even though Jordan was resistant to the idea, it was the plan.

Even if he didn't make the move permanent, it was obvious he would be there frequently and for potentially long stretches of time. It made sense for him to have a home base there rather than always staying at the hotel. I still didn't know how to feel about it. So instead of trying to come up with an emotion, I swallowed hard.

"Do you still think it'll only be six months?" I asked.

"I don't know. Everything is still up in the air. But maybe you could come check it out sometime soon. I think you would really like it here. The area around the apartment is really nice. It's great for walking around and people-watching. I think you would enjoy it. Then, if you did, maybe you would stay for longer."

He was trying to be nonchalant about it, but the question hung heavily between us. It reminded me of the argument we had before he left. Just like then, I wasn't willing to back down.

"I just started getting settled in Astoria," I said. "Moving out here from New York was huge. I'm still trying to get used to it and really find my way here. I'm really comfortable and happy here, and I'm not ready to just pick up and move all over again. Besides, I like having my own place. I never have before. I've always been surrounded by people and suffocated by what they want from me."

"You think I would suffocate you?"

"That's not what I'm saying, Jordan," I said. "This isn't about you. This is about me. I told you from the beginning leaving New York and coming all the way out here was about me reclaiming my life. I didn't want to be controlled anymore."

"So, now I'm controlling, too," he said.

"Stop it. You're twisting my words. I just said this isn't about you. I just can't be expected to make decisions like this so fast, or to just give up everything I've started to build here already. I wasn't expecting any of this. Right now, I just need to take one step at a time," I said.

Jordan let out a long breath. "I know. I'm sorry. It's just... Never mind. You're right."

His words fell off into tense silence. We tried to pick the conversation back up, but it was weird and awkward. Finally, I told him I was going to take a nap, and he agreed he needed to get ready to go to the bar. We stumbled our way through a tense goodbye and got off the phone.

I curled up on the couch and brought the blanket down over me, just wanting to close my eyes for a little while. It seemed the tiredness Samantha warned me about was setting in more now, and I didn't want it to catch up with me too much. I had only just relaxed when someone knocked on the door.

It couldn't be Jordan. As dramatic as that would be, I doubted he would have that whole conversation with me while on his way to my house and not tell me. The payoff of showing up at my door wasn't really enough to justify that.

Wrapping the blanket around myself, I went over to the door and peeked out. I was surprised to see Becca and Ava standing outside. They smiled at me when I opened the door, but their expressions turned to concern when they saw the blanket.

"Are you okay?" Ava asked.

"What's wrong?" Becca asked.

I shook my head. "I was just resting a little. I'm fine. What are you two doing here?"

Becca glanced over at Ava. "We just thought we would stop by and check on you. See how you're doing."

"Come on in," I said. They followed me inside, and I brought them into the living room. "Anybody want some tea? Ava?"

"Sounds good," she said. "This little one is causing me some trouble this time around. It wasn't so bad last time."

"I'm with you there," I said. "I mean, I don't have any prior experience, but so far, it's a doozy."

The women laughed as I headed into the kitchen to put the pot on to heat. I could hear them in the living room talking about Becca's pregnancy and the symptoms she went through. She laughed, saying how she didn't believe Tyler didn't catch on. She was sure there were days when it was so obvious.

It made me feel good to hear them in there. Not just because I didn't feel so alone in my situation with Jordan and the baby, but also because of the friendship I'd found in them.

I filled a tray with the pot, cups with tea bags, and a plate of cookies and brought it into the living room. Setting it on the coffee table, I curled back into the corner of the couch and draped my blanket over my lap.

"So," Becca said, looking at Ava, then at me. "Have you told Jordan yet?"

"Ah, so now the truth comes out," I said with a teasing lift of my eyebrow as I poured hot water into my cup. "The real reason you came over here."

"No, we really did want to check on you," Becca started.

"Yes," Ava said, nodding.

"I told him," I said.

"So?" Ava asked. "How did it go? How did he react?"

I let out a sigh, some of the humor draining away from me. "I mean, he took it better than I could have imagined. Really. There was a misunderstanding with the phones, and he actually drove all the way back here just to talk to me about it. He was really sweet and supportive. Said he was happy about it."

"So why do you look less than pleased?" Becca asked.

"Because he's still in Portland," I said. "I know I'm being selfish and maybe a little ridiculous. But I just hate that he's there. And he has no idea when he's going to come back. He told me today he got an apartment."

Ava nodded. "I heard about that. But just because he thought he would be more comfortable having his own place than being in the hotel all the time."

"And you're allowed to be a little selfish right now," Becca said. "It's not like you're just clinging to him because you're needy. You want him here because you're carrying his child. That makes sense. I can't even imagine having Tyler away from me while I was pregnant. Even when he didn't know. I just wanted him around. Even when I acted like I didn't."

Ava laughed. "I remember those days. At least you told him. I'm really glad you didn't try to hide it. I know it wasn't easy, but you did the right thing. And I'm really glad Jordan took it so well. I figured he might. I've known him pretty much his whole life. He's a good man."

"Yes, he is," I said. "I just miss him. And even though he's only ninety minutes away, he's so busy right now, he can't really drop things and come back when I want him to."

They nodded empathetically and sipped their tea as I poured out everything that happened between us and Ethan's threats. There wasn't any hesitation, nothing holding me back from telling them everything. I realized then just how close I had gotten to these two women. Other than Samantha, they were the closest, truest friends I had ever had.

But when they looped back to talking about Portland, I moved the conversation on as quickly as I could. I didn't want to talk about him wanting me to move to Portland or my hesitation. I needed to figure out what I thought about it first.

35

JORDAN

Another long night. Another cold sweat. Another nightmare that woke me up when it got too real and I felt like screaming and thrashing at things that turned out to not be there. I sat up, my chest heaving as I tried to take in enough oxygen to fill my lungs. My eyes darted around the room, looking for the shadow men that had just been chasing me in the dream. Listening for the cries of the baby locked in the room alone. Searching for Hannah's body.

None of them were there. I knew that. But I had to try, or else I would go mad.

I got out of the bed and looked around, opening the sliding door and stepping out onto the balcony. I was only wearing boxers, but I didn't care. Being on the middle floor of a hotel at seven in the morning meant that I was likely invisible to the people going about the beginnings of their day. I sat down on the cold concrete and put my head in my hands. I had to get a grip. I had to figure this out.

It had been two weeks since I had been around Hannah. In those two weeks I might have slept through the night once.

When Hannah was by my side at night, I would sleep all the way through. I didn't have nightmares with her. I barely dreamed at all. Usually, I would fall so deeply into sleep that the next thing I was conscious of was waking up, smelling her skin and kissing her shoulder or the top of her head. Without her, I was a mess.

Our last real conversation was me telling her I was getting an apartment and asking her to move in with me. I knew it was a lot. I knew it was soon. But she was carrying my child. The rules were out the window, and we were making it up as we went along. But she acted so weird when I asked.

She was independent, and I knew that. I loved that. But for the past two weeks, our conversations were brittle and depthless. They felt more like checking in, making sure the other was alive. None of them lasted more than five minutes before one of us would find a reason to get off. Usually, it was either that we were going to work or going to bed. As much as I wanted to talk to her, I couldn't think of anything to say. Everything I wanted to say would start a fight.

She was going to share her space with a baby soon. Why couldn't she share a space with me? I turned it over and over in my mind but never brought it up. It had to be enough that I got to talk to her at all.

Matt was able to move into his apartment almost immediately, but I had to wait the two weeks for mine. It meant I was at the hotel alone, and that made it worse. Being at an apartment alone was one thing, but a hotel was something wholly different and far lonelier. It meant coming into a building full of people, all on vacations or work trips or dates. All of them with someone to hold or with a purpose for work. For me it was just surviving until the next day.

I helped Matt move in and then went to the store to get

a couple of air mattresses. Matt's place was already furnished, but mine wasn't, and I didn't plan on putting a bunch of stuff in it. Matt chose a two-bedroom spot and had a bed for me in case I needed to stay for some reason, and I returned the favor by buying an extra mattress for him. He laughed at the idea, but I could see he appreciated it anyway. It was a token, but it was something to show him I thought about him, too. We were there for each other.

Now that he seemed to be getting along and had people to talk to, things were moving along pretty well for him.

I wished I was happy. But I couldn't be, not with Hannah back in Astoria. Not with me moving into an apartment I didn't want in a city I didn't want to be in.

It was pretty early in the day, and I had already made my call to Tom. There wasn't much to move, so I figured I would be done and set up before Tom called me back. My furniture was simply the air mattresses, a futon that I found at a thrift store three buildings down that was twenty bucks, a nightstand, and a television. I didn't watch a lot of TV, especially since I was usually at work when anything good was on, but having it there meant I could plug in my streaming stick and watch stuff to go to bed to. Or, more often, I could put it on in the background when I was awake so I didn't feel so alone.

When everything was inside, Matt headed back to his own place to get ready for work, and I hooked up the streaming stick to get something on while I put away my clothes in the closet. It was a studio, so everything was in one big room, aside from the bathroom and the closet on one wall. I preferred it that way if I was alone. I could see everything. If I woke up in the middle of the night, there were no rooms for me to assume someone was in. Less broken doorknobs that way.

I had only just started getting my clothes in the closet when my phone rang. I ran to grab it off the nightstand where it sat charging, hoping it was and simultaneously hoping it wasn't Hannah. I wanted to talk to her. I wanted to have fun with her over the phone. But I didn't want to hear that distance in her voice, that hesitation of knowing that I wanted her there with me and she didn't want to come.

Instead, Tom's name flashed across the screen. I swiped to open it and cleared my throat.

"Hey, Tom."

"Jordan, what's up? I saw you called," he said.

"You know, I don't really remember why I called," I lied. Suddenly with him on the phone with me, it didn't make any sense to talk to him about it. I couldn't tell him about Hannah being pregnant right after I signed a lease on an apartment. What was he going to do? How could he fix it? He couldn't. All it would do is put him in an awkward position and make him feel guilty.

"Oh," Tom said. "Because I heard your voicemail and it seemed like you wanted to speak to me about something important. Is everything okay?"

"Yeah." I paused. How much was I willing to lie to my brother? How much was I willing to lie to myself? "I'm just missing home, I think. Not used to not having everyone around. Look, I've got to get going. I still need a shower before I head into the bar."

There was silence on the other end for a moment. "Alright," he said, finally. "If there was something going on, you could tell me, you know."

"I know."

"Well, if you happen to remember what it was," Tom

said, "just call me back on the cell. If I don't answer, call the office number and have them page me."

"Will do," I said. "Thanks, Tom."

"Sure. Have a good one," he said, and I hung up.

I stood staring at the closet for a few moments before tossing the hanger back on the air mattress and going to the door to put on my shoes. I was halfway down the street before I realized exactly what it was I was doing. I was knocking on Matt's door before I knew what I was going to say.

"Hey," Matt said as he opened the door. His expression fell from pleasantly surprised to worried when he got a look at my face. "What's going on, dude?"

"Can I come in?"

"Mi casa, su casa, come on," he said, and I walked inside. He shut the door behind me as I paced in his living room. "Jordan, what's going on, man?"

"I think... I think I need to take a few days off to get my stuff. Like, really pack it all up and just make the move up here, you know? Looking around my room, it was nuts, man. I can't live with air mattresses and a futon. I need to just bite the bullet and move up here, like you did." The words all spilled out of me without much of a breath between them. Matt stared at me with his hands on his hips. It was his Superman stance, and I used to make fun of him for it all the time. Anytime he was presented with something he didn't know how to handle, he stood like he was a superhero and waited until he figured it out.

"Sure," he said finally. "I think I can handle that. Do you need to leave now?"

"No, I can close tonight. I think I'll leave in the morning, though," I said.

"Alright," Matt said. "I can handle that. No problem.

We have a good staff. I should make it a couple days without you, but you better come back."

I laughed. "I will." I didn't know if I believed it, but I said it anyway.

Later that night, I helped close the bar with little fanfare. Business was down from the past week or so, but still busy. The novelty of being brand-new had mostly worn off. Matt didn't seem worried, so I didn't stress it. I had other things to do.

That night, more so than any of the others, I had a hard time sleeping. When I did, I felt like I could smell Hannah's skin beside me, and I slept like a rock. But I kept waking up to her not being there beside me on the rapidly deflating mattress and struggled to go back to sleep.

36

HANNAH

I put down my paintbrush and took a step back so I could take in the entire mural. A smile came to my face. It was finally finished. I had to admit, there were a few moments there when it felt a little touch and go. So much had been going on in my life, I worried I might not be able to accomplish what I hoped I would when the library asked me to do the piece.

But I kept pushing through, and I had finally just put the final strokes in place. It wasn't what I had in mind when I first started. Things changed, and my plans grew and altered as the weeks in Astoria marched on. It felt like the longer I lived there and the more I got to know the town, the better I was able to understand what I was creating.

Aside from that, it resembled what I'd first concocted when I was making the sketches. It felt like so long ago that I saw looking at a blank wall and drawing out my ideas. The images I showed off to Becca were far different than what I ended up with, but I was happy with the final results. It was even better than I had imagined.

I needed to add another coat of sealant spray to make sure the paint remained intact for as long as possible. But that would have to wait until the next day. The first coat needed a chance to dry and cure, so I decided I would return the next morning to truly finish it off.

"It looks amazing," a woman said as she walked past holding the hand of her little child.

I remembered her as one of the mothers I had seen a few times before while working on the project. I smiled at her.

"Thank you," I said. "I'm just finished it up."

She nodded. "I've been watching the progress. It's great."

"Thank you so much."

The little girl tugged on her hand, trying to compel her to the playing field. She laughed and waved at me. I returned the wave and watched them walk away before packing up my tools. I was still smiling from the compliment when I got into the car and drove home.

Thinking about nothing more than the rumbling of hunger in my stomach, I unlocked the front door. I was considering indulging a particularly strong craving for Indian food as I walked into the house when I noticed something out of the corner of my eye. Stopping in my tracks, I turned to look.

The movement I noticed was Ethan flipping a pregnancy test around in his hands as he sat on the couch and stared at it. My breath caught in my throat, and heat shot up the back of my neck and onto my cheeks. My heart felt like it was going to burst out of my chest, and cold sweat broke out on my skin.

Instinctively, my hand went to my pocket to find my

phone. Only, it wasn't there. I remembered I'd stuffed it into my bag along with my paints. That meant it was in the car. My hand moved out of my pocket and brushed briefly across my belly. Thinking about the vulnerable, fragile baby inside, my fear shifted to anger.

"What are you doing here?" I asked, demanding his attention. "Get out of my house."

Ethan looked up at me coolly, unaffected by the intensity of my voice. He glanced down at the pregnancy test again, then at me, holding it up.

"What's this?" he asked.

"You went through my drawers? How dare you."

It was the only way he could have gotten the test. As shocked and unsure of my emotions as I was the day I found out I was pregnant, I still wanted to remember it. I'd kept one of the tests I took and tucked it away in my drawer as a memento. Now, Ethan was holding it.

His face still devoid of emotion and his body language disturbingly calm almost to the point of being subdued, he looked at the plastic stick again.

"There's no result on it," he said.

"They fade."

I couldn't believe this was happening. It was too surreal to be standing there in my living room, explaining the function of a pregnancy test to Ethan. I still couldn't figure out how he even got into my house. Now I was wondering what else he had gone through, how much more he violated my space.

"So?" he asked.

It wasn't an entire question, but I knew exactly what he was asking. Part of me hesitated. If I denied it, maybe it would be safer. But on the other hand, maybe not. Besides, I was tired of bending to him. He didn't control my life anymore. He wasn't even a part of it. I wanted him gone, and he needed to face reality.

"I'm pregnant, Ethan."

His eyes widened, and he put the test down before standing up like he was going to take a step toward me. I held my ground even though I wanted to get as far away from him as possible.

"I can't believe it," he said. His tone surprised me, sounding almost happy. "This is incredible."

"What?" I asked.

"We're going to have a baby," he said.

I shook my head adamantly. "No, Ethan. No, we are not going to have a baby. I'm having a baby. You aren't the father."

"Of course I am."

"Listen to me. This is not your baby. This is Jordan's baby," I said.

He shook his head, a look approaching maniacal on his face. "That's supposed to be our child. *We're* supposed to have children together."

"No. We aren't. I broke up with you. It's over between us. It has been for a long time. You need to move on and leave me alone."

"I can't do that, Hannah. Especially now. You're pregnant, and I'm going to make it right," he said.

He was starting to really scare me. There was something off about his tone. He didn't sound like he was thinking clearly.

"What are you talking about?" I asked.

"You don't need to worry," he said. "This is all going to be just fine. I read somewhere that if a woman is married to someone other than the biological father, it doesn't matter. When the baby is born, the husband is automatically the father. It's on the birth certificate and everything. No one has to know anything else."

"We aren't getting married," I said. "You're being completely crazy."

Ethan took a threatening step toward me. His eyes flashed and his expression became angry and bitter. He made a menacing movement that put him between me and access to the front door. I couldn't get out of the house, but I needed to get away from him. I ran as fast as I could to my room and slammed the door shut.

My hand shook as I locked the door, then ran into the bathroom and locked myself in there. If I'd been able to fit into the linen closet or in the cabinet under the sink, I probably would have gotten in. I wanted to put as much space and as many obstacles as possible between Ethan and me.

He pounded on the door to my room so hard it felt like the house was shaking.

"Open this door right now," he screamed.

He pounded even harder, then let out an exasperated sound. Things went quiet for just a moment, but I didn't move.

"Hannah," he said in a quieter tone. "Hannah, please. Let me in. I just want to talk to you. I came all this way to find you. Doesn't that mean anything to you? I missed you so much and was so worried about you, I had to find you. I searched for you, and I came out here to get you and bring you home.

"I know things haven't been perfect between us, but we could be a family. You can't really think that guy is any good for you or for the baby. You don't even know him. And he owns a bar. What kind of life can he give you and a child? I could make sure both of you have everything. You and I have so much history. We know each other. We know everything about each other," he said.

"I do know you, Ethan," I said. "And that's exactly why there are two locked doors between us."

"Damn it!" Ethan shouted, slamming his hands against the door again.

The sound startled me, making me cry out, but I swallowed any more reaction. I didn't want to give him the satisfaction, and I didn't want him to think he was breaking me down. He went back to pounding his fists against the door and screaming. Soon, the sounds got louder, and I realized he was kicking the door. He was trying to break the lock.

I stepped back from the door and pressed one hand to my stomach, praying the lock held up. But what then? I didn't think he was going to give up this time, but there was nothing I could do. I couldn't get away.

The bathroom window was too small for me to climb out of. I didn't have my phone. There was no way for me to get out and away from the house or for me to call for help. I was stuck there with nothing to do but pray he didn't get in.

For the next several minutes, Ethan went through the cycles a couple more times. He would yell and scream, pounding on the door until my teeth rattled. Then he would change back to trying to talk to me calmly and nicely. As soon as he realized that wasn't working, he would go back to kicking and pounding.

Suddenly, I heard another voice boom toward the front of the house.

"Hannah?"

"What the fuck are you doing here?" Ethan demanded.

His voice wasn't coming through the door at me anymore. A loud bang made me scream, and a second later there was another. Voices grunted and shouted, but I couldn't understand what they were saying. Another loud bang came right before a crash that sounded like walls were coming down. I stood with my back against the counter, my hands over my mouth.

Then there was silence. That was almost more terrifying than the loud sounds and shouting. My heart jumped into my throat at the sound of something hitting the bedroom door.

"Hannah?"

I nearly sobbed at the sound of Jordan's voice.

"I'm here. I'm fine," I said.

"Call the police. I have him," he said.

I scrambled to unlock the door and ran out into the bedroom. With my phone in the car, my only option was to get to Jordan's phone, forcing me to go out into the rest of the house. I did and found Jordan holding Ethan down on the ground. One shoe was lying on its side in front of my bedroom door. Apparently, that was what hit it to get my attention.

"I need your phone," I said.

Jordan nodded and indicated his pocket. I hated to get that close to Ethan, but I knew Jordan had him. That didn't stop Ethan from growling and trying to grab at me when I crouched down. I fished the phone out of his pocket and called the police.

They were there within a few minutes, but it felt like hours. I stood near the front door, staring at Ethan, and waiting for any sign of him moving. Finally, the police arrived and dragged Ethan away in handcuffs. One came back after stuffing him into the back seat of the car.

"You should really consider getting a restraining order against him, Hannah," he said.

I nodded. "I will."

"And we'll be back to take pictures and notes of all this damage so we can include it in the police report."

He walked out, and the second the door closed behind him, I crumbled, sobbing, into Jordan's arms.

37

____

JORDAN

I had been awake on and off for a while. For once, it didn't bother me. It wasn't nightmares or stress that was keeping me awake this time. It was contentment. I wanted to spend every single second with her that I could awake. I wanted to be conscious of how I breathed in her scent. How she felt in the crook of my arm. All of it.

Her head rested on my chest, and one leg was draped over mine. She looked so peaceful. I watched her sleep, her deep, full breaths rising her back off me and then sinking back into me. She was wearing one of my T-shirts, and it dwarfed her. The arm draped over me twitched in her sleep, and she smiled.

I brushed a strand of hair gently over her ear, and she stirred. I frowned at first, not wanting to wake her, but she slid her head up to my shoulder and smiled at me through drowsy eyes. I smiled back and kissed her nose.

"Morning," I whispered.

"Morning," she said as she stretched.

"How are you feeling?" I asked.

"I'm okay," she said, but then suddenly her eyes went

250

wide. She was up and running to the bathroom before I knew what was happening, and when the door slammed shut, I figured it out. I knew it was miserable, but a part of me smiled anyway. It was part of being pregnant. If I could switch with her so I did the unpleasant parts, I would. But she was carrying our baby. Anything was worth that.

The fan in the bathroom turned off, and I could hear her brushing her teeth. When she was done, she opened the door sheepishly and made her way back into the bed, curling up beside me. I patted her on the backside and kissed the top of her head.

"I like getting back in bed with you," she said.

"Does it make you feel any better?" She nodded. "Good. So, I have a question."

"What is it?"

"When do you want to tell everyone?" I asked.

"Now, if you want," she said.

"Really? You're okay with that?"

"If you are," she said. "I don't want to hide it anymore."

"Do you mind if I call my mother?"

"Go ahead. I want to hear her reaction, too," she said.

I opened my phone and found Mom's contact info and clicked it. She picked up on the third ring and sounded groggy when she answered.

"Jordan? Is everything okay?" she asked.

"Late night, Mom?"

"Oh, you know," she said in the way that she used to dismiss any critique of her newly found late-night shenanigans. "It was that damned Martha again, dragging us all around to different places."

"Uh-huh," I said. "I'm sure it was all Martha's fault."

"Well, it is," she grumbled. It sounded like she was still

in bed, which at nine in the morning for Mom was like getting up after noon. "Anyway, how are you, son?"

"I'm doing great, actually," I said. "I had some news for you."

"Well?" she asked when I didn't come right out with it. "What is it?"

"Hannah and I are going to have a baby."

The squeal was so loud I had to hold the phone away from my ear, and Hannah began laughing.

"Oh, my baby boy, I am so happy," she exclaimed. "Is Hannah there? Did I hear her? I thought you were in Portland."

"I came back for the night," I said. "But yes, she is here."

"Let me talk to her," Mom said, apparently already done with talking to me. I handed Hannah the phone, and she giggled as Mom gushed about the new grandbaby on the way. I lay back and listened to them giggle with a smile on my face. When she was done, Mom forgot to even talk to me again and hung up, promising to call her again later that day.

"I think the next person I call should be Matt," I said. "But if you want to tell the girls to tell my other brothers, that's fine."

"How did you know I told them?" Hannah asked, shocked.

"I didn't. I guessed. But you just confirmed it," I laughed. "It's okay. Tell them to spill the beans."

Hannah got up to grab her phone and then tucked back into bed beside me, texting Ava. I called Matt's number and waited for him to pick up. When he did, he sounded rougher than Mom did.

"What?" Matt asked as a way of greeting.

"Hey, brother," I said. "I have some news that can't wait."

"Are you sure?" he asked. "I am really tired."

"It'll only take a second," I said. "Hannah and I are having a baby."

"That's nice," Matt said, not registering it. Then it sounded like he took a deep, sharp breath. "Wait, what?"

"Hannah's pregnant. I am going to be a dad," I said.

"Oh, no, not you, too," Matt said, suddenly awake. "I mean, congrats and everything, but dammit."

I laughed. "Your time will come, little brother."

"Well, this is great news," Matt said, sounding a bit apprehensive, "but if it's possible, I need you back here tomorrow. We were swamped last night, and it looks like tomorrow will be just as bad. And Lamont got deployed. He leaves tomorrow."

"Oh, I didn't know Lamont was active duty," I said.

"Yeah, I forgot to mention it to you," Matt said. "Thought you two could bond over that. Now you won't get a chance."

"Well, I'll get my stuff together today and I'll head back tomorrow afternoon."

"Sounds good," Matt said. "See you then. And tell Hannah I said congratulations."

"Will do," I said, hanging up.

After getting dressed, we headed down to the mural to take a look at the almost finished product. Pulling in, it was immediately stunning. My eyes were drawn to it the entire time I walked toward it, and I gathered her up in a side hug as we stared at it.

"This is amazing," I said. "Like, seriously amazing."

"Thank you," she said. "I'm really glad you're here. I wanted you to be when I do the final coat of the finisher."

"Let me get the blanket," I said. I ran back to the car and grabbed the blanket we used for picnics and brought it over. I only had a few water bottles in the car with me, so it was a paltry spread, but I sat in the grass and watched her finish it up. When she was done, she turned to me.

"It's finished," she said. She ran over to where I sat and jumped into my lap. We stayed there staring at her mural for quite a long time. Finally, Hannah pulled up her phone and checked the time. "Looks like we better get going if we're going to make it to work on time."

"I don't think anyone would fault us being a little late," I said, grinning.

"Mr. Anderson," she said teasingly. "We can't do that to them."

"I know. Come on."

After the fanfare that was us coming in the doors of The Hollow and being greeted by hugs and handshakes, we got on with the business of running the bar's night service. It felt nice, if disorienting, to be back in the old bar, and I was having a decent night when I noticed something seemed to be bothering Hannah. It wasn't glaringly obvious or anything, but as the night progressed, she seemed less enthusiastic, and her face went from her normal constant smile to a more reserved, pensive look.

I was heading back to the kitchen for expo when she came out of the employee restroom. I gathered her up in a hug, and she squeezed me tightly as I kissed her head. Then I pulled her out at arm's length and studied her face.

"You okay?" I asked.

"I just don't want you to leave is all," she said. "I miss you too much when you're gone."

"I understand," I said. "I miss you like hell, trust me. It drives me absolutely bananas every single day, and now that

I know you're carrying our baby, it's even more so." I took a pause for a moment before I continued. "I really want you to come with me."

I expected the upset face, or the shift in tone that had come from her the other times I mentioned it. But this time, none came. Instead, she nodded and fell back into my arms for another hug. I held her tight and swayed with her.

"I just need some time to think about it," she said.

"That's fair," I said. "We don't have to talk about it again tonight, okay?" She nodded again, against my chest. "We can just focus on having a good night at work and then curling up together in bed. Nothing else. Deal?"

"Deal," she said, nodding again against my chest. Then she pulled back and placed a kiss to my lips and then to my cheek. "I've got to get back to my tables," she said and walked away.

38

HANNAH

Whuen I lived in New York, rarely did a day go by when I didn't think about how nice it would be to live on my own. I was a full-grown woman and had no idea what it was like to not live with other people. I had no concept of having my own place, my own life.

And it wasn't just the people. It was the noise. New York was never quiet. Even my parents' opulent home filtered in the sounds of the city. There was constant noise, constant reminders of the chaos that made up the city that, quite literally, never sleeps.

For a lot of people, that represented vitality and excitement. There were times when I felt that way about it, too. It was exciting. Thrilling to be a part of it. But it was also exhausting. Having that much constantly happening, that many people watching, drained me. I dreamed of a time when I was away from all that and could just exist in my own bubble.

Now my bubble was starting to feel really lonely.

I was sitting in my house alone again. What was once a welcome peacefulness was now just too quiet. The idea of me getting used to him being gone and it feeling better eventually was totally out the window. These last few days were by far the worst. I missed him and felt out of sorts without him around.

We still hadn't worked out our living situation. He was in Portland and I was in Astoria, and we didn't know when or if or how that was going to change. In truth, that was all on me. Jordan had no question about whether he wanted me in Portland with him or not. He tried again to convince me to go, and again, I hesitated.

I didn't know what the hell was wrong with me. He was in Portland. That wasn't going to be changing anytime soon.

Jordan loved what he did. He didn't relish the idea of going to Portland, and he never wanted to leave Astoria, but he also wasn't going to turn his back on his business and not fulfill his responsibilities. All the brothers had an important role in keeping the growing empire going. They were all working to support themselves, their families, and most importantly, their mother.

I had to come to terms with the idea that he wasn't choosing them over me. He wasn't choosing his career over me. But if I demanded he come back to Astoria or not be a part of my life, I would be forcing him to choose me over them.

It was a sobering thought.

Yet, I still couldn't bring myself to commit to going with him. Sitting there alone in my house, trying to get into terrible afternoon TV, I couldn't really figure out why. I could go to Portland and have Jordan and our growing relationship. Instead, I stayed here and had my couch and people on talk shows screaming at each other.

Not an equal trade.

But then why couldn't I work it out with him? Why couldn't I just take the leap?

If I was being honest with myself, I knew it was because things still weren't really cemented with Jordan. We had never really said what our relationship was or how we felt about each other. We had managed to hit all kinds of milestones and plan for others while deftly skating around any actual confirmations.

That was what was holding me back. Without that confirmation, I didn't know where I stood.

Muting the women screaming at each other over the head of the TV psychologist, I picked up my phone. Samantha answered on the fourth ring.

"I didn't think you were going to answer," I said.

"I'm sorry. I was doing an emergency afternoon bath."

"For yourself?"

"Partially," she said.

I was just going to leave it at that. I didn't really need to know the full story.

"Am I fundamentally flawed?" I asked.

"That was a really serious question to throw at me right after *Sesame Street*," she said. "What's going on?"

"I'm home alone," I said.

"Aren't you usually? I mean, unless you're at work."

"That's the point. Why? Why am I here alone when I could be in Portland with a really amazing guy?" I asked.

"Do you really want me to tell you what I think?"

"Yes."

She took a deep breath. "You're scared."

"That's your revolutionary insight?"

"Yes. Sometimes the simplest thing is what makes you think the most. Now it's the question of what you're afraid of. I haven't gotten a phone call or an elaborate feathered-filled box asking me to be a matron of honor. If I don't miss my guess, that means Jordan and you are still not defining anything. You haven't established what your relationship is," she said.

"That would be correct," I said.

"And that scares you. For better or worse, you are used to being in a committed relationship. You are used to the stability. Without that, you feel like you don't have a footing. You don't know where you stand in his life, and you don't know if you should put yourself out there if he hasn't. After all, you've been through a lot, even more recently. So, why should you make yourself so vulnerable?" she asked. "Am I close?"

"Yeah," I said with a resigned groan. "That's pretty much what I was thinking. We haven't talked about it. Not at all. I don't know if we're a couple. I don't know how he feels about me. It's making me really uncertain about everything."

"Then maybe you should go to Portland and talk to him. You can't just sit around and wait for him to pop by again, only to turn back around and leave right after the conversation," she said.

Samantha was right. This was what I had to do. Thanking my best friend for being the one to talk some sense into me, I got off the phone and went into my bedroom to pack a bag. When I was packed and ready, I drove to The Hollow.

Ava looked up at me questioningly when I walked in. "You aren't scheduled for tonight, are you?"

"No. And I might need to be unscheduled for a couple of days," I said.

"Why? What's going on?" she asked, sounding worried.

"I need to go to Portland. I have to talk to Jordan."

Ava smiled. "It's about time. Go. We have everything handled here. Don't worry about it for a second."

"Thank you," I said.

She hugged me tight, and I jogged toward the door.

"Hannah?" she said.

I turned around to face her.

"And if you need to be unscheduled permanently, we have that handled, too," she said.

I smiled. "Thank you."

The drive to Portland was only ninety minutes, but I spent every minute of it wondering what was going to happen when I got there. Lingering trauma from being with Ethan for so long had me wondering what I might find at the bar. Jordan tried to get me to move with him, but he didn't really push very hard. Maybe that was because he didn't actually want me there. Maybe he was already building another whole existence in Portland and I didn't factor into that equation.

I forced those thoughts out of my mind as I got to the city. I couldn't let myself spiral right now. Ethan was gone. Out of my life for good. He would have a long time in jail to think about everything he did, and when he was out, he wouldn't be allowed anywhere near me.

The GPS guided me to the bar, and I took a few seconds to admire it. Though it was obviously an older building, I was impressed by how well they seemed to make it look like The Hollow in Astoria. It was like it had been there all along.

I glanced in the visor mirror and smoothed my hair before getting out. I felt strangely nervous walking inside, but as soon as I saw Jordan behind the bar, that all melted away. I waited for him to look over in response to the bells over the door. When he did, his eyes widened.

"Hannah!" he said, obviously shocked to see me. He ran around from behind the bar and scooped me into a hug. "What are you doing here? Are you okay?"

I shook my head. "No. I'm not. I miss you. I miss you so much, Jordan. But I'm scared."

"Scared? What do you mean? Did something happen with Ethan?" he asked.

I gave an exasperated sigh and shook my head. "No. It doesn't have anything to do with him."

"Come on," he said. "Let's go in the back and talk."

He gestured at Matt to indicate we were going in the back, and Matt nodded. As soon as we were in the office, I threw my arms around him again. I just needed to be close to him, to feel him near me.

"I'm scared because of what I feel for you, Jordan," I said. "This isn't something I've ever felt before. I didn't even know if it was possible. But I don't know what you feel for me."

He looked at me incredulously. "How can you not know that? How can you not know how I feel about you?"

"Because you've never said it?" I said. "We've never said what our relationship is, or if we even have a relationship. We've never talked about our feelings. I keep holding myself back because I'm trying to protect myself."

"Hannah," he said, taking my hands and holding them tight as he looked into my eyes. "I love you. I've loved you for a long time."

"You do?"

He nodded. "Yes."

"I love you, too," I said.

Jordan pulled me close, and his mouth dropped down to mine in a deep, passionate kiss. When he stepped back from me, both of us were breathless.

"I hate this, but I have to go back to work," he said. "We're shorthanded already. I'm sorry."

"Don't say you're sorry. It's your job. I'm here. I'll wait for you," I said.

"You will?"

"I have a bag in my car, and Ava gave me permission for a slumber party."

Jordan grinned. "Oh, did she?"

"Maybe not those words exactly, but the sentiment was there," I said.

We walked back out to the bar, and I slid onto one of the booths. Jordan poured me a pineapple juice and put a bowl of snack mix in front of me.

"Nice touch," I said.

He shrugged and grinned before going back to work.

I sat there watching him work for almost an hour before Matt gave me an incredulous look.

"Hannah, are you just going to sit there, or are you going to do your job?" he asked.

"My job?" I asked.

"You are on official Hollow grounds. Your skills and responsibilities transfer," he said, then gave me a playful smile. "Come on, the cocktail waitress insisted on a break, and we really need the help."

I smiled at him. "Sure. I can help."

I fell right into the rhythms of the bar and found myself really enjoying working there. It was the same vibe as the other location, and yet different in a way I couldn't really define.

We worked hard through the rest of the night. Jordan kept plying me with juice, water, and food, but I was feeling great by the end of it all. Like being near him just gave me a new surge of energy.

After we closed the door and locked it, I looked around and realized I couldn't find Jordan. In the office I found him filling out some papers at his desk. As I walked toward him, a calendar on the wall caught my eye. It had all the shifts marked with who was going to be working and when. And my name was on it.

"What's that all about?" I asked, pointing to my name on the calendar.

"Matt asked if you were going to do your job," he said.

"Yeah."

"Well, that's really your job. It's been waiting for you from the beginning. We knew you would come here eventually," Jordan said.

All I could do was laugh and melt into his lap for a kiss. I felt so happy and peaceful. There was nothing left to worry about anymore.

39

JORDAN

I hadn't slept in the bed I'd bought for the apartment before Hannah came, and I was glad for it. The first time I slept in it, I had her curled in my arms like she was supposed to be. Granted, the studio apartment wasn't going to work out, and I had already called the landlord and asked if there was another room. I got voicemail, but I remembered him saying weeks ago that they had multiple two-bedroom apartments available on the same floor. While I didn't relish the idea of moving all my furniture again, I would do it happily if it meant I got to have Hannah there with me.

I rolled over and curled around her, and she wiggled her hips into me. Natural physical reactions took over, and she turned to look at me over her shoulder. One eyebrow cocked, she smiled at me, and I smiled back. I shrugged.

"How are you feeling this morning?" I asked, wary of how the mornings were sometimes difficult for her.

"Feeling good," she said.

"How good?"

"Really good," she purred.

"Oh, really now," I said, sitting up a bit and gently guiding her jaw around so I could brush my lips against hers. One of her hands slid down and grasped my cock through my boxers. "That good?"

She nodded, and I pressed my lips down for a deep, emotional kiss.

Soon, that kiss turned hungry. Hungry for affection, for closeness and release. My tongue slid into her mouth and played with hers. She returned my exploration eagerly, and my hand slid up her shirt. Filling my palm with her breast, I moved my lips down her neck to her collarbone. I kneaded into her chest as she gasped when I reached the sensitive area in the crook of her neck.

Moving down, I helped her remove her shirt entirely and tossed it away. I took her sensitive nipple into my mouth and slowly, reverently caressed it with my tongue. My hand slid down her stomach until it reached her panties and dipped inside. She was wet and ready for me already, but I wanted more. I wanted to show her just how much I'd missed her all this time.

I moved across her chest to the other side, taking her nipple into my mouth while my middle finger explored her slick folds until it found her clit. I rubbed in a circular motion as she moaned, and I sucked on her breast. Then, I moved down the center of her stomach, pulling her panties down and away as I did. She reached for me, and I scooted so that my legs were facing the opposite way as hers. Hannah placed her hand on my cock and stroked it through the thin boxers.

Groaning as her fingers wrapped around my staff, I slid my tongue along her lips and heard her moan as well. She pulled my cock through the hole in my boxers and used her tongue to sweep up the bottom of it, then swirl around the head while I paid attention to her clit. She stroked me as she sucked on the head of my cock, and I teased her clit with the tip of my tongue and slid a finger inside her.

Brushing the tip of my finger along the upper walls, I found a spot that made her squirm and paid it extra attention. Soon, her breathing hitched and she writhed as she fell into a climax, diving her lips deeply over me while moans escaped her mouth. Her moans vibrated over my staff, and I rocked into her, feeling the tension building up around me as well.

When her body stopped convulsing, I pulled my hips away from her and slid around. Pulling my boxers off, I tossed them away as I positioned myself between her thighs. She arched her back up, and I took her breast into my mouth again as my cock slid through her folds until it reached her opening. I teased her clit with the head before sliding into her slowly. She was slick and ready for me, and I drove deep into her pussy.

Rocking my hips back and then thrusting deeper, I took my time in slow, measured movements. There was no hurry. There was nothing but time now. We had each other forever.

I sat up on my knees as I continued my slow motion of rocking into her and admired her body. She was so beautiful, and I let my fingers roam across her body as I gained speed. Hannah reached up and pulled me down by the back of the neck until our lips pressed in again, and I could feel her rocking underneath me, begging me to go faster, harder.

Obliging, I began to thrust deeply into her at a much quicker pace. Her mouth opened as she closed her eyes and let her head fall back into the pillows. I pressed my closed fists on either side of her as I mounted her and thrust over and over again. She crossed her ankles over my ass as I slammed into her with gaining intensity.

Suddenly, she opened her eyes, and they bored into mine. She bared her teeth as an aggressive need rose between us. I began to slam into her harder, faster, and she cried out. Then, pressing up on her elbows, she maneuvered until we switched and she was on top of me. Her hips took over the motion, and she pounded down on top of me. She sat up, pressing her hands into my chest for leverage as she rode me, and I admired her beauty again. There was nothing in the world sexier that I had ever seen than watching her ride me, knowing I was pleasuring her as much as she was pleasuring me.

I reached up and grasped her breasts, and she moved one leg so her foot was planted on the mattress beside me. It gave her better positioning to slam my cock deeper into her, and she slid her fingers down until she could touch herself. Swirling her middle finger over her clit, her mouth fell open and she continued to slam onto me. I could sense that we were both nearing completion, and I grabbed at her ass with one hand to guide her into ever harder, faster thrusts.

I groaned deeply as she rode me and felt a desire for control build up. Hannah's eyes bored down into mine, and I pulled her with me into a seated position until my back was against the wall. There, I grabbed her ass and pulled her hard down onto me. She placed her hands on the wall to steady herself as I took a breast into my mouth and guided her motions.

The tension was at a breaking point, and I knew I was extremely close. I pushed until she fell on her back again, and I lay down on top of her. Her legs wrapped around my back, and I buried my face in her neck. Both hands reached down to get under her ass, lifting it and squeezing as I slammed into her as hard as my hips would let me. The groans turned to a growl, and I could feel her release underneath me.

Her body vibrated and shook, and she screamed out as I raised my voice with hers. The overwhelming rush flowed through me, and I exploded into her, my body locking up as I came hard and shook as I emptied myself deeply inside her. When I was spent, I crashed on the bed and curled her into me again, pulling the covers over our naked bodies in satisfaction.

We lay back, catching our breath for a few minutes before she rolled over onto my chest. Placing a kiss and sighing contentedly, she turned so she could stare at me. I was doing the same, just taking in her beauty.

"I'm very glad you decided to move in with me," I said.

"I am, too," she said. "I only hesitated because I was afraid. What if things don't work out being here?"

I sat up and pressed my lips into hers, and she rolled so she was lying in my lap, looking up at me.

"They will," I said, "I promise you that. Because I love you."

"I love you, too," she said, and we shared another sweet kiss.

A thought crossed my mind, and I sat with it for a moment before saying anything.

"You know, I can keep my place in Astoria," I said. "That way we will have a place to stay when we visit home."

She sat up quickly, her eyes wide and a grin breaking across her lips.

"Really?" she asked.

"I don't see why not," I said. "It's not like we won't be going down there all the time. It's where Mom and my other brothers are. It would be nice to have a place we can stay that still feels like home."

"We could spend holidays there so we could be close to your mom," Hannah said, getting excited. "It would be our little getaway."

"I like it," I said. "Do you? Do you really?"

"I do. I love it." She threw her arms around me, and I smiled.

"Good, because I love it, too. And I love you."

"I love you, too, Jordan," she said, and we kissed once again.

I lay back in the bed with her and held her tight. I never intended on letting go.

EPILOGUE

HANNAH

I drew in a breath, then realized I was holding it and forced it out of my lungs. My eyes squeezed tight, I tried to do what the birth coach had taught me and focused on my happy thought. The only problem was, I couldn't really remember what my happy thought was in that moment.

The only thing going through my mind was the pain. It started when Jordan and I were out at a romantic dinner he'd surprised me with to mark the last week of my pregnancy. With our baby girl due in seven days, we were taking as much time as we could to just soak each other and this experience in.

And partway through my plate of incredible portobello mushroom ravioli with sun-dried tomato garlic cream sauce, it became pretty clear our daughter wanted to join the party.

My first contraction wasn't that bad. Just a pain that was different than the Braxton-Hicks contractions I had been having for a couple of weeks. I ignored it and kept enjoying my dinner and talking with Jordan about the future. Then a few minutes later, another pain came. This one was a little more intense. By the third one, I had to stop and catch my breath when the pain hit me.

It was Jordan who decided it was time to get to the hospital. There were so many emotions as we piled into the car and made our way. He got on the phone and called the doctor like we'd been instructed to do, telling her we were on our way and my contractions were only five minutes apart.

Things were happening fast. I was so excited to know I would soon be welcoming my daughter into the world and seeing her little face for the first time. But it would be a lie if I didn't also admit to being nervous and even scared about labor. I did all the preparation I could. We went to labor classes. We learned the breathing patterns and focus techniques. We did the exercises. All that was left was actually doing it.

I thought I was completely calm about the situation. Now that it was happening, it didn't feel quite that way. Jordan reached over and held my hand, reassuring me with just that touch. It was enough to bring back my focus, and by the time we were at the hospital, I felt in control again.

In the maternity ward, they got me in a gown and hooked me up to monitors to check on the baby. Everything was going great, so I got up and started pacing the hallways. I knew from the beginning I wasn't going to be the type of woman who had the patience to lie in bed throughout labor. I needed to be up moving and letting gravity do its job.

Two hours of painful contractions later, I felt a gush of water. My eyes widened, and Jordan laughed almost like he was just realizing how real this was. The nurse wandering the halls with us rushed us back to the delivery room so the doctor could check me.

"Alright. Looking good. Won't be long now," she said.

"Really?" I asked.

"You can do this. Just keep focusing. Your baby will be here in no time."

Less than two hours after that, she was in my arms. It all seemed like a blur, almost like it didn't happen. But the sweat running down my face and my exhausted muscles reminded me it did. I had never felt happiness like it before. It was more than I ever could have imagined.

We took the next few hours to be selfish and just relish our new little family together. Then just as I expected, as soon as we invited everybody, they swarmed the recovery suite, eager to meet the new little one. Even Matt had gotten on the road and was there to greet his new little niece. Ava cradled her own newborn in one arm and mine in the other, and I felt my heart swell. I knew they would grow up so close, and I couldn't imagine anything better.

Samantha arrived less than an hour after everybody else. I had Jordan call her in the midst of my labor, and she got the first flight she could. It was amazing to see her standing there with my daughter in her arms. My worlds had come together twice now. The first time was horrific with Ethan trying to wedge his way in again. This time, it was everything I ever could have wanted.

I woke up in the middle of the night to find Jordan sitting in the hospital rocking chair, cradling Bella. They looked so sweet I didn't want to say anything and ruin the moment. Only a few seconds later, she started to fuss, and he looked over at me. I smiled.

"Bring her over and I'll feed her," I said.

He settled her into my arms so I could feed her, and as my hand rested on her back, I felt something under the first layer of blanket. Sticking my fingers down into the swaddle, I pulled out something hard. I gasped when I saw it was a gorgeous diamond ring. I looked up and found Jordan on one knee.

"Are you serious?" I asked, tears in my eyes.

He nodded. "Yes. I had the ring ready to propose at dinner, but those plans changed."

I laughed and looked down at the happily suckling baby. "Yes, they did."

"Hannah, will you marry me?" he asked.

"Yes."

He jumped to his feet and came over to slip the ring on my finger and kiss me.

The End